Crime Conspiracy

Crime Conspiracy

A Buck Taylor Novel

Chuck Morgan

Printed in the United States of America

First printing 2020

ISBN 978-1-7348424-2-5 (eBook)

ISBN 978-1-7348424-1-8 (Paperback)

ISBN 978-1-7348424-3-2 (Large Print)

LIBRARY OF CONGRESS CONTROL NUMBER

2020912579

Dedication

To my faithful readers. I am not sure I will ever be able to find the words to tell you how much your continued support means to me.

Contents

Chapter One

Dee Hightower put her pen down, closed her test booklet and sat back in her seat. She felt good about the test, and it showed in the huge smile that now crossed her face. It had been six long years of online, night and weekend school at Fort Lewis College in Durango, Colorado, but with the completion of this final test, she could now relax. In two weeks, she would receive her diploma and then she would start the job search effort to put her new psychology degree to use. She hoped to land a job working for the Bureau of Indian Affairs so she could use her new degree to help her friends and neighbors on the Ute Mountain Reservation, where she had lived her entire life.

More importantly, she could quit working at the grocery store in Cortez. It wasn't like she hated the job—after all, it helped put food on the table and a roof over the heads of her husband, Ronnie, and their three children—but it wasn't part of her dream. Dee Hightower was going places, and no one was going to stop her. She was the first member of her family to go to college, and she planned to make them proud.

Dee gathered up her test booklet, grabbed her backpack and dropped the booklet on the professor's desk. She had completed most of her classwork over the last six years on the internet, but tonight she'd had to drive the sixty miles from Towaoc to Durango so she could take the test in a classroom setting. She shook hands with the professor, thanked him for being her mentor all these years and headed for her car. It was late, and she hoped to get home before the kids went to bed.

She called her husband to let him know she felt good about the test and to tell him she was leaving. Anytime over the last six years she'd had to make the drive, she would check in before leaving campus, so Ronnie wouldn't worry. He never liked her making the drive alone, especially at night, but he understood that this was important to Dee, and he wasn't going to stand in her way.

Dee said goodbye to some of the classmates she had become acquainted with over the years, thanked them for the invitation to head to a pub downtown for a few celebratory drinks and headed for her car.

She started the car, sat back for a minute and took a deep breath. She had finally done it. She was now a college graduate, but instead of feeling happy, a shiver went up her spine, and she felt uneasy. She felt like she was being watched. She looked around the mostly empty parking lot but didn't notice anything out of the ordinary.

"Geez, Dee. Get a grip. You just graduated college. Take a break and feel good about what you've accomplished," she said to herself.

She shook off the odd feeling and pulled out of the lot, never noticing the van that pulled out of the dark space at the far end of the lot. Dee drove through downtown Durango, jumped onto Highway 160 and headed west. She checked her watch. She should make it home just as her husband was getting the kids settled into bed. Focused on the road ahead, she never looked back as she climbed out of the valley.

As was her routine, when she reached the small town of Mancos, she sent Ronnie a text to let him know where she was. She still had a half tank of gas, so she didn't need to stop at the convenience store just inside the town limits. She cruised through town and headed for Cortez, the next town, and then home. She was making great time.

* * *

Ronnie Hightower woke with a start and wiped the sleep out of his eyes. He had gotten the kids settled down early tonight and had a couple of beers while he waited for Dee to get home. He must have fallen asleep on the couch. He checked his watch and saw that it was a little after one a.m. He looked around the living room and didn't see Dee's backpack anywhere. He stood up and headed towards the bedroom. Maybe she came in, saw him sleeping and headed for bed so as not to disturb him. He pushed open the bedroom door, and the bed was still made.

He pulled out his phone and checked for messages. The last text he had was from nine p.m., which was the one Dee sent from Mancos. She should have been home hours ago. He stepped outside and saw his truck in the gravel driveway, but not Dee's old Subaru. He dialed her number and listened as it rang and went to voice mail. It wasn't like Dee to miss saying good night to the kids.

Ronnie called his sister-in-law, Jessie, who lived two blocks over, told her that Dee hadn't come home and asked if she could come over and keep an eye on the kids, so he could head towards Mancos and see if he could find her car. Though the Subaru was old, he kept it running in tip-top shape, but anything could have happened. Within fifteen minutes, Jessie, followed by five pickup trucks, pulled into the driveway and parked next to Ronnie's truck. Ronnie's brother Sam and several of his friends parked their trucks along the street. They got out of their trucks and formed a circle at the end of the driveway. Ronnie could always count on Jessie to be ahead of the curve, and she was this morning. She had started calling around, and soon they had a search party formed. By the time they left the house, six more cars and trucks had joined the group.

Ronnie told them what he knew; his neighbor and best friend, Scott Sage, a Montezuma County sheriff's deputy, gave everyone their assignments, and the search for Dee Hightower began. Scott called the sheriff's office and asked them to put out a BOLO on Dee's car and to ask the La Plata County sheriff's office to check the highway between Durango and Mancos.

By eight a.m., the searchers started arriving back at the Hightower home, and the news wasn't good. There was no sign of Dee's car anywhere. Jessie fed everyone a breakfast of eggs and bacon, with plenty of coffee, and those who could stay gathered around the kitchen table and pulled out their maps. Scott Sage called the sheriff's office and spoke with the sheriff, who promised to get every deputy and reserve deputy in the county working on the search.

Ronnie tried to remain calm as he got his kids ready for school, but he broke down when he called his boss at the Montezuma County Public Works Department. His boss promised to get Dee's information to all the county road crews and told Ronnie to take the day off and to call if he needed anything.

After breakfast and some strategizing, the remaining searchers, augmented by several new additions, headed out again and began working the back roads. The biggest hurdle was that there were a lot of back roads, forest service roads and trails throughout the county, and Dee could be anywhere. Everyone started with positive thoughts, but as the day wore on, those thoughts diminished, and by nightfall, everyone feared the worst. Dee Hightower had vanished off the face of the earth and now joined a long list of missing Native American women.

Chapter Two

Professor Dale Carmichael turned off Highway 160 at the sign for Big Meadows Reservoir State Wildlife Area and followed the gravel road to the parking area and boat ramp, where he pulled to the side and parked. Carmichael and his students had left Denver earlier that morning, and they were thrilled to get out of the van and stretch. It had been a long drive, and the students walked around the parking lot trying to work the kinks out of their legs and backs. Unkinked for the most part, and ready to get on the trail while they still had a few hours of daylight left, they started to unload their gear from the back of the van.

It was a beautiful early spring day, warm with just a bit of a chill in the air, and there wasn't a cloud in the sky. A perfect Colorado bluebird day and a great time of year to set out on a two-week adventure in the Weminuche Wilderness Area, but this wasn't a vacation. The professor and his team of PhD candidates were here as part of a wildlife survey jointly commissioned by the U.S. Fish and Wildlife Service and Colorado Parks and Wildlife. Their assignment was to prove or disprove the existence of "ghost grizzlies" in the wilderness area.

Grizzly bears were thought to have been

extirpated from the state of Colorado in the 1950s. The last one had been spotted and killed in 1952, until a lone female grizzly attacked an elk hunter and outfitter in the San Juan National Forest, near the Colorado–New Mexico border, on September 23, 1979. The hunter, using an arrow to stab the bear in the throat and the heart, survived the attack with quite a tale to tell, but it reopened the possibility that grizzlies still lived in the Colorado mountains. The official government response was that grizzlies no longer lived in Colorado. Over the years, there had been scattered reports by hunters and hikers of grizzly sightings in the Weminuche Wilderness. Those reports were unconfirmed, but the number of sightings had increased of late, and the agencies were concerned that perhaps a stray grizzly had slipped into the state and was now making itself at home in the area.

It would not be too much of a stretch to believe this could happen. Just recently, while state agencies, conservation groups and ranch and farm organizations were debating the possibility of reintroducing wolves into the state, a pack of six or seven wolves was spotted in northern Colorado. It seems they reintroduced themselves into the state while no one was looking. This gave conservation groups a boost and started more people talking about reintroducing other animals, including grizzlies, into the state. The debate was heated on both sides, so finding the truth about grizzlies in Colorado was high on the agencies' priority lists.

The locals referred to the bears as "ghost

grizzlies," and they were listed as "officially unconfirmed." The recent rash of sightings led the two government agencies to join forces and quietly arrange for Professor Carmichael to set up a study to try to put an end to the speculation. With the increased use of the Continental Divide Trail through the Weminuche Wilderness, the government decided to err on the side of caution. The last thing they needed was for an encounter between a grizzly and a hiker to end in the death of a hiker. That would be bad for the tourist industry. The agencies were hoping that the survey would give them a clearer picture of the status of grizzlies in the area, and hopefully confirm that there were none around.

Professor Carmichael placed a placard on the van's dashboard, noting that the van was there on official United States Forest Service business and indicating they would be returning to this location in fourteen days. As any good hiker should, he also gave his itinerary and hiking route to his assistant at the University of Colorado in Boulder, and to Bill Wagner, his contact at the USFS. He gathered his students together, had everyone check one another to make sure nothing was falling out of their backpacks, checked his weather app one more time and headed south along the reservoir towards trail 843. They intended to connect with trail 839, which would lead them to the Continental Divide Trail at Archuleta Lake. If all went well, they would make camp for the night at the lake.

Professor Carmichael did not doubt that his team

could make the five-mile hike and reach their first night's destination at Archuleta Lake without any difficulties. He had chosen each student carefully, and strength and endurance were two of the most important attributes he looked for. They were going to be hiking on mostly improved trails, but the terrain in the Weminuche was as rugged as it gets, and they would spend several days off the trail and roughing it. All of his students, like himself, were seasoned backpackers and were members of the campus hiking club. They were all physically fit and emotionally mature, but this was not going to be an easy hike in the woods. They were going to have to go where the grizzlies would possibly be, and that was going to use every skill they had.

His team was made up of four students from the animal behavior department at the university. Kendra Jackson was tall and dark skinned with a shaved head. She was smart, with an IQ bordering on genius, and she played point guard for the university basketball team, the Lady Buffs. Her biggest asset was that she had already completed the one-hundred-mile-long segment of the Continental Divide Trail from Pagosa Springs to Silverton, Colorado. The very same segment they would be hiking over the next fourteen days. Her knowledge of the trail and the area should prove to be invaluable.

Robert Meyers, average height with dark curly hair, and Sandra Moore, short and stocky with short blond hair, spent their summers working as interns in the bear habitat area of the Denver Zoo. Their familiarity with bear behavior was valuable. Grizzlies were only a possibility in the area. However, black bears were a sure thing, and it was still early enough in the season that many of the bears were just emerging from hibernation and encounters with humans could prove problematic.

James Tulley was built like a football player but had never played. Growing up, he grew tired of being picked on for being the smart kid, so he made a promise to bulk up, which he did, almost to excess. He was also an expert in the use of trail cameras and would be handling the majority of the electronic surveillance for the survey.

The fifth member of the team was Dom Rivera. He had black hair that he wore high and tight, and he had a weightlifter's build. He looked like he would be more at home on a military base than on a college campus. He didn't talk about himself on the ride down from Denver and stayed a ways back from the group as they passed the southern end of the reservoir. He had been a late addition to the group, and the only thing Professor Carmichael knew about him was that he was a handyman at the university, and he was on a mission.

The last member of the group was Lum Gladstone, a local guide and outfitter. He'd left the reservoir three days before on horseback, with two pack mules, to set up their first base camp at Goose Lake. Lum would act as guide, camp cook and security for the group. He also carried all their cameras and electronic gear as well as their food supply. He was forty years old, tanned and weathered and had been guiding in the area since he was in his teens. Lum didn't believe they would find any grizzlies in the area, as he'd never seen one, but the survey sounded interesting, and the money was good this early in the season, so he was happy to sign on.

The team, tired and ready for a good night's sleep, reached Archuleta Lake just as the sun was setting. They set up camp, used their camp stoves to cook their meals and settled in for the night. Tomorrow was going to be a long, hard trek.

Chapter Three

Buck Taylor sat on the bank of the Gunnison River, about a half mile south of the new footbridge that led to the Lucy Taylor Memorial Riverwalk, and watched his grandson, also named Buck, practice casting his fly into the wind. It was a skill they had been working on for the last hour or so and a skill that would come in handy on days like today when the wind was more than just a light breeze.

They had spent the better part of the morning cutting up broken tree limbs in Buck's backyard. The late spring snowstorm that hit the state a week ago had dumped a foot of heavy wet snow on trees that were just beginning to leaf out, which led to a lot of broken branches in the area. Since Buck had some time between cases, he had asked his grandson to help him cut and stack the limbs and branches in exchange for some time on the river working on different casting techniques. Besides his family, there were only two things that got Buck fired up: a good investigation, and time on a river, any river, fly-fishing. Buck's fishing gear was never out of reach and had a special place in the back of his state-issued Jeep Grand Cherokee.

Buck finished tying a small bead head nymph to his tippet and sat back to admire the newest and final addition to the Riverwalk. The new open-air gazebo was large enough for family gatherings and also was slated to host concerts and plays for the folks of Gunnison. The gazebo and the Riverwalk itself were a gift to the city from Hardy Braxton and his wife, Rachel. It was their way to pay tribute to Buck's late wife, Lucy, who had died after a five-year battle with metastatic breast cancer.

Buck and Hardy had grown up together in Gunnison and had been on-again, off-again friends their entire lives. They played football for the Gunnison High School Cowboys, and in their senior year, they broke every defensive record the state kept track of. Many of those records still stood today. They were known as the "wrecking crew," and their skills earned Hardy a college scholarship and a position in the National Football League until a knee injury ended his career. Hardy was now one of the richest men in the state after taking his father's small rodeo stock business and turning it into one of the largest stock suppliers in the world. A rodeo or western show didn't happen anywhere in the world that didn't include bulls and horses from Braxton Bucking Stock. That small business led to multiple other businesses, including energy exploration, retail and hotel development. He was also Buck's brother-in-law, having married Lucy's younger sister the year after Buck and Lucy were married.

Buck was grateful for the gesture, and the Riverwalk was a big hit with the people of Gunnison as well as the tourists and fishermen, who got to try their luck in the gold medal waters where

Buck and his grandson now stood. Buck's youngest son, Jason, had been the architect of record and construction manager on the project, and part of the plan included the river improvements that took this from a great fishing area to an incredible fishing area.

Buck's thoughts were interrupted by the loud splashing as his grandson hooked into another decent-sized rainbow trout. Buck could see the huge smile on his face as he scooped the fish up in his net and held it up for Buck to see.

Buck nodded his approval, stood up and waded into the middle of the river. Even though he loved to fish here, it made him sad. He wished Lucy could be here with him, sitting in her wheelchair on the small handicapped dock, watching him fish. He thought back to that Sunday morning when the family had gathered for a private ceremony at the little dock to scatter Lucy's ashes in the river. When they finished and turned to go, they were stunned to see several hundred of their neighbors and friends standing silently behind them in the park. Word had gotten out about their private service, and everyone turned out to pay tribute to Lucy. The affair turned into a huge party, with plenty of food and drinks. Lucy never wanted any kind of service, but Buck figured she would have loved this spontaneous outpouring of love. He wiped the tears from his eyes, cast his fly into a small spot behind a boulder and hooked a nice trout.

The afternoon flew by quickly, and as the sun was setting, they called it quits and headed for

Buck's Jeep. They were in the process of stowing their fishing gear when Buck's phone buzzed. He checked the number, looked at his grandson and shrugged his shoulders.

"Yes, sir," he said.

"Hey, Buck. Hope I didn't catch you in the middle of anything?" said Kevin Jackson.

Kevin Jackson was the director of the Colorado Bureau of Investigation and Buck's boss. He had been the youngest person ever appointed to head up the CBI when he was tapped by Governor Richard J. Kennedy to run the agency. He'd spent the early part of his career on the administrative side of the Colorado Springs Police Department and was highly regarded by the law enforcement community. He was not only an effective manager but a seasoned investigator in his own right. Buck held the man in high regard.

"No, sir. Just wrapping up an afternoon of fishing with my grandson."

"Well, hope the fishing was good, but I'm gonna have to tear you away for a while."

"No problem, sir. What's up?"

"The governor got a call from the sheriff in Montezuma County. He has a missing Native American woman, and he has asked for our help, specifically your help. She's been missing little over a week with no trace. You know the governor has been concerned about the rash of missing Native American women around the country, but this one hits too close to home. This is the tenth woman to disappear in Colorado in the past four years, and this makes the third one in Montezuma County. The governor wants some answers. He told the sheriff you and Bax would be there tomorrow afternoon."

"No problem. I'll head out first thing in the morning. Have you already called Bax?"

"Yeah, she'll meet you at the sheriff's office tomorrow as soon as you can get there. Knowing her, she's probably halfway there already. I emailed you a couple of files. Look through them and use what you need."

"You are right about Bax. She has been aching to get involved in this situation since it first came to her attention a few years back. With a little luck, maybe we can get to the bottom of this."

"Great. Keep me posted on progress and yell if you need anything. This is now at the top of the governor's priority list."

The director hung up, and Buck hooked his phone to his belt. He looked at his grandson.

"Thanks for today. You were a huge help, but now it's time for me to go to work. Let's finish loading up the gear, and I'll run you home."

In response, he got a huge hug from his grandson. They hopped in the car, and Buck pulled out of the parking lot. A quick five minutes later, Buck pulled into the driveway and parked behind the Gunnison Police Department SUV that was parked there. His oldest son, David, stepped out onto the front porch and waved them in.

David was a police officer with the Gunnison Police Department. He looked a lot like his dad when his dad was his age. Slightly taller than Buck and slightly heavier, but the resemblance was striking. Unlike his father, David still moved with the ease of a young man.

David was a sergeant and the night shift supervisor. He liked working the night shift and had been a patrolman on that shift for many years. He enjoyed the calm and quiet of the small mountain town in the early morning hours.

Buck could smell the barbecue ribs cooking on the grill as he walked around the house and into the backyard. Judy, David's wife, was just setting them on the picnic table, and she waved for Buck to grab a seat. She put a cold Coke on the table in front of him. Little Buck, excited about spending the day with his grandfather, talked through most of the dinner. Mostly about the fish he had caught. He finally ran out of steam when he finished his slice of homemade apple pie, and he raced off to watch television.

Buck sat back, contented, and took a long swallow of Coke. Buck's Coke consumption was legendary, and everyone who knew him kept him well supplied. Finished with his meal, he told Judy and David about the missing woman in Montezuma County and that he would be gone for a couple of days. Judy, as always, promised to check in on the house, and he stood, stretched and bid them a good night. He walked through the house, gave each of his grandkids a kiss and hug and headed for his car. He had a long drive ahead of him in the morning, and he wanted to get an early start.

Once he got home, he spent an hour looking over the files the director had emailed him, packed his go bag for a couple of days' stay and headed for bed. He thanked the river spirits for allowing him to spend time with his grandson and for allowing them to catch a bunch of fish, and he fell asleep, thinking about Lucy.

Chapter Four

If you asked Buck, he would tell you that he fell in love with Lucinda Torres the first day of their senior year in high school. Lucy, on the other hand, would always tell people that Buck stalked her all senior year before she gave in, mostly to shut her friends up, and agreed to go to the movies with him. She had always considered him just another jock, another football player who was too full of himself. What she found on that first date was a shy, unassuming gentleman, for lack of a better word, who, it seemed, cared more about pleasing her than bragging about his prowess on the football field. She would tell people it was love at first sight that had taken a year to accomplish. From that day forward, they were inseparable.

During senior year Buck had been approached by several college football scouts who wanted to sign him to play for their schools. Gunnison High School was a pretty small school back in 1978, and Buck and his family were amazed at how many schools had recruited him, but for Buck, college just wasn't in the cards. Buck hated school and spent a lot of time getting himself out of trouble instead of getting an education. When he found something that interested him, he had no problem learning all he could about the subject, but regular schoolwork just bored him. After several long heartfelt discussions, first with Lucy and then with his parents, he had decided to join the army after graduation. Surprisingly, no one was surprised.

Buck spent four years after high school in the army, and by the time his enlistment was up, he had been promoted to First Sergeant. He spent three years of his enlistment in the military police and really took to police work. That was when he decided to apply for a position with the Gunnison County Sheriff's Office. Since he was already well known in the county, he had no trouble getting a job as a deputy. He proposed to Lucy on the night he received the call that he had gotten the position. His life and career were set, and he made the most of his time with the Gunnison County Sheriff's Office, eventually becoming the undersheriff in charge of the Investigation Division and coming to the attention of the Colorado Bureau of Investigation.

Buck had worked with the Colorado Bureau of Investigation on several cases inside the county and had earned the respect of the investigators he had worked with. As twilight started to fall on Buck's career, he knew that unless he wanted to go into politics and run for sheriff, he had reached the highest position in the sheriff's office that he could obtain. He loved his job, but when the offer came in from CBI, he sat down with Lucy and had a long heart-to-heart talk. He'd spent seventeen years in the sheriff's office and always figured he would retire from that job. They had three children, two in high school and one not too far behind, and he was a well-respected member of the community. Did he have the right to disrupt all their lives and pick up and move someplace else and start all over? The kids had friends, Lucy owned a small deli/ice cream parlor, and they had a good life. He could stick it out for another ten years and retire, and they could travel and see the world like they had always planned. Twice he turned down the offer from CBI, although more and more, he felt like he was trapped behind a desk instead of doing what he loved, which was investigating crime.

The final offer came directly from Tom Cole, then-director of the Colorado Bureau of Investigation. Buck always remembered that day. The Denver Broncos had just lost another game, the third one in a row, and his friends had all packed up and headed home, when there was a knock at the front door. Now, anyone who lives in a small community knows that no one ever uses the front door, and no one ever knocks. Who could this possibly be this late on a Sunday evening?

Buck answered the door and was surprised to see the director of the Colorado Bureau of Investigation standing on his front porch. The director smiled and said, "Before you close the door in my face, please listen to my offer."

Buck invited him in, and he and Lucy sat on the couch and listened as the director laid out his plan. He was opening a new branch office in Grand Junction, Colorado, that would house five agents and a small forensic unit. Buck could continue to live in Gunnison but would have to report to the office in Grand Junction twice a month. Otherwise, he would be free to work out of his house. There would be no disruption in his life other than having to spend some time on the road as his investigations warranted. He would work alone, but he would have the resources of all the branch offices at his disposal.

Before Buck could say a word, Lucy said, "Buck, this is what you have been waiting for, a chance to be a real investigator again. You have to take this." That was one of the things that made him love Lucy every day. She always knew what he was thinking, and she always understood what drove him. She had nailed it this time. Buck looked at the director and replied, "Well, I guess it's settled, looks like you have a new investigator on your team."

That was nineteen years ago, and Buck never looked back.

Chapter Five

Buck made the drive from Gunnison to Cortez, Colorado, the county seat of Montezuma County, in a little under four hours. Luckily, most of the recent snow had melted, so the drive was uneventful. He turned right off Highway 160, drove north on North Mildred Road for a couple of blocks, turned left onto East Driscoll Street and pulled into the parking lot for the Montezuma County Sheriff's Office. The first thing he spotted was Bax's gray Jeep Cherokee, so he pulled into the space next to it, got out, grabbed his backpack and headed for the front door.

Buck wasn't an imposing figure, but when he was on a crime scene, or running an investigation, there was little doubt to anyone around who was in charge. At six feet tall and one hundred eighty-five pounds, Buck was in the best shape of his life. He looked like he could still play football for the Gunnison High School Cowboys.

He wore his salt-and-pepper hair, which had a lot more salt than pepper in it, longer than the style of the day, and considerably longer than when his wife of thirty-four years, Lucy, was still alive. Today he wore a short Carhartt ranch jacket over a T-shirt and jeans. He had the jacket zipped up two-thirds of the way to hold off the chill from the cool north wind. Even though the calendar said it was spring, winter hadn't completely let go yet, and with memories of the snowstorm the week before, Buck knew the weather could change for the worst at any time.

He presented his credentials to the deputy at the front desk and was buzzed through the office door. He passed through the back office area and found Bax sitting in a small conference room with Sheriff Reuben Garcia and a young deputy Buck didn't know. Sheriff Garcia stood up and, with his hand extended, met Buck at the door.

"Hey, Buck. It's been a long time. Thanks for making the drive down."

Reuben Garcia had been sheriff of Montezuma County for as long as anyone could remember. Buck had first met him almost twenty years ago, and he still looked the same as he did the last time Buck saw him. Sheriff Garcia was five feet ten with a decent build, a full head of white hair and a gray mustache. His handshake was firm.

"No problem, Reuben. What's it been, about five years since we had that murder in Dolores? You look good."

"Good memory, Buck." He pointed to the young deputy, who rose and reached out his hand. "This is Scott Sage. He was the first deputy involved in the disappearance. I thought he might be able to help."

Buck shook hands with the deputy and then walked over and set his backpack on the table next to Bax. CBI agent Ashley Baxter worked with Buck on a lot of interesting cases, in between working on her own cases. At thirty years old, she was one of the youngest agents in the Grand Junction Field Office, and she valued the time she got to spend with Buck because she learned so much about running an investigation. Bax was also a whiz at doing deep background searches, a talent Buck did not share, so he relied on Bax to help him out. They worked well as a team and had found themselves collaborating more and more as the years rolled by.

"When did you get here?" asked Buck.

"I came down last night. The sheriff was kind enough to let me sit here and go through the files of the missing women."

The sheriff and Deputy Sage sat down, and Buck pulled his laptop out of his backpack and fired it up. While he waited, he said, "Reuben, why now? These disappearances have been going on for a long time. I understand the urgency with these cases, but why bring this one to the governor?"

The sheriff got a sad look in his eyes. "This one's personal, Buck. Dee Hightower is my goddaughter."

Buck looked at Bax and then back to the sheriff. "Okay, Reuben, then we'd better get started."

Bax clicked on an email, and Buck's computer chimed with an incoming message. Bax had created the digital case file and sent the link to Buck. He smiled. He was known around the CBI office in Grand Junction as a technological dinosaur and considered himself lucky that his grandkids could help out when he screwed up the TV remote. He always appreciated it when Bax took care of the computer work.

CBI had gone digital a couple of years back, so instead of having a blue binder for each case, Buck just had to open a program on his laptop. The new case was automatically assigned a case number, and Buck would list everyone who needed access to the file and send them email invites. All evidence, lab reports, photos, etc. that were part of the case would be uploaded into the file, and anyone who needed access just had to open the file. That was a lot better than the old system where everything was placed in the binder by hand, and Buck would spend half his time trying to track down who had the binder.

For a tech dinosaur like Buck, this made his life so much easier, and he had ready access to anything he needed. He opened the chronology page, which was the first page in the file. Nothing was ever entered into the file without a note being entered in the chronology first. The chronology kept track of everything that happened in the investigation. Buck was meticulous about his case files and had never lost a case in court, in all his years in law enforcement, because something was missing from his files. He noted that Bax had already uploaded the three missing person files into the case file. He would read through those later at the hotel, but now he wanted to hear it firsthand.

"Reuben," he said. "Can you give me the rundown on this most recent disappearance?"

The sheriff took a sip of water from his glass and sat a little taller in the seat. "Eight days ago, Scott here called me to let me know that Dee hadn't come home from school. She has been taking classes at Fort Lewis College, mostly online, but this was a final exam, so she had to take it on campus. She left the campus at close to nine p.m., texted her husband, Ronnie, when she reached Mancos and said she would be home before he put the kids to sleep. Ronnie must have dozed off, and when he woke up about one, Dee wasn't home. He called his sister-in-law to come watch the kids so he could go look for her, and Jessie—that's the sister-in-law—called a bunch of people, Scott included, and organized a search party." The sheriff looked at Scott, who continued.

"That morning, we covered all the main roads between Durango and Towaoc, but by sunrise, there was no sign of her or the car. We went back out after breakfast and started working on the side roads, but still nothing. I called the sheriff and asked him to put out a BOLO for her car, and Ronnie called his boss at the county road department, and he promised to let all the road crews know to keep an eye out for her. Since then, we've continued to search, but so far, nothing."

"We've hit a dead end, Buck," said the sheriff. "That's when I called the governor and requested your help. I don't know what else to do."

"Tell me about Dee."

Sheriff Garcia sat back and thought for a minute. "I've known Dee all her life. Her father was a deputy here for years. Died of a heart attack when he was thirty-five years old. Dee was twelve at the time. She took it hard. Had some problems in school, growing up, but she graduated, got a decent job at the grocery store and married Ronnie. They have three kids, and it looked like she was putting her old life behind her. She spent the past six years attending classes online and at the campus on weekends. She took her final exam the night she disappeared. She will get her diploma next Saturday. We are all looking forward to a big party."

"Reuben, is there any chance she got tired of it all and just called it quits and headed for parts unknown? Maybe a boyfriend someplace, drugs or a desire to get free of the reservation?"

"Nah, Buck. She's not that kind of girl. She worked too hard to get her degree, and she loves Ronnie and those kids. Nah. No way she ran."

"Okay," said Buck. "What about the husband. Any chance he's not telling you the whole story?"

Scott answered before the sheriff. "No way. He loves Dee. Sure, they had their ups and downs, but who doesn't? I grew up with Ronnie. There's no way he would hurt her or the kids. Just can't see it."

Buck looked at Bax. "Why don't you head over to the grocery store with Scott and talk to her coworkers? Also, talk to some of her friends in town here. I'm sure the sheriff has a list in the file of everyone they've talked to. Let's see if anyone remembers anything more. I don't want to talk to the people in Towaoc until we've ruled out everyone here. I'm going to head over to Fort Lewis College and talk to her teachers and see if I can get a line on any friends she might have there.

Let's meet back here at around five, and we can go have a chat with her husband and some of the neighbors.

"Reuben, can you get me a list of all motor vehicle stops that your guys and the Cortez Police made that night? Also have someone check all the businesses that front Highway 160, and let's see if anyone has any video of that night. Check banks, ATMs, gas stations. You know the drill."

Buck closed his laptop and stood up. "Reuben, we will do our best to locate Dee. She's our priority, but I don't want to forget about the other missing women. We are way behind on this, and we need to move fast."

Bax closed her laptop and grabbed her backpack while the sheriff and Scott stood. They shook hands with Buck and Bax, and everyone headed out.

Once outside in the parking lot, Buck turned to Bax. "You went through the files on the missing women. Other than the fact they were all Native American, anything stand out?"

"Nothing that jumps out initially—different ages, different educational backgrounds, different family lives. I'll call Paul and have him start running deep background on them and see if anything pops. This is not going to be easy, Buck. Native American women have been disappearing for years, and no one gives a shit. We need to figure this out."

"We'll do our best. Have Paul run deep background on Dee and her husband, Ronnie. Have him get a warrant for their phones and tear apart their social media lives. Let's make sure there's nothing hiding. Also, be careful what you share with Scott. We don't know much about him, but I want to make sure he's not too close to this thing and gets in the way. Call if you need me."

They each stowed their backpacks in the backs of their Jeeps and headed out of the parking lot. They had a lot to do, and none of it was going to be easy.

Chapter Six

Dee Hightower was tired, cold and hungry. She was also sore in all the wrong places. The repeated rapes were taking their toll, and the cold floor was sapping what little strength she had left. She had no idea where she was or how long she had been here. All she knew was that she missed her husband and children, and she hoped this nightmare would end soon, one way or another. The idea that her family had no idea where she was drove her crazy, but she knew if she was going to get out of this, she needed to stay strong. One day this would end, and when it did, she would kill the people who did this to her. She wasn't a violent woman, but she remembered the things her grandfather had taught her about hunting and skinning animals, and she hoped one day she would be able to use that knowledge to gut these bastards.

She pulled the old horse blanket tighter around her shoulders. She wanted to be grateful to the shorter guy for getting her the blanket, but she also wanted to keep the fire burning in her soul. She was not going to give in to these guys for the cost of a shitty, old blanket that smelled like it had never been washed. A chill ran up her spine, and she pulled her naked legs up under the blanket.

Dee flashed back to that night after class. She

remembered shrugging off a feeling that she was being watched as just the relief of completing her final exam. She knew her family would be so proud of her for the accomplishment. The first family member to ever go to college, let alone graduate. Had she missed her graduation? She felt like she'd been tied to the bed frame for weeks. Was anyone looking for her? Did anyone care that she was missing, or did they just write her off as another native woman who ran off and left her family? She knew that was what a lot of people thought every time another woman from a reservation went missing. That she had grown tired of living a hard life and headed to Las Vegas or Los Angeles in search of a different, better dream. But she wasn't like that. She loved her family and her life with Ronnie, and she wanted to use her degree to make things better.

She looked around, trying to pick out small details of her surroundings in the nonexistent light. Over the last who knew how many days, her night vision had become more acute, and she could make out details she hadn't seen before. It looked like one wall was rock, like she might have been in a cave, but then the other three walls seemed to be made out of wood. Wherever she was, there was no sound from outside until she heard the metal bar being removed from the door and one or both of her captors would enter. They would bring her the one meal of the day, but she wouldn't be allowed to touch it until she had serviced them. After the first couple of times, she set it into her head to not fight them; she could still feel the bruises on her cheek and her arms. She hated giving in. Hated the smell that accompanied them—they smelled like something had died—and she hated hearing them as they grunted and groaned while penetrating her, sometimes vaginally and sometimes anally. It was the latter she hated the most, but the taller fella enjoyed that way the best.

She had no idea where her captives were at any minute, and she would sometimes sit on the cold floor or that gross old mattress for what seemed like hours before they came back. She wondered if maybe they had jobs, but she had no way of knowing. The only change in that routine had happened a while back when a woman brought her nightly meal. She'd tried to engage her in conversation, but the woman handed her a mask and told her to put it on, or there would be hell to pay. The woman didn't say another word. She wondered what the cost of hell was since what she was going through was worse than anything she could imagine. She could tell that the woman had turned on a light because she could see little flashes through the face mask. The woman handed her a bar of soap and a bucket of cold water and told her to wash herself, and then she toweled off with a towel that felt worse than the old blanket.

After the woman left, she ate her plate of gruel or whatever crap they were serving her, and then both of her captors came in and spent a long time with her. She figured they liked her nice and clean. She was lost in her thoughts when she heard the metal bar being removed and the door open. The dirt floor made it difficult to distinguish footfalls, but when the big fist grabbed her by her hair and turned her over the end of the bed frame, she knew it was the taller guy. He pulled the blanket off, threw it on the floor, unzipped his pants and slammed into her. She wondered what she had done to deserve the violence, but the pain was intense, and she thought she was going to pass out. After what seemed like an eternity, he pulled out, zipped up his pants and, without saying anything, left the room and replaced the bar on the door. Dee lay on the bed and cried.

For the first time since her capture, she prayed that she would die. She thought about her children and never getting to see them grow into the people she knew they would become. She wondered if they would do all right, growing up without a mom. She wiped the tears from her eyes, pulled the blanket closer and prayed to God that he would end her torment. She closed her eyes and cried herself to sleep.

Chapter Seven

Professor Carmichael and his team set out early the next morning after a hearty breakfast of freeze-dried eggs and bacon and a pot of thick, dark coffee. The nighttime temperature had dropped into the twenties, but most of them didn't find it too difficult to handle, and the coffee made the morning chill bearable. The hiking that day was arduous, but they didn't travel anywhere near the distance they'd intended. The time they spent looking for bear scat along and off the trail had taken a toll on their schedule, and by the time dinnertime rolled around, they estimated they still had five or six miles to go to their base camp at Goose Lake. They decided to stop for the night and make camp.

The day had been mostly uneventful, but as darkness settled in, they reflected on the odd occurrence that had happened a couple of hours before. They had stepped off the Continental Divide Trail and onto a small side trail to check for scat. They also thought it might be an excellent place to set up a trail camera. So, while James Tulley, with camera in hand, went off to find a suitable location along the trail, the others separated to search a larger area. Kendra Jackson was the first one to arrive back at their rendezvous point, and commented that she felt like she was being watched. As several of the others arrived, they told of having the same feeling. Everyone was a little spooked, and Professor Carmichael tried to allay their fears by gathering them all around to examine some of the scat they had found. They were marking the locations where the scat was found on the topographic mapping program when James Tulley came rushing up to the others looking like he'd seen a ghost.

"James, you okay?" asked Professor Carmichael.

James took a sip from his water bottle and looked around nervously. "I saw something in the woods. Not sure what it was, but it was big and looked like it was wearing a heavy coat. It was just standing there, fifty or sixty feet away, just watching me." James's hands shook.

"Probably just a bear, dude," said Robert Meyers. "They're all over up here. You need to get a grip."

"It was no fucking bear. This thing stood on two legs and just watched me through the trees," said James

"Maybe it was bigfoot," said Sandra. She had also reported feeling like she was being watched, but she let her laughter overcome her anxiety. James just glared at her.

Professor Carmichael, sensing that it might be a good time to get moving, loaded up his backpack and hoisted it onto his shoulders. The others did the same, and they headed back to the main trail. He could sense the tension in his group and hoped it would pass with time, but he could feel his students looking around with a little more intensity as they hiked. He noticed that he also kept a closer eye on the woods around them, and he tried to shrug off the uneasy feeling that sent a chill up his spine.

The group knew they weren't going to get to the base camp before dark, so they decided to camp along the trail. They built a larger fire than they had the night before, and everyone was quiet as they ate their meals and finally settled into bed.

Tucked away in his tent, still shaken by what he had encountered, James Tulley lit up a marijuana blunt and pulled up the satellite feed from the trail cameras he had set out along the way and flipped through the pictures one at a time. He froze when the first picture came up on the first camera. There in the distance was a tall fuzzy shadow. He felt a shiver run up his spine as he checked the other two cameras. He was stunned to see the same shadow in the distance on each camera.

He stared at the shadowy figure in the woods. One camera might have been a fluke or a smudge or something, but to have the same figure appear on all three cameras? That was too much of a coincidence. And then a sobering thought hit him like a ton of bricks. He had placed each camera about a mile and a half apart as they hiked the trail. Whatever this thing was in the pictures, it was following them.

Chapter Eight

Buck cruised down Highway 160 and entered Durango from the west. He turned left on US 550 and headed north. His destination was just up the hill, Fort Lewis College, but first, he wanted to stop and see an old friend. At Seventh Street he turned right until he got to Main Avenue, then turned left and pulled into the first parking space he found. Just down the street was his lunch destination—the La Bon Cafe.

Buck didn't speak a lick of French, but he knew one thing: the La Bon Cafe was neither La Bon, whatever that meant, or a cafe. What it was, was a twenty-foot-wide hole in the wall, sitting between a local bookstore and a real estate office. Mostly it was a bar with about fifteen stools and six small tables along one wall. It was dark, musty and usually smelled like stale beer, amongst other fine cooking aromas. However, what it lost in atmosphere it made up for by having the best burgers in Durango.

Jimmy Palumbo looked up from where he was wiping the bar down after the lunch rush and blinked twice when he heard the front door open. He walked around the bar and gave Buck a huge bear hug. The last time Buck had seen Jimmy, Buck was in the process of wrapping up a huge drug bust at a local shipping company. It turned out to be one of the biggest drug busts in the country, and Buck, with the help of the La Plata County Sheriff's Department, had pulled together a team of local, state and federal law enforcement folks to pull it off.

It was also a week Buck would never forget. Before coming to Durango, Buck had been working a triple homicide in Teller County. Two of the prime suspects in the murders traced him to Durango and ambushed him in his hotel parking lot. If it hadn't been for some quick thinking, incredible luck—maybe his late wife looking out for him—and the help of Jess Gonzales, the special agent in charge of the DEA office in Grand Junction, Buck wouldn't be here today.

Jimmy Palumbo now here was a real character. Jimmy was a bear of a man. Six feet six and two hundred seventy pounds a good bit of it still muscle. He had gray hair tied up in a small ponytail and a neatly trimmed gray beard. He was dressed as always, in jeans and a T-shirt that usually had a rude saying on it, but which was unreadable today because of the full apron he wore. Jimmy and his girlfriend, Loraine, were the proprietors, bartenders and, as he liked to say, "head chefs of this fine establishment."

Jimmy was a transplant from Detroit by way of Southern California. At least that was the story most people heard. Although no one ever got the real story. It was told, mostly as a legend, that Jimmy once rode with the Hell's Angels in

Southern California and had to bug out when things got a little hot with the law. Most of the people who knew him believed the story, since he looked the part. He had tattoos on every piece of visible skin, and he had a light scar on the side of his face that was only visible when he shaved off his beard, which hardly ever happened. However, Jimmy's appearance and his bloodstained apron made for quite a picture.

There was a soft side to Jimmy as well, which only the locals got to see. Each year around the holidays, Jimmy would open his place and serve free food to the homeless and less fortunate. A charity event never happened in town that Jimmy wasn't a part of. And if anyone suffered an illness or a disaster, Jimmy was the first one in line to lend a hand, whatever it took. Deep under all that outside bravado was a simple man with a heart of gold.

Buck grabbed a seat at the bar, and Jimmy threw a huge burger patty on the grill. Jimmy never asked you your order. If you were sitting at the bar or a table, you were there for a burger. That's all he sold. He didn't have chicken or salads, and he sure as hell didn't have anything gluten-free or vegan. Jimmy was all meat and French fries. Sometimes this surprised the tourists, but the locals all knew the program, and at lunchtime, the bar was usually packed, and Jimmy would be standing behind the bar at the open grill, sweating, regaling folks with tall tales and cooking up a storm. Loraine usually was at the register, taking in cash and handing out to-go orders. They were quite a team.

Jimmy set a cold bottle of Coke in front of Buck then turned back to the grill.

"You back in town on a case?" asked Jimmy.

"Not in Durango. Working a missing person case in Montezuma County."

"That missing Native American woman? Read about it in the paper. Happened, what, about a week or so ago? You got any leads?"

Jimmy flipped the huge burger, dropped a couple of slices of cheddar cheese on it and listened to the sizzle. When it sounded just right, he placed it on a plate with a massive pile of fries and set it down in front of Buck.

Buck knew that whatever he said to Jimmy would stay right here. He had first met Jimmy seventeen years ago during a homicide investigation. Buck was still new to CBI, and he was working with his mentor, Phil Mitchell, a grizzled, seasoned veteran of forty years of police work and one of the best investigators Buck had ever worked with. One night he and Phil accompanied two Denver homicide detectives to interview a known drug dealer about his possible involvement in a recent murder. This was only going to be an interview, and it should have been simple, but it went south in a big hurry. The guy they went to interview was waiting for the cops with a couple of his friends and had no plans to go back to prison.

As soon as they walked into the location and announced themselves, all hell broke loose. The Denver homicide detectives were both hit and seriously wounded; Buck dove for cover behind a desk, but Phil wasn't that lucky. The first round went in just under his armpit, where his ballistic vest didn't cover. The second round hit him in the neck. The coroner would later say that either round would have killed him instantly. Buck was pinned down and returning fire when this mountain of a man, who looked like one badass biker, came charging in, firing his weapon at the drug dealer and his friends. At one point, a bullet raked across his cheek, leaving a deep bloody gash, but he kept shooting.

By the time the cavalry arrived, the four bad guys were dead. Buck had been hit twice in the chest, but the vest had protected him. It still hurt like hell. The big guy who saved him hadn't been wearing a vest. He was lying against another desk, with blood dripping down the side of his face and three gunshot wounds in his chest and right arm. Buck had been putting pressure on his chest wound when the ambulance arrived. Every day since, he thought about how Jimmy Palumbo's heartbeat kept getting weaker and weaker the harder he pressed to slow the flow of blood.

Jimmy, as it turned out, was a ten-year veteran of the Denver Police Department and had been working undercover with the drug gang for the past two years. He wasn't even supposed to be at the location that night. He had forgotten a gift for Loraine at the office. He went back for it and had just walked in the back door when he heard the detectives announce themselves at the front door, and the shooting started. He had no choice but to get involved.

Jimmy was in recovery for ten days and in rehab for ten months before he was told he could go back to work. The doctors said that if it hadn't been for Buck, Jimmy would have bled out. Jimmy never forgot that. By the time rehab was over, Loraine had convinced Jimmy that maybe a change of scenery was in order. Jimmy agreed reluctantly, but he never once looked back. Jimmy and Loraine ended up in Durango after bouncing around Colorado for a few years, fell in love with the town and bought a small closed restaurant and bar.

Jimmy grabbed another can of Coke and set it on the counter. Buck filled him in on what they knew so far, which wasn't much, and said that he was heading up to the college to interview her professors and possibly some friends if he could find any.

"Any chance she's a runaway?"

"I'm keeping an open mind about that. Bax is convinced this is connected to all those other Native American women who have disappeared over the last decade. We're gonna need a lot more evidence for me to be convinced. You hear anything, give me a call. Right now, I'd like to find her unharmed, but after eight days . . ."

Buck checked his watch, downed the last of his Coke and stood up. Jimmy would never charge Buck a dime, so he pulled a twenty out of his pocket and laid it on the bar.

"Put that in the charity jar, will ya?"

"Will do. And Buck, stay safe, okay?"

Buck walked out into the sunlight and headed for his car. With a full stomach, he was ready to go to work.

Chapter Nine

Buck's first stop was the college registrar's office, where he picked up a copy of Dee's college transcript and a list of her teachers and their schedules for the next two hours. She'd carried five classes this last semester, and four of the teachers were on campus today teaching. With directions to the first classroom, he headed across the campus.

After several missteps, he found Professor McNally sitting in an empty classroom grading papers.

"Excuse me, Professor." He held up his credentials. "Buck Taylor with the Colorado Bureau of Investigation. Mind if I ask you a few questions about Dee Hightower?"

The professor looked up, set his red pencil on the desk and waved him in. He was a thin man with balding silver hair, and he wore thick square glasses. His eyes were bloodshot, and he looked like he hadn't slept in a couple of days. He pointed towards the chair opposite his desk, and Buck sat down.

"Dee Hightower, huh? Word around campus is she ran off. I don't believe it for a minute. Dee was one of my best students. Never any sign of trouble, and she worked her tail off, what, with school and raising three children. Since you're here, something must have happened to her. Was she involved in some kind of crime?"

"Dee may be the victim of a crime. That's what we are trying to figure out. She's been missing for several days, and we're talking to anyone who might have seen her recently. According to her schedule, she took your class on Saturday mornings, but I understand she was here the night she disappeared to take a final exam. Do I have that correct?"

The professor thought for a minute. "Yes, that would be correct. All of my classes took their finals on the same night."

"Did Dee have any issues or problems with any other students or faculty? Any issues that concerned her that might help me get a line on her disappearance?"

"I don't get to know my students that well, Agent Taylor. They don't confide in me like they do some of the other, younger teachers. Dee worked hard, turned in quality work and got excellent grades. We never really spoke about her personal life. The only reason I know she had a family was because each student was required to give a little introductory speech about themselves on the first day of class. I wish I could offer more assistance."

Buck stood up and handed the professor one of his business cards. "If you happen to think of anything else, no matter how small, please give me a call. Thanks for your time."

He walked out of the classroom and looked at

the next name on his list. He headed off in search of Dee's next teacher.

Two hours later and frustrated, Buck sat on a bench sipping from a can of Coke he bought from a vending machine in the administration office. He looked over his notes and scratched his head. He had to be missing something. He'd spoken with four teachers and five students who were in Dee's weekend classes, and no one knew much about her. They all heard she disappeared on her way home after the final exam, but other than that, they knew little of her personal life. She didn't stick around after her weekend classes were over. She was never seen at any of the clubs downtown that were popular with the students. Most of them assumed that since she was older than the other students, she didn't feel comfortable mingling with them.

The one thing everyone noted was that Dee was a solid student. She never skimped on her projects, she was smart, and if you were teamed up with her for a project, you were guaranteed an A.

He had one teacher left to speak with, but he didn't think that would go anywhere. This teacher taught one of Dee's online classes, so other than on the computer, there would be little personal contact between them. He pulled his laptop out of his backpack and opened his navigation program and plugged in the teacher's address.

Buck closed his laptop, finished his Coke and stood up.

"Are you the cop looking for Dee?" asked a soft female voice.

Buck turned around and spotted a young girl coming towards him, carrying a heavy backpack and looking at her phone. She had long blond hair and wore a flowered blouse and ripped jeans.

"That would be me," said Buck. "And you would be?"

She walked up to the bench but kept a safe distance. "Do you have some kind of ID?" she asked.

Buck pulled his ID out of his pocket and held it so she could see it. She didn't look at it, but he got the feeling that someone had told her to always ask for ID as a safety measure. He put his ID back in his pocket.

"What's your name?" he asked again.

"Simone."

"Well, Simone. Do you know Dee Hightower?"

He waited while Simone looked in every direction except at him, and then she sat on the arm of the bench.

"Dee helped me out sometimes. She was like a big sister. Someone I could talk to, and she would help with my work. We had one class together on Saturdays, but she would always answer her phone when I called."

Buck waited as Simone gathered her thoughts. "I can't believe she's missing."

"Simone, did you talk to Dee last Saturday? Do you know if she was bothered by anyone?"

"She argued with Mr. Armstrong."

"Simone, did this argument happen last Saturday, and do you know what it was about?"

Buck pulled out Dee's class schedule. There was no Mr. Armstrong listed as a teacher for any of her classes. He put the list back in his pocket.

"No," said Simone. "The Saturday before. She was upset, and I told her not to drive until she calmed down. She had a long drive home, and she was shaking."

"Simone, who is Mr. Armstrong? He's not listed on Dee's class schedule."

She looked confused. "He's not one of her teachers. He was supposed to be helping her get into grad school at CU, but she missed a couple of admissions deadlines, so she couldn't start in the fall. He forgot to tell her about the deadlines."

"Is he a faculty adviser?"

"No, he works in the admissions office. He was helping her on the side. I told her that he was only trying to get in her pants, but she always saw the good in people. I think he's a creep."

"Simone, did the argument get physical?"

"I saw her slap him in the face before he stomped off. He was yelling something at her as he left. She wouldn't tell me what he said, but it upset her."

Buck pulled out his notebook and wrote down Simone's contact information. He thanked her for talking to him, and he grabbed his backpack and headed for the admissions office. This was an interesting development. He wondered who else might have known that Dee was looking to get her master's degree.

The admissions office was locked up tight by the time he got there. He made a note to himself in his notebook to call them in the morning. He was interested in who this Mr. Armstrong was and why he was acting as an adviser. He headed back to his Jeep, pulled out of the parking lot and headed down Eighth Avenue. Just as he got to Eighth Street, he had a crazy idea. He turned around and slowly drove back past the homes along Eighth Avenue. He spotted what he was looking for on the third house, and he pulled over to the curb and slid out.

The door was answered by a petite older woman with short gray hair. She looked at his ID, introduced herself as Elenore Williams and invited him in.

"Ma'am, I see you have one of those camera doorbells on your house. Do you pay the extra money to store the images from the doorbell on the cloud?"

It occurred to him that he almost sounded like he knew what he was talking about. This whole cloud thing was something he had only just recently learned about.

Mrs. Williams asked him to wait one minute, and she called a man's name up the stairs. The man turned out to be a boy who couldn't have been more than twelve or thirteen. She introduced her grandson Mathew to Buck and asked him about the cloud storage for the doorbell. He offered to access the storage for Buck, and they sat down in the living room while he ran and got his laptop.

Mathew sat next to Buck and pulled up a web page for the doorbell. He entered his password and pulled up the video storage from the camera.

"Can you go back to last Saturday between, say, seven and nine p.m. and see what cars drove by the house?"

"Sure can," said Mathew, and he clicked a couple of keys and found ten video files that had been recorded between those times. They hit pay dirt on the fourth video: Buck could see an old Subaru as it passed under the streetlight at the end of the driveway. They continued, and two minutes later, a white utility van, like the kind painters or plumber use, drove by. Buck could see two shadows through the windshield but couldn't make out features. He asked Mathew if he could forward the two video files to one of his coworkers, and he gave him the email address. Buck thanked Mathew and Mrs. Williams and headed for his Jeep.

He called Paul Webber and told him to expect the file and what he was looking for. He also asked him to see if he could run a computer check on Mr. Armstrong, who worked at the college. He didn't have much to go on, but he knew Paul had worked with less. He never knew how Paul or Bax found the information they were looking for on the computer, and he never asked. A friend of his once told him that sometimes things are better left unsaid, and when it came to computers, he always followed that advice. He slid into his Jeep and headed back to Cortez. Maybe today hadn't been a total waste of time.

Chapter Ten

Bax and Deputy Sage walked in through the sliding door of the grocery store and asked the clerk behind the service counter to call the manager. There were pictures of Dee on posters at the front of the store, with a description of her and the car. The number was a special line that the sheriff's department used for situations just like this. Bax had spotted the same posters in other stores and on every pole and building they passed. It seemed like the entire county was involved in the search.

The manager, Dolores, was a black woman of medium height with a full head of cornrows. She asked them to follow her, and she led them to a door at the side of the service counter. Inside the tight space was a large safe, an old metal desk and three office chairs. The fluorescent lights were bright enough to make Bax squint for a minute until her eyes adjusted. They each grabbed a chair in front of the desk, and Dolores sat behind the desk.

Deputy Sage spoke first. "Thanks for taking a minute, Dolores. I know you're busy."

"Not a problem, Scott. Dee is one of our family, and we will do whatever we need to, to help find her."

Bax clicked on the recording app on her phone and set it on the desk. "Dolores, can you tell us about Dee? The kind of employee she is, who her friends here are. Anything you think might be important or not."

"That's easy, Agent Baxter. Dee is a dream employee. She works her ass off. She doesn't complain when she has to stock shelves instead of working a register, and she's always willing to pick up an extra shift or switch shifts with someone else. I wish I had ten more like her."

"How long has she worked here?"

"She started right out of high school. I was the assistant manager back then. I remember when I interviewed her. She was very poised for a high school student with no work experience. I remember she promised me that if I were to hire her, she would never let me down, and she never has."

"Anything unusual happen the week before she disappeared? An argument with an employee or a customer? Lack of focus, nervous, concerned about something? Anything that was out of the ordinary."

Dolores thought for a minute. "Now that you mention it, the Saturday before she disappeared, she came in and she looked upset. I asked her about it, and she told me it was nothing important. I know she was in class all day, so if something happened it had to have been either at the college or on the way back here. I have no idea what it might have been, but it was odd. She was always so upbeat."

"I don't want you to take this wrong, but I have to ask. Have you noticed anything missing from the registers, and did anyone here pay more attention to her than you might think reasonable?"

Dolores laughed. "Dee was the most honest employee you could ever meet, but just in case, the sheriff had us do a complete financial audit after she went missing. Everything was in perfect order. Not a dime missing. As far as someone paying attention to her, I assume you are thinking romantically or sexually. The answer would also be no. Most of the older women working here have happy marriages, and the men I have here are either in high school or are retired. Besides, Dee loves Ronnie, and those kids are her entire life."

"Thanks, Dolores. We'd like to talk to some of her coworkers, especially the ones she was close to. Can we borrow this office for a little while, and can you direct her friends to us?"

Dolores told them that wouldn't be a problem, and she stepped through the door. A minute later, there was a knock on the door, and a middle-aged Native American woman stepped into the office and took Dolores's chair.

Maxine Graywolf had started a couple of weeks before Dee, and they became good friends. They often took lunch or dinner together, and they talked a lot while they were working. Bax went through the same kinds of questions with Maxine that she'd asked Dolores and got the same answers. Then she asked her about the Saturday before she disappeared.

Maxine gathered her thoughts before she spoke. "Something was bothering her, but she wouldn't say what it was. I asked her a couple of times if Ronnie and the kids were okay, and she told me to stop worrying. I respected her wishes and didn't ask again, but after dinner, when she came back to the register, her eyes were bloodshot, like she had been crying. I asked her again what was going on, but she completely ignored me for the rest of the shift. We didn't work together again until Monday afternoon, and by then, she was back to her old self, so I didn't ask further. Do you think if I had pushed her harder that she might not be missing?"

"Maxine. There's no way to know that," said Deputy Sage. "I don't want you to think that way."

They talked for a few more minutes, and then Maxine headed back for her shift. She said something that Bax thought interesting as she was walking out of the office.

"You know. If you're serious about the missing women, you might want to talk to the guy who runs the *Dolores Weekly Chronicle*. He's been interviewing people for years about the missing women, and I've heard he has gathered a ton of information. He might be willing to share."

Bax thanked her, but before she could ask Deputy Sage about the newspaper guy, the next employee was at the door, and this was the way it went for the rest of the day. By the time they were finished interviewing every employee, and even a couple of customers who wanted to help, the day was shot, and they were no closer to figuring out where Dee was.

They agreed to meet at the sheriff's office at

nine the next morning, and they would head over to interview Ronnie Hightower and some of his neighbors. Deputy Sage said good night and pulled out of the parking lot. Bax headed for the hotel. Buck had sent her a text and told her he was back, and that they should meet for dinner.

Before she pulled out of the parking lot, she pulled out her phone and called Paul Webber.

Paul answered right away. "Hey, Bax. What's up?"

"Paul, can you do me a favor? Can you pull up everything you can find on the *Dolores Weekly Chronicle* and see if you can get some background on the guy who owns it?"

"Is this guy a suspect?" asked Paul.

"No. But he might have some information about the missing women. One of the women we spoke with today said she heard he has been working on this for a long time and might have some useful information."

"No worries, Bax. Let me see what we can dig up, and I'll send you what we find."

"Great," said Bax. "How are the background checks coming?"

"I should have the phone logs tomorrow afternoon. The judge signed the warrant this morning. I sent some stuff to your email earlier today, and I also sent some stuff to Buck. Call if you need anything else."

Bax hung up and pulled her Jeep out of the parking lot. Tomorrow was going to be another busy day.

Chapter Eleven

The camp Lum Gladstone had decided on was in a small valley about a mile and a half northeast of Goose Lake, along Fisher Creek. It was an idyllic location with good tree cover, and the creek provided clean drinking water. Lum had chosen this valley after scouting the area over the three days he'd waited for the professor and his team of students to arrive. His biggest reason for choosing this area was the large amount of bear scat he'd found here. Just the day before, he had run off two black bears—a momma and her cub—and he saw several recent signs of predation.

The team had arrived with no further incidents, and everyone settled into their assigned tasks. The next couple of days were filled with scat collection, placing camera traps around the area and using a drone to look for active bears. They spotted several black bears in the area, but so far nothing that looked like a grizzly. The plan the professor and Lum had worked out over dinner the night before was to spread out and venture into some of the other valleys along the creek. They would continue to use the camp as their base camp, but the professor wanted to cover as much ground as possible in the short window they had to work in.

Professor Carmichael had passed out the day's

assignments following breakfast, and Lum had issued bear spray to each student and given them a brief safety lecture about hiking in bear country. As they spread out to their assigned areas of study, Lum cleaned up the camp. He planned to set out on foot and check on each group during the day. If they got to their assigned locations, the farthest he would need to travel was about six miles out and back. For a man with Lum's experience, that was a piece of cake. He spent a minute before setting out listening to his weather radio, which worked sporadically at best even though it was linked to a satellite.

"Professor," said Lum. "We may need to look at our schedule. The weather service is calling for a snowstorm. Should hit here about midnight tonight."

"How much snow are they predicting?"

"Couple inches right now, but you never know in these mountains. Could be nothing, could be a lot. I'd like to have everyone start back earlier than we planned so we can get the camp prepped."

"Good plan, Lum. Let's get them all back here by seven tonight. That gives us enough time to get ready?"

"You got it, Professor." Lum grabbed his coat and rifle and headed out. The professor looked at the sky. There wasn't a cloud to be seen, and everything was perfect, but he trusted Lum to make the right decision when it came to the safety of the group.

The professor started entering data from the trail cameras they had positioned over the past couple of days and read the notes Sandra Moore had made about her examination of the scat. There was nothing unusual in her notes. The scat contained mostly berries and some small rodents, but nothing significant. He sat back and scratched his head. Something was off, but he wasn't sure what it was. Everything they had uncovered so far said black bears were inhabiting the area, but the elk carcass Robert Meyers had stumbled on yesterday afternoon said larger predator. The elk was a good-sized buck and appeared healthy and fit. It had been brought down by a vicious attack, as the deep lacerations across its throat indicated.

The professor pulled up the pictures Robert had taken and enlarged them on his screen. He looked closely at the deep cuts and tears in each picture. Every bone in his body said this was not a black bear attack. He knew there were mountain lions in the area as well. Two had been spotted yesterday, but he thought it would be difficult for a lone mountain lion to bring down an elk that size. He looked at the pictures again and felt confident that this kill had been made by a tier-one predator. He wrote up his notes and put his laptop aside. He decided to take a look at the carcass himself, so he grabbed his map, GPS and bear spray and headed out.

Two hours of hiking led the professor to the GPS coordinates Robert had used to mark the location of the carcass, but as he looked around, he saw that there was no carcass. He did notice some blood on the ground, but where was the elk? If Robert's estimate was right, the elk weighed a couple hundred pounds, and bears don't typically carry off their kill; they just eat it where it falls. He figured a lion could have dragged it off, but he thought they would have torn it apart and just taken select pieces. There was no sign of dismemberment.

Not wanting to waste the hike, he started walking around the area, looking under downed trees and behind boulders. Having had no luck locating what was left of the elk and after bagging up a couple of samples of scat he found, he was ready to head back to camp, when he got this odd feeling. The first thing he noticed was the silence. The wind had kicked up, and the sky had started to fill with dark clouds, but it was the lack of bird or insect sounds that threw him. Everything around him had grown silent.

The feeling of paranoia came on without any warning. It was like a sound, but not a sound from the outside world. This sound was like a low hum, and it felt like it came from inside his head. He put his fingers in his ears and blew out through his nose in an attempt to clear his head, but it didn't help. The panic increased at the same rate the headache increased. He looked around, trying to get his bearings. The pain was intense, and he wondered if he was having some kind of brain aneurysm. Nothing was making any sense, and he was having trouble focusing. His eyes hurt, and his vision blurred, and then he saw shadowy creatures coming out of the woods towards him. He needed to hide, so he started running and ducking behind trees, but the creatures were still coming.

His entire body felt like it was on fire, and he pulled off his jacket so he could scratch his arms to try to stop the itching, but nothing he did would make it stop. He ripped off his shirt and found a stick on the ground and started ripping at his skin with the stick, leaving bloody streaks down his arms and across his chest, but the burning continued. He felt like his blood was boiling, and he couldn't make it stop. He raced into the woods, crashing through the undergrowth and tearing his exposed skin even more. He was having more trouble seeing, and he fell into a deep ravine and slammed his head into the tree.

* * *

Lum got back to camp with Kendra just as the first snowflakes started to fly. The wind had kicked up throughout the afternoon, and the storm hit a lot earlier than predicted. Kendra had been in the valley farthest from the camp, and as soon as he got there, he knew something was wrong. She was sitting on the ground with a look of fear in her eyes. She looked up as he approached and asked him if he heard the humming. Oddly enough, he'd had a strange tingling across his body the entire afternoon but shook it off as nothing to worry about. Once he saw Kendra, he got concerned. He got her to her feet, grabbed her backpack and headed back towards camp. He didn't like the look of the sky, and he was worried about Kendra. She appeared dazed or confused. Halfway back to camp, he had to take her arm and help her move. Then his vision got blurry, and he felt hot.

James, Robert, and Sandra had gotten back to camp before them and were huddled in one tent. They could sense that they were being watched and they had tied down the rain tarp, so they couldn't see outside, which meant whoever was watching them couldn't see inside. They huddled in their sleeping bags. Robert was sitting up in his bag, and he held his Swiss Army knife out in front of him to fend off anyone or anything that came through the tent flap. His eyes were as wide as saucers, and he looked from side to side as if trying to focus on the threat.

Lum was able to calm everyone down for the moment. He put Kendra in the tent with them, and then he went in search of his satellite phone, and the professor. He stopped for a minute and tried to clear the fog from his head. He hadn't seen Dom in the tent with the others. He ran over to Dom's tent and flung open the flaps. The tent was empty, and it occurred to his foggy mind that he hadn't seen Dom in his assigned area earlier in the day. He tried to think about what to do, but he was getting nowhere. He ran to the professor's tent and looked inside. It, too, was empty. None of this was making any sense. Where were Dom and the professor? Had they gone off together? Had someone or something abducted them? His mind raced, but no answers were forthcoming.

The snow was coming down hard and fast, and the wind made visibility impossible. Lum raced to his tent and found his phone, but he couldn't get anyone to answer him. He might have had better luck if he'd turned it on, but his mind was racing and getting nowhere fast. He needed to find the professor. He dropped the phone onto his sleeping bag, next to his rifle, and headed off deeper into the mountains. As he left camp, he thought he heard his horse whinny, but he didn't have time to check on her or the two mules. He had a job to do. He had people to find. He pulled his hat tighter onto his head to keep it from blowing away in the wind, pulled up the collar on his open coat and ran off deeper into the valley.

The storm raged all night, and by the next morning, there was over two feet of heavy, wet snow on the ground. The valley looked beautiful in the early morning light, but there was no one around to see it.

Chapter Twelve

Dom Rivera knew what he was searching for; he just had no idea where to find it. He had been searching for years, and this seemed like his best shot. When he'd joined Professor Carmichael's team, he knew he would need to break away from the group and search on his own. He just picked the worst day to do it.

Even though he was there to help with logistics and serve in a security capacity, he was essentially a gopher. He wasn't a PhD student like the rest of the team; he wasn't a college student at all. He had spent five years in the army, before receiving an "Other Than Honorable" discharge. He never discussed what led to the OTH, but it made it difficult to get a job. He'd been doing odd jobs around the campus when he got to talking with Professor Carmichael.

He had heard the professor was mounting a small expedition into the Weminuche Wilderness, and he had a strong need to get there himself. He offered to help the professor with whatever needed doing in exchange for being made part of the team. When he explained his reason for wanting to be on the team, the professor agreed to help him with his search and made the decision to keep Dom's background, and his reason, quiet. This was a two-week trip, and he needed to keep a certain amount of harmony amongst his team. He was concerned his students might see Dom in a different light if they knew why he was there.

That morning before the team woke up, Dom had grabbed his GPS, his Google Earth photos and his topo map and headed out of camp. He had two reasons for heading out that morning. The first was part of his job. He had seen the pictures from the game cameras of the mysterious creature, or whatever it was, that seemed to be following them, and he took it upon himself to see if he could figure out whether it was a creature, or if it was some kind of defect in the cameras. He planned to backtrack to the last camera and see what he might find in the area where the image had appeared.

The second reason was personal. Dom never knew his grandfather, but over the years, he'd heard stories of a self-taught engineer who was involved in some of the most cutting-edge technology of his day. His grandfather had been an engineer for AT&T back in the sixties and seventies. He was supposedly working on a top-secret program with the military when he disappeared while on a helicopter flight in the area around Creede. His family had no idea why he was even in the Creede area since he worked at Bell Laboratories in Denver. The helicopter was never found, and the military were not the most cooperative people when it came to looking for his body. Dom's parents wanted closure and never got it, so Dom had decided to take on the challenge of finding the chopper after his dad died.

His grandmother never spoke of his grandfather's work. Dom had been reviewing some of her financial records in preparation to sell her house and move her to a memory care unit in a local nursing home when he stumbled on a mystery. His grandfather had had a one-hundred-thousand-dollar life insurance policy, which was a lot of money back then, but that money wasn't used to pay off their mortgage after he disappeared. Dom couldn't find any mortgage information at all. It was like the money suddenly disappeared, and his grandmother was unwilling to offer an explanation.

He knew his grandparents were not wealthy people and that their only real asset was their home, but when he looked through his grandmother's financial records, two years back, he discovered an account worth over a million dollars. He was stunned, and no one in the family, including his parents, could explain where all that money had come from. His grandmother was no help in finding out anything about the account since she had very few lucid moments anymore.

Dom started wondering if the money was some kind of payoff, to keep her quiet about what her husband was working on. He decided to try to find the helicopter and maybe get some answers. It was tough going at first because there was no information anywhere to explain why an AT&T communications engineer from Denver was traveling in a helicopter in the mountains of

Colorado. Over the years, Dom filed numerous Freedom of Information requests but got nothing from the military. He tried AT&T, which had by now broken up into numerous phone companies and was equally stonewalled.

The use of online satellite mapping services made his search easier, and he spent countless hours looking at satellite images of the areas around Creede. He settled on three possible locations from images that appeared to show some kind of metallic objects, and he decided to investigate those areas. That was the arrangement he worked out with the professor.

Dom wished he had checked the weather before he left camp. They had talked about a snowstorm coming in, but he figured he'd be back in camp before it hit. It hit earlier than expected. He had backtracked to the location of the last camera but found nothing in the area that could explain the fuzzy image in the pictures. He did see a huge black bear, but she was too far off. It was the biggest bear he had ever seen—not that he was an expert on bears—so he decided to steer clear and head for the coordinates from his search.

He reached the coordinates by midafternoon and realized that he was a long ways from camp. He hadn't brought anything with him other than his coat, a backpack with some water and a couple of snacks. He looked at the dark gray clouds and knew his time was limited. He dropped his backpack at the edge of a clearing and started his search.

The snow started an hour later, and once it

started, it never stopped. Cold and frustrated, he looked at his meager finds. He'd found a couple of pieces of what looked like curved plastic and a couple of small pieces of metal that looked burned, but he didn't find what he was looking for. He put the pieces in his backpack and started hiking. He hoped he would make it back to the camp before the worst of the storm hit.

The snow worsened as the late afternoon wore on, and he decided that his best bet was to find some kind of shelter and wait out the storm. With the wind howling and the snow falling in sheets, he realized he was hopelessly lost. He was also having trouble seeing. The snow blindness hit him all of a sudden, and he stopped walking and realized he was in real trouble. He kept stumbling around looking for shelter through blurry eyes, never realizing he was walking in circles. Unable to go any farther, Dom sat down in the snow, with his back to a tree. He said a silent goodbye to his family and closed his eyes.

* * *

The hikers who found his body told the Forest Service ranger they encountered on the trail that had the man traveled straight ahead for another fifty yards, he would have found a pile of rocks that created a small sheltered area, and he might have survived the storm.

The search and rescue team reported that the area around the body was littered with debris from what looked like a small helicopter crash. The information was passed on to Bill Wagner, who had checked Forest Service and FAA records and found no information about any missing helicopters in that area, going as far back as the 1950s. He noted the crash site and the coordinates in his report and noted that a preliminary search of the area did not find any human remains. He wrote it off as another unidentified crash site.

Chapter Thirteen

Buck and Bax sat at a table for four in the back corner of the small restaurant. Bax had her laptop open on the table next to her bottle of beer, and Buck had his notebook out and was sipping from his glass of Coke.

Paul Webber had uploaded the video clips from the doorbell camera Buck had sent him to the case file, along with a note that he had sent it down to the tech guys to see if they could improve the image. He was able to determine that there was no one in the car with Dee Hightower when she left the college. The utility van had dark tinted windows, so making out faces, or even accurately determining if there were one or two people in the van, was proving difficult.

Bax was looking through the deep dive material Paul had loaded into the case file. He had gotten a lot of information in a short time, but she wasn't sure if any of it was going to be useful. She was just about to turn her laptop around so Buck could see what she was looking at when the waitress brought their meals. She closed the lid. The burritos were large and looked delicious. They both dug in and made small talk while they ate.

Bax slid her plate away, opened the cover on her

laptop and pulled up the data from Paul. She turned it so Buck could see it.

"We don't have their phone records yet, but their social media posts are mostly pictures of kids and food. Looks like Dee is quite the cook. There's a couple of posts from Ronnie looking for thoughts about gifts for their upcoming anniversary, and some rather bland political comments. Nothing crazy."

"Did Paul get anything off the dark web?"

"Not so far. That might take a little longer. He also ran her name to see if anything popped up that wasn't on their pages. A couple of crude comments about her being missing: you know the kind. Probably ran off with another guy. That kind of stuff, and a couple of negative posts about Native Americans, but nothing I would call suspicious."

"Was he able to look into Scott Sage?"

Bax clicked a couple of keys. "Sage spent four years as a marine, right out of high school. He joined the sheriff's office five years ago and has a spotless record. All in all, seems like a decent guy. Married, two kids, and oddly enough, no social media presence."

Buck changed the subject. "Anything from the interviews at the store and with her friends?"

"Nothing that gives me pause. Everyone liked her; she was a hard worker. Only thing that stood out was that she seemed upset to her friends the Saturday night before she disappeared. She wouldn't talk to anyone about it, but they thought she had been crying?"

Buck looked up from his apple pie and vanilla ice cream. "I got the same story from a friend of hers at the college. Said she argued in the parking lot after class with Mr. Armstrong. According to the young woman, Armstrong is not a teacher, but works in admin, and was supposedly trying to help her get into grad school. The young lady said that from where she was standing, it sounded like she missed a couple of delivery dates for her application. I tried to track this guy down, but the admin office was closed. I asked Paul to see what he could find."

"So, it doesn't sound like we made much progress today, other than the videos. And at this point, we don't know if those are helpful or not."

"Yeah, not too much. Tell me about this newspaper guy."

"All I have," said Bax, "is that he owns the *Dolores Weekly Chronicle*, and he has been researching the disappearance of the Native American women for some time and is supposed to have a large collection of information. I was going to run up and see him tomorrow morning. Thought we could head down to Towaoc when I get back and talk to Ronnie and his friends."

"Okay. Let's call it a night and see what tomorrow brings. I'm gonna read through the files on the three missing women tonight. I'll look through everything Paul sent, and we can cover this more at breakfast in the morning."

They stood up and each placed a twenty under their plates. They thanked the waitress as they headed towards the door, climbed into their Jeeps and headed for the hotel.

Chapter Fourteen

Buck sat at the desk in his hotel room and read through the entire case file. He also read the reports the sheriff had given them about the two other missing women. He took a drink from his now-warm Coke and sat back in the chair. Something wasn't making sense. The little bug that ran around in his brain during an investigation was there, but it wasn't dancing around, more like just sitting there on the periphery. He hated when that happened. He picked up the first report and then set it back on the desk. Maybe he was looking at it all wrong. He closed his eyes and cleared his head.

After a few minutes, he opened his eyes, and the problem was right there in front of him, and he knew what he had been doing wrong. He had been looking at the victims as Native American women, and they were all lumped together into the mystery of hundreds of native women who had vanished. He'd let all the stories, theories and conjectures cloud his judgment. What he needed to do was look at each woman as a separate victim—not clouded by being Native American, but just a female crime victim. He pulled up the file on Dee Hightower and started reading again, only this time he didn't see her as Native American, just as a woman.

Another two hours passed before he put down

Dee's file. He felt he had a better handle on who she was, and that made him smile. Now what he needed to do was reread the other reports but follow the same investigative track. He felt better about how the day had gone now that he had a little more clarity. He took out his notepad, tore off the page he had started for each woman and began again.

He didn't realize how late it had gotten when he stopped reading the last file. He looked at the clock and knew he should get some sleep, but he felt he was on to something, and the little bug in his brain was moving around a lot more than it had earlier that evening.

Dee Hightower was much more than a Native American woman. She was a devoted wife and mother, a hard-working employee, a good friend, a top-notch student and a woman with drive and ambition. She wanted to take what she had learned in college and put it into practice helping other women on the reservation who might be going through troubling times, and she wanted to take her education to the next level. This woman was not content to just sit on her ass. She had something to prove.

The woman who'd disappeared from the county a year or so before was none of those things. She was unemployed, a high school dropout who had repeatedly been in trouble with the law. She was younger than Dee by seven years, and she had two children by two different men, and both children were being raised in the foster care system. She'd disappeared after a long night of drinking and drug use, and she was last seen in the company of several men, heading for a party they'd heard about. She arrived at the party okay but was never seen again.

The third woman had disappeared three years before Dee. She was barely a high school graduate, passing through her senior year by the skin of her teeth. She was living with a guy ten years her senior, and they had two children. She was underemployed, working as a part-time cleaner at a restaurant in Cortez. She smoked a little dope, did an occasional line of coke and drank a lot. She disappeared one night after fighting with her . . . Buck wasn't sure what to call him. Boyfriend didn't seem to fit. Maybe common-law husband, lover or something else. He wasn't sure what the appropriate title was nowadays. Anyway, they had a fight that caused some of their neighbors to take notice, and everyone agreed she left the house on foot. No one, including her man, knew where she was headed, but when she didn't come home the next morning, people began to worry. For some odd reason, it took her man four days to call the Cortez Police and report her missing. No sign of her was found in the area, and she joined a long list of the disappeared.

Buck sat back in the chair. The only thing these three women had in common was that they were Native American. From everything Bax had told him over the past year about these women, Dee didn't fit the profile. The little bug was dancing now, and Buck knew he was on to something. Dee Hightower didn't disappear because she was a

Native American woman. She disappeared for a different reason altogether, and now he had a case he could work. All he had to do now was figure out what that reason was.

He closed the case file, shut down his laptop and finished his Coke. He showered and crawled into bed. With any luck, he could still get a couple of hours of sleep.

Buck's alarm clock went off way too early, and he wanted to shut it off and grab a few more hours of sleep, but he had to meet Bax for breakfast and then head down to Towaoc and interview Ronnie Hightower. He got up, shook the empty can of Coke next to the bed to see if there was anything left, showered and dressed. He clipped his badge and gun to his belt, grabbed his light CBI nylon jacket and headed out the door.

Bax was already sitting at the back table at the restaurant when he walked in. He smiled at the hostess and headed for the table. Before he sat down, the waitress brought over a glass of Coke and a heaping plate of scrambled eggs and bacon. Buck smiled at Bax, thanked the waitress and sat down.

"Thanks for ordering for me."

"No worries. I was doing some thinking last night, and I think we have been looking at this case all wrong. I don't think this is related to the other disappearances."

"Shit, Bax, great minds. I stayed up half the night rereading the files because nothing about this case was making sense to me. The only common denominator is that all the women were Native American, but I don't think that's a factor in this case."

Bax took a forkful of eggs and washed it down with black coffee. "Do you think I was too focused on the Native American connection and slowed us down?"

"Look, Bax. The missing women are something you have been following for a long time, and you finally got the chance to investigate a recent disappearance, instead of women who have been missing for years. It made sense to start there. We needed to cover that part of it, but you have good instincts, and no one can ever fault you for not looking at all the facts. Now we need to figure out the way forward."

"Do you think I should still talk to the newspaper guy in Dolores?"

"Yeah. From what you said, he's been looking into these disappearances for a long time now, so we might get some good insight out of him. Besides, we still have those other two women to look into, so we might as well use the time we have down here to check out those cases as well."

They discussed each of their reasons for not believing this disappearance was part of a larger pattern, and they brainstormed what they hoped to gain by interviewing Ronnie and some of their friends. They were just settling their bill with the waitress when Bax's phone rang, and she answered it.

"Hold on a minute," she said, and she pointed

a finger towards the door. Buck nodded, and she walked out. Buck left a generous tip for the waitress and got a big smile in exchange as he grabbed his and Bax's backpacks and headed towards the door.

Bax was just hanging up as he stepped onto the sidewalk. Her face was hard to read.

"What?" said Buck.

"They found Dee's car. That was Scott Sage. We need to go. I'll text you the GPS coordinates. Scott said it's in an easy spot to miss."

She grabbed her backpack, and they headed for the Jeeps. Buck pulled out his phone, looked at the coordinates and slid into the driver's seat. Bax was already pulling out of the parking lot with her flashers on.

Buck called the CBI office in Grand Junction and told them to roll the forensic unit. He gave them the coordinates Bax had sent him, then he started his Jeep, hit his flashers, and pulled out of the lot. The coordinates, according to the navigation system, looked to be in the middle of nowhere. He scrolled the map in all directions and couldn't find any roads in the area. He hit the gas and caught up to Bax, and they headed south from Cortez on Highway 491 towards Towaoc.

Chapter Fifteen

The drive seemed to take forever as they cruised along on gravel roads that had numbers like 254 and 256. It felt like they had driven a hundred miles and Buck was certain they were lost until he spotted a cloud of dust, and as they came over a small rise, he spotted a procession of pickup trucks of all makes and sizes, each truck full of men and women, many carrying rifles. The procession turned through an old barbed wire fence and started down a road. Well, not much of a road. More like two bare dirt strips through the scrub. It must have been an old farm road.

He spotted the flashing lights of a Montezuma sheriff's SUV as the procession of trucks fanned out in the empty scrub field, parked and everyone climbed out. Bax pulled alongside the SUV, and Buck pulled in next to her. He climbed out of his Jeep, grabbed his backpack and headed to where Scott Sage and another deputy were trying to hold back an ever-moving wave of humanity.

Buck was able to get ahead of the crowd and, using his most authoritative voice, yelled for everyone to stop moving.

"This is a crime scene," he yelled. "You have just destroyed any tracks we might have found on the way here. Stop moving and get off the trail."

The crowd stopped moving and stepped away from the two-track trail.

"Deputy," he said, looking at Deputy Sage. "Hold everyone back until we see what we have. Where's the car?"

Deputy Sage pointed towards a ravine that looked like it ran all the way to the base of Ute Mountain. Buck looked around. Ute Mountain, or the sleeping Ute Mountains, stood out like a monument over the flat scrub fields. His first thought was that whoever dumped the car had to know the area. They were literally in the middle of nowhere.

Ute Mountain is the tallest peak in a cluster making up the Ute Mountains, a small mountain range visible for miles. Although less than ten thousand feet tall, Ute Mountain is listed as the eighth most prominent peak in Colorado because of its isolation.

One of several Ute legends has it that the mountain range is the body of a warrior God who is sleeping with his arms crossed, recovering from wounds he suffered in a great battle against "the Evil Ones." The mountain range is still considered a sacred place.

Buck and Bax left the deputies to deal with the crowd and, walking slightly off the two tracks, headed in the direction Deputy Sage had pointed. They found the car on its side at the bottom of the ravine, about a hundred yards from where Buck had stopped the crowd.

Making a wide circle around the car so as not

to disturb any prints or tracks they might find, they walked around the car, taking pictures. Bax found the first set of boot prints and took a series of close-up photos. She set a marker next to the prints and continued. They met back at their starting point.

"We need to check the car and make sure Dee isn't in it. We are not going to be able to hold that crowd off for much longer. Those folks want to help, but they are not going to sit still."

Buck walked back up the ravine a ways and crossed over to the far side. He figured whoever had dumped the car most likely did it from the track, so if he went down to the car from the other side, he shouldn't disturb any evidence.

"Bax. Use your phone on video and follow me from there."

Bax nodded, set her camera to video and waved for him to go ahead. Buck slid into the ravine, climbed up the opposite side and walked back to the car. He climbed down the side of the ravine and stopped at the car. Looking up at Bax to make sure she was filming, he looked in the side windows that were facing the sky. The back hatch had flipped open when the car hit bottom. He got down on his stomach and slid under the hatch. He slid back out, climbed back up the far ravine wall and followed his trail back to Bax, dusting himself off as he went.

"The car's empty. No sign of her phone or laptop." They heard someone approaching and turned to see Deputy Sage followed by a fair-skinned man of about thirty-five or so, with black hair pulled back in a long ponytail.

"Agents, this is Ronnie Hightower. I tried to stop him, but he insisted, so I thought it best that I come with him."

Buck looked at Ronnie and then at the deputy. "No worries, Deputy." He walked up to Ronnie and reached out his hand. "Buck Taylor, CBI. Mr. Hightower, can you confirm that this is your car?"

"Yes, sir." He paused for a minute. "Is my wife in there?"

"No, sir. She's not."

Ronnie Hightower looked relieved. If his wife wasn't in the car, then she might still be alive. He had to believe that for the sake of his kids. Buck asked Bax to stay with Ronnie, and he asked the deputy to follow him.

"Can you get Ronnie back to your office so we can interview him?"

"Sure can," said Deputy Sage.

"Good. Have the other deputy stay here until the forensic team arrives. It will be a couple of hours. Make sure he keeps all these folks back. There is nothing they can do here. Who found the car?"

"Couple locals, out dove hunting. I know them both, and they are stand-up guys. I recorded their statements and sent them on their way. We can bring them in if you want to talk to them, but they don't know anything other than what you see."

"Okay. Download their statements and send them to Bax's phone. Let's head back to the office and talk to Ronnie."

They walked back to where Bax was talking softly to Ronnie. "Ronnie," said Buck. "Deputy

Sage is going to bring you back to the sheriff's office so we can find out some more information about your wife. In the meantime, I have a forensic team on their way down to go through the car and see if they can find anything that will help find Dee."

"Buck, what do you want to do with this crowd?" asked Deputy Sage. He pointed down the road towards the pickup trucks. "They all want to help. Dee is family."

Buck thought for a minute and looked around the area. "Can you get a couple more deputies or reserve deputies down here? Let's start a search. Use the car as the center point and cover all directions out about a mile. I know these mountains are sacred to the Ute people. Are there any official or unofficial ceremonial sites near here?"

Deputy Sage walked off towards the crowd and spoke with an older gentleman standing by the closest truck. They spoke for a few minutes, and then he walked back to Buck.

"The chairman says there are a couple of sites, some that are no longer used. He will take a couple of trucks with him and head out to search those areas."

"Great. One more thing. Make sure they understand that they are not to touch anything they find that is out of the ordinary or doesn't belong there. Same with the searchers here. Anything they find, mark it and leave it for the forensic guys."

Deputy Sage walked back to his patrol car and called the office. He walked back to Buck, stopping first to talk with the other deputy. "Sheriff will have a dozen people here in about an hour. In the meantime, Chris"—he pointed to the other deputy—"will get this group organized and start the search."

Ronnie nodded his head and walked off with Deputy Sage. He looked devastated, like a man without hope. Buck had seen a lot of family members look that way after finding out a loved one had been involved in a crime, and it never got any easier. He felt terrible for Ronnie, and he hoped they could find a happy ending somewhere out here in the vast emptiness. At least that's what his heart was telling him. His head, on the other hand, wasn't as confident.

Chapter Sixteen

Buck had just pulled into the parking lot at the sheriff's department when his phone rang. The display on his entertainment console said Kevin Jackson.

"Yes, sir," said Buck.

"Hey, Buck. How are things going in Cortez?"

Buck filled him in on the investigation so far and explained the conversation that he and Bax had had at breakfast and their belief that this abduction was not part of the larger missing women's cases. He also told him about finding Dee Hightower's car.

"Any reason to believe that the car being found near Ute Mountain might change your thoughts that this is not part of the larger problem?"

"I still don't think so, sir. Ute Mountain is still sacred to the Utes, and whoever dumped the car knew the area, but it doesn't change the fact that Dee Hightower doesn't fit the profile. We could certainly be wrong, but I think we're on the right track now. We'll have to see what the forensic team finds. That will give us more insight. We are getting ready to interview the husband."

"Any reason to doubt his story?" asked the director.

"Not so far. He seemed genuinely broken up when we found the car. Paul is still running background, and we are waiting on their phone logs, which we should get today, but like everything else, we will treat him as a suspect until we can clear him."

"Okay, now, the reason for my call. Can Bax cover this case for a day or two?"

"Yes, sir. I can call Paul and have him run down here to give her a hand if needed. What's going on?"

"Good. The governor got a strange call from one of the county commissioners in Mineral County. A group working on a survey of some kind got caught in the snowstorm last week, and they have four dead and three missing. The autopsies came back a little odd, and I guess it's attracted a lot of attention, which has descended on Creede. He'd like you to run up there and see if there is anything we need to deal with or if the locals can handle it."

Over the last couple of years, Buck had become the "go-to" guy when the governor needed a case handled with discretion. Buck had made the governor look good on several occasions, and he was now in high demand. Both the governor and Director Jackson knew that Buck would never get involved in anything political, and they both accepted the fact that he would follow the evidence, wherever it led him, and he would not tolerate any interference. They were both okay with that, and so far, they hadn't violated that trust.

"Sir, in what way were the autopsies odd?"

"I'll send you copies of the reports. I'd rather you look at them yourself. If you don't think there's anything there, let me know and head back to Cortez. If there is something there, then go ahead and sort it out. Let me know what you need once you get there, and I'll get it taken care of. And Buck, be careful."

The director hung up, and Buck sat back in his Jeep and thought about the conversation they'd just had. It wasn't like the director to be so cryptic. Buck wondered what kind of odd things he was going to find in the autopsies, and he wondered who was descending on Creede.

Buck grabbed his backpack, entered the front door of the sheriff's department, flashed his credentials and was buzzed through the lobby door. He found Bax, Deputy Sage and Ronnie Hightower sitting in a conference room. He had called Bax on the way back to Cortez and asked her to set him up in that room instead of an interview room. He wanted Ronnie comfortable.

Buck set his backpack on the floor next to the conference room table and pulled out his notebook. Bax had her laptop open and was accessing a recording app.

They offered Ronnie coffee, water or a soft drink, but he refused. Buck pulled a bottle of Coke out of his backpack and set it on the table.

Buck explained that they were going to read Ronnie his Miranda rights and then just have a conversation about him and Dee and their life together. Ronnie nodded.

Bax read him his rights off the Miranda card, slid a consent form in front of him and asked him if he was okay talking to them, or did he want a lawyer present? He was about to answer when a large Native American man wearing a suit and a white Stetson pushed open the door. He wasn't large in the sense of being overweight but stood six inches taller than Buck and had at least sixty pounds on him. He set his briefcase on the table and looked at the form in front of Ronnie.

"He won't be needing that form, young lady. My name is James Windsong, and I will be representing Mr. Hightower during this inquiry. I understand the urgency of the situation, but I want to make sure my client's rights are protected, as I am certain you do as well." He sat down in the chair next to Ronnie and removed a small voice recorder from his briefcase, turned it on and set it on the table. "You may begin your questioning, Agent Taylor, but I will stop Mr. Hightower from answering anything I find troublesome."

Buck had dealt with way too many lawyers during his career in law enforcement, so the sudden appearance of Mr. Windsong didn't bother him. What did concern him was, when had Ronnie had time to call an attorney, since he was with Deputy Sage the entire time, from when they left the abandoned car until they got to the station? He looked at Bax, and she gave him a slightly raised eyebrow, so she must have been thinking the same thing.

Buck went through the formality of identifying everyone in the room for the audio recorders and then sat back in his seat.

"Ronnie—can I call you Ronnie?" He looked at the attorney, who nodded. "I know you've been over this with a lot of people, but could you tell us about the night Dee disappeared?"

Buck had pulled out his laptop and opened the original police report that was taken by Deputy Sage on the morning following the disappearance, when this became a police matter. He already knew what was in the report, having read it several times, and he would look at it only if something Ronnie said didn't jive with the report. Otherwise, his focus would be on Ronnie.

Ronnie explained about getting the text from Dee that she was on her way home from Durango. He said that when he got her text from Mancos, he got the kids settled into bed. He knew she would get home before they fell asleep, and he didn't want her to have to deal with getting them ready for bed. He sat down in front of the TV and didn't have any recollection of falling asleep until he woke up around one a.m. He checked his bedroom to see if Dee had come home and decided not to wake him. He checked the garage for her Subaru and then called his sister-in-law to see if she could come over and watch the kids so he could look for Dee's car. His sister-in-law quickly organized a search party of their friends and neighbors, and then she and Scott, Deputy Sage, showed each volunteer where to search. By morning they hadn't found her car, so they began again after breakfast with additional searchers.

Ronnie stopped to catch his breath and asked for a glass of water.

"Ronnie," said Buck. "Do you often fall asleep on the couch when your wife isn't home?" The lawyer started to stir, and he looked at Buck, then he looked at Ronnie and nodded.

"Sometimes. I worked on a paving project that day and came home wiped out. I had a beer with dinner, and it must have hit me harder than I thought."

"You must be pretty proud of Dee, what with graduating college? That's quite an accomplishment. Did you have any concerns with her taking classes at Fort Lewis?"

"Not really. Most of her classes were online, so she worked on them while the kids were in school. It was just this last semester when she had to take a couple weekend classes that weren't offered online. Since she was on campus during the day, I guess I never really thought about it."

"Did she have any concerns during the week or so approaching her disappearance? Anything bothering her, any problems at school?"

"Not really," said Ronnie.

"What about her behavior in the weeks before. Anything about her different? You know. Less talkative, lack of focus, easier to piss off. Anything like that?"

Ronnie thought for a minute and then told them that he hadn't noticed any change in her behavior. Buck asked a few general questions about the kids and school and Ronnie's job, and then he got to the questions he felt were most important.

"Ronnie. I need to ask you three questions that might be hard to hear. You can talk with your attorney before you answer, but when you do answer, I need you to be as honest as possible."

He waited a second to see if the lawyer was going to object, but Buck figured the lawyer knew these were coming. Ronnie nodded okay.

"Ronnie, is it possible that Dee left on her own? Could she have a boyfriend or girlfriend, or could she be involved with drugs, or something else?"

Ronnie looked at the attorney, who nodded. "No, sir," he said. "We have a good marriage, and she would never leave our kids."

"Okay, Ronnie, that's good. Is there any chance that Dee might try to hurt herself?"

Ronnie got visibly upset. "You think Dee killed herself?"

The lawyer put his hand on Ronnie's shoulder. "It's okay, Ronnie. They have to ask."

Ronnie looked at the lawyer and then at Buck. "Dee would never hurt herself. We're Catholic. It goes against our religion."

Buck's next question came fast before Ronnie had a chance to calm down. "Did you kill Dee or hurt her in any way?"

Ronnie bounced out of the chair. "Fuck you, man. You think I killed my wife?" The lawyer was out of the chair and had his arms wrapped around him. He looked at Buck. "Can you give us a minute?"

Buck, Bax and Deputy Sage stepped out into the hall. Deputy Sage did not appear pleased, and he glared at Buck. "This was supposed to be a conversation, not an interrogation. What the hell?"

"Scott," said Bax. "We wouldn't be doing our jobs if we didn't ask the hard questions. I know Ronnie is your friend, but you need to calm down and be a cop. You're not here as his friend."

The lawyer stepped out into the hall. "He's calmed down. Can we wrap this up soon? He's pretty fragile right now."

They walked back into the room. Ronnie was sitting calmly, wiping tears out of his eyes. He looked at Buck and Bax. "I'm sorry, sir, about the outburst. I didn't hurt my wife in any way or cause her to leave. I love her with all my heart." Tears fell from his eyes, and he used a napkin to wipe them.

"Thanks, Ronnie. That's all we need for now."

He closed his laptop and placed it in his backpack while Bax did the same. They shook hands with the lawyer and left the room. Buck led Bax into a small empty office and closed the door. They discussed the interview for a few minutes, both agreeing that Ronnie probably had nothing to do with the disappearance, and then he told her about the call from Director Jackson.

"What do you think is going on in Creede?" asked Bax.

"I have no idea. If all goes well, I should be back sometime tomorrow. You gonna be okay here?"

"Yeah. I'll be fine. I am going to run up and talk to the newspaper guy, and I'll call Paul and see if he has anything on the phone logs or on the video of the van you sent him."

"Good. Keep things close to the vest around Sage. I'm concerned about what led Ronnie to call a lawyer, and my gut says it was on Sage's advice. You need anything while I'm gone, go to Reuben. I'll call you tonight."

Buck stopped by the sheriff's office to let him know he'd be back as soon as he could, then he walked out to his Jeep and pulled out of the parking lot. He had no idea what he was walking into.

Chapter Seventeen

Buck slowed down as he turned onto Main Street from East Seventh Street. It had been several years since he had been in Creede, Colorado, and he was stunned by what he saw. Creede is the county seat of Mineral County and usually has a population of about three hundred, but today the streets were packed with people. There seemed to be tents in every open space and lots of RVs and vans with stickers about bigfoot, UFO abductions, chemtrails, gun rights, and every kind of conspiracy you can imagine.

He followed Main Street until he came to the Mineral County Sheriff's Office, parked in the dirt lot across the street and walked over. He found Sheriff Carl Butcher sitting in his office with a black plastic walking cast on his foot, propped up on a small embroidered stool.

The sheriff looked up from his computer screen. "Buck Taylor. My god, it must be ten years since I saw you last."

He started to stand, but Buck waved him down, walked into the office and shook hands. "Carl, what happened?"

"Broke my damn ankle playing catch with my grandsons. Tried to show off some of those old high school moves, with 'old' being the operative word.

Planted my foot and tried to zag, but my foot stayed where it was. Clean break. Doc says a couple of weeks, and I should be good as new. They told me they were sending someone from your office, but they didn't say it was you."

"I was in Cortez on a case and was the closest person available. What's with all the people in town? Looks like one of those Comic-Con conventions you see on the news. The director said something about odd autopsy reports for a couple lost hikers and that there were a lot of people around, but he didn't tell me any of this."

"Yeah," said the sheriff. "Guess he wanted you to be surprised. Grab a chair. Can I get you anything?"

"How 'bout I get you something? Coke still in the little refrigerator, and you want another coffee?"

Buck took the sheriff's cup and walked out to the little refrigerator in the corner. Grabbed a Coke, poured a cup of coffee and headed back to the office. He set the cup down, took a big gulp from the Coke can and sat down.

"Where's Brenda? She wasn't at the counter when I came in."

"She ran out for a late lunch. She'll be back in a bit. So how ya been? Heard about your wife passing a couple of years back. You doin' okay?"

Buck filled the sheriff in on the last couple of years and about Lucy's death after battling metastatic breast cancer. After all this time, he still found himself getting choked up, even though they'd known it was coming. He still missed Lucy every day. They say that time heals all wounds, but Buck wasn't sure that was the case when you lost your closest friend. He decided to change the subject.

"So, what's going on in town? The director was unusually cryptic on the phone."

"Couple weeks back, a group of college students from CU and their professor, fella by the name of Dale Carmichael, headed into the Weminuche to look for grizzly bears. They were supposed to be gone two weeks. They never showed up after the big storm, and we mobilized our search and rescue team, hooked up with the Forest Service and went looking for them."

He slid some pictures he'd printed off over to Buck. "Those are pictures of the campsite we found. Place was destroyed by the heavy snow." He handed Buck a couple more pictures. "These are the four bodies we found." He gave Buck a minute to look at the pictures.

The front door opened and in walked a tall, ramrod-thin, young fella wearing jeans and a flannel shirt. His blond hair hung loosely under his straw cowboy hat, and he had a sheriff's department badge clipped to his shirt. The sheriff waved him over.

"Buck, this is Eddie Shelley, part-time deputy, part-time guide. He led the search for the hikers. Eddie, Buck Taylor, CBI."

Buck stood up and reached out his hand.

"Nice to meet you, Agent Taylor."

"Please, call me Buck. Nice to meet you as well."

"I was just filling Buck in on what you guys found up there. Pull up a chair," said the sheriff.

Buck sat back down and looked at the pictures. He looked up at the sheriff. "Why are they buried in the snow, and where are their clothes?"

The pictures Buck held showed what appeared to be three different people, all lying partially covered by snow and all in various stages of undress.

Eddie pulled out his phone and opened his gallery, flipped through some pictures and handed Buck his phone. "Most of the clothes were in the tents, some of it was ripped and it was scattered around like they tore it off for some reason."

"Where was the fourth body found?" asked Buck.

"The fourth body," said Eddie, "was found in one of the tents. The tent was crushed by the snow. That body was fully clothed, but we found him holding an open Swiss Army knife, like he was trying to defend himself against something."

Buck looked at the next picture on the phone, which showed the body under the crushed tent.

"How many are still missing?" asked Buck.

The sheriff took over. "We're still looking for Carmichael, one student named Rivera and Lum Gladstone, their guide. Lum is local, and his family would like some answers."

Eddie took back his phone and flipped to another picture. He handed it to Buck. "We found Lum's rifle and satellite phone lying on his bedroll in another crushed tent. It wouldn't be like Lum to leave either one. He was way too careful. He also didn't protect his horse or the two mules from the weather. One of the mules was dying when we got there. We had to put it down."

Buck was just about to say something when the front door opened and in walked a bald man with a gray Van Dyke beard. He wore cargo shorts, a button-down shirt and Teva sandals. He headed straight for the office.

"Sheriff. Are you sure you don't want to . . ." He stopped short when he saw Buck sitting in the chair. "Pardon me, Sheriff. I didn't realize you had company."

"It's okay, Luther. This is Buck Taylor, CBI."

Luther looked Buck up and down. "CBI, huh. Looks like someone is finally taking this seriously." He reached out his hand.

"Luther Strange," he said. "You've undoubtedly heard of me. My blog and podcast, Strange Revelations, is carried in over fifty countries and has over twenty million followers."

Buck shook his hand and looked at the sheriff and then back to Luther. "What's a podcast?" The sheriff held back a chuckle.

Luther looked at Buck like he had two heads, and then he smiled. "You can see for yourself. I am on my way to do a live podcast from the meeting room at the Community Church. Since the sheriff is reluctant to be interviewed, I would love to interview you."

"Well, Mr. Strange. That would be a short interview. I just got here and have no idea what's going on," said Buck.

"The invitation stands if you're not afraid of the truth." Luther turned and walked out of the office.

Buck looked at the sheriff. "What the hell was that?"

"Luther has lived here for years. All those people in town are here because his podcasts have brought them in. He is into whatever conspiracy theory is current, and he has convinced his followers that we are hiding information about alien abductions, or bigfoot or whatever wacky thing he is on about this week. He's mostly harmless, but I think he believes the crap he sells."

"Is he crazy?" asked Buck.

"Crazy maybe, but last year he cleared around a half million bucks from all his sponsors. I'd like to be that crazy."

Buck let out a low whistle. "Are you hiding a conspiracy, Carl?"

"I wish I knew. That's why you're here. To help us figure this out."

Chapter Eighteen

Buck stood up and threw his Coke can in the recycle bin. He was gathering up his papers when the front door opened, and a deputy Buck didn't recognize walked in with two guys wearing green camo coats and hats. Both men were in handcuffs, and the deputy had two AR-15s slung over his shoulder. He told the men to stand still and be quiet.

The sheriff stood up and gingerly walked out of his office. "What's going on, Bob?"

"We have a right to carry our guns. The Second Amendment . . ." bellowed one of the men.

Bob, the deputy, pushed the loudmouth into the counter. "I told you to knock that shit off."

The sheriff walked up to the counter. The deputy handed Eddie the two rifles and he made sure the chambers on both guns were empty before he locked them in the gun safe in the sheriff's office.

"Fucking idiots," said the deputy. He looked at Buck. "Pardon my language. These two geniuses walked into the grocery store wearing face masks and carrying the rifles. Scared the shit out of everybody in the place. Thought it was a robbery. All these crazies in town, and everybody's a little jumpy. When I got there, eight people had guns trained on them. They're lucky they didn't get killed."

"We have a right," said the biggest one. The deputy told him to shut up. The sheriff looked at the two men.

"Fellas, let me clue you in about this county. There are about eight hundred and fifty people that live in this county, and about eight hundred and forty of them carry guns. We are all about Second Amendment rights, but we are not about stupid." He looked at the deputy. "Bob, lock them up. They can have their guns back when they're ready to leave town, which will be right after breakfast. In the meantime,"—he looked at the two camo dudes— "you're gonna spend the night with us, just for being stupid. Eddie, call Jackie over at the Moose Café and let her know we are going to need dinner and breakfast for two."

The big guy started to object, but the sheriff cut him off. "Right now, we are gonna keep this friendly. You're gonna have a nice dinner and breakfast on the county and have a warm place to sleep. One more word from either of you and I will call the judge, and we'll book you for resisting arrest, for starters. So, are you okay being our guest, or do you want me to make this ugly?"

Both men just nodded, and Bob and Eddie walked them to the back of the office to the holding cells.

The sheriff looked at Buck. "Just what I need. Do you believe those guys? Geez."

Buck grabbed his backpack and the pictures from the sheriff's desk. "I'm gonna check in at the motel and read through the reports tonight. What's our plan?"

Eddie walked back over. "I'd like to meet you here at six. I can get us fairly close by truck, but we're still gonna need five or six hours to get to the campsite. You okay on horseback?"

"I can ride. How far out were these guys?"

"About as far as they could be," said Eddie. "The Weminuche is almost five hundred thousand acres of some of the wildest and most isolated land in Colorado. They were right in the middle of it. According to Lum's wife, he figured it would take him eighteen hours to reach the area they planned to use as their base camp."

"Can we fly in?" asked Buck.

"Yeah. There's some flat ground near Goose Lake. Take us about an hour, maybe hour and a half from there to hike in. We'd need a chopper," said Eddie.

Buck pulled out his phone, pushed a speed-dial number and waited. "Hey, Buck. You in Creede?" said the director.

"Yes, sir. Got in about an hour ago. Interesting place right now. Sir, I need a favor. Can you get a chopper up to the airstrip here, first thing in the morning? The site is a long way in, and it would save a ton of time. Might need it for a day or two."

"No problem, Buck. I'll make some calls and text you when I know whose chopper you're gonna have. I know this case is a little odd, but we need to keep this as low-key as possible."

Buck looked out the door and down Main Street.

"With all due respect, sir. I think that ship has sailed. I'll do my best."

"That's why you're there, Buck. Thanks." The director hung up.

Eddie looked at the sheriff. "Man, must be nice to have that kind of pull."

"One thing you need to know about Buck," said the sheriff. "He doesn't mess around. Now I'm gonna head home for supper and to take a pain pill. Foot is killing me."

The sheriff headed back to his office. Eddie turned to Buck. "Bring a sleeping bag and a warm coat. There's still some snow up where we're going. Also, bring a long rifle if you got one with you, or I can get you one of ours. Winter was dry before the storm last week, and the bears are out and as thick as mosquitos. And just as hungry."

"No problem. I'll see you at the airstrip at six."

Eddie headed back towards the holding cells, and Buck stepped out onto Main Street. The town looked like a giant street festival. There was loud music coming from several directions, and the various smells from food cooking on grills were enticing. It also reminded him he hadn't eaten in a while.

He threw his backpack into the back of the Jeep and walked down Main Street towards the Moose Café. He lost count of all the different conspiracy theories he saw on bumper stickers and signs, taped wherever someone could find space. He stepped into the cafe and found an empty seat near the back by the window, so he could watch the crowds. The waitress took his order and returned with a glass of Coke. He sipped while he thought about the deaths of the four students.

"What would lead four otherwise healthy students to tear off their clothes and run off into a blizzard? And where was the guide? He left his gun and phone in his tent. Why would he do that?" he thought to himself.

He was checking messages on his phone when a shadow crossed his table. He looked up just as a guy sat down. "You the cop investigating the murders?"

Buck just looked at him. He was dressed like an average person, except for the beads he wore around his neck and the ball cap that read don't trust anyone. "The government is testing a new weapon in those mountains, and those students were guinea pigs." He looked around to make sure no one was watching, and then he slid a paperback book across the table to Buck. "The Dyatlov Pass incident was real." He stood up and left as fast as he had arrived.

Buck looked at the book and stuck it in his pocket. The waitress brought his burger, and he was just about to bite into it when a woman with stringy blond hair dressed in clothes most homeless people would throw away sat down. She slid a small pamphlet across the table and left. Buck's first thought was, "Shit. I just want to eat my dinner in peace."

He looked at the cover of the poorly printed pamphlet. "The Bigfoot Murders" by Dr. Eugenie

Cash, PhD. He left the pamphlet there and ate his burger. He spotted a couple of teenagers heading his way, and he glared at them until they turned around and left.

He finished his dinner, paid his bill and left the waitress a nice tip. He didn't figure that with this kind of group in town she would get much in the way of tips. He stepped out into the cool evening air and headed for his Jeep. It seemed like every person he passed tried to hand him something, from small books to poorly written stories stapled together. As he reached the sheriff's office, he paused at his Jeep and dialed Paul Webber. He knew it was late, but he hoped he might catch Paul at the office.

"Hey, Buck. I was just going to call you. You're famous."

"What? Okay, before we get to that, I need you to run a background search for me. The guy's name is Luther Strange. He's a—"

"Blogger and has a podcast heard around the world, at least according to him," said Paul.

"You've heard of this guy?" asked Buck.

"Yeah, I try to listen to him every day."

Buck was stunned. "The guy traffics in conspiracy theories. What don't I know about you, Paul?"

Paul laughed. "It's not like that. I keep tabs on his theories and his guests. It keeps me sane, but I have gotten some interesting information out of his blogs and podcasts. Why do you want me to background him?"

"I met him today in Creede, and he seems a little off."

"I can do that, but he's the reason I was going to call you. His live podcast from Creede today was about the dead and missing hikers. He had on some interesting guests, but my question to you is: Has the coroner released the tox screens yet?"

"Not yet. We should have the preliminaries tomorrow. Why?" asked Buck.

Paul hesitated a minute. "Because he has them. He revealed them on his show today."

"Fuck. How do I find the podcast?"

"I'll text you the link. Just click on it. In the meantime, I'll run a background check. Oh, I almost forgot the other reason I was calling you. We may have something on the white van. We're running a couple of things down, and I should have it tomorrow. I'll send it to Bax so she can look at it while you're in Creede."

"Thanks, Paul."

Buck hung up and dialed Bax. She answered right away. "Hey, Buck. How are things in Creede?"

"Nutty," said Buck. "I'll fill you in later. How'd things go with the newspaper guy?"

Bax filled him in.

Chapter Nineteen

Bax headed for Dolores as soon as the interview with Ronnie Hightower and his lawyer ended. She had asked Deputy Sage to head back to Ute Mountain and supervise the search. She was concerned, as she knew Buck was, about Ronnie contacting the lawyer while in the car with Sage. She had no issues with anyone asking to have a lawyer present during questioning, even just a friendly conversation. What she was concerned about was when one of the investigators on the case went behind her back and suggested it to the person being interviewed. What he did wasn't illegal, but it was a bit unethical. It undermined her and Buck and made it even more clear that Scott Sage was too personally involved in this case.

She thought about the interview while she drove to Dolores. Ronnie's answers were right in line with the statement he'd given Deputy Sage on the morning of the disappearance. They were maybe too much in line with the statement. She was sure that Deputy Sage had coached him on the way back to Cortez. She didn't think Ronnie had anything to hide, but if he didn't, why did he need coaching? Maybe she was just overreacting and looking for more things to blame on Sage.

She rolled down the window to clear her head,

and the cool air did the trick. She slowed down as she entered the town of Dolores, Colorado, population just a shade under one thousand people, and one of three municipalities in Montezuma County. She followed Railroad Avenue until she spotted the sign for the *Dolores Weekly Chronicle* on a small brick building next to the post office. Next to the newspaper was a small coffee shop, so she stopped in and picked up a small iced coffee and sat for a minute at one of the tables along the sidewalk. She enjoyed watching the people as they went about their daily lives. With her job, it was nice, once in a while, to see people who had not been victimized. It kept her grounded.

She finished her coffee, tossed the cup and walked to the front door of the Chronicle. As soon as she opened the door, she knew she was in a newspaper office. The sounds. The smells. It brought back memories of her earlier years when she would go to work with her dad on the weekends. Those were fun times. The bell above the door clanged, and a voice yelled out from the back.

"Be right there."

Bax took a minute to look at the pictures that were hanging on the wall. She spotted the man she assumed must be the owner, since he was in each picture, shaking some politician or other dignitary's hand or accepting some kind of award. He was a tall, distinguished-looking man, and she smiled as she could see the progression of time through the hairstyles and clothes in the pictures. She stopped at one picture that caught her attention. He was standing at a bar with a crowd of eight men and two women gathered around him, and everyone had a drink and was toasting his accomplishment.

"That's me and the gang from the *Chicago Tribune*, right after I won . . ."

"The Pulitzer," Bax responded without turning around.

"You've either got good eyes, or you've seen one before." He stepped around the wooden counter and extended his hand. "Winston Lowell, proprietor, at your service. My friends, most of whom are long gone, called me Win."

Bax turned from the picture and shook his hand. "Ashley Baxter, Colorado Bureau of Investigation. My friends call me Bax. Pleased to meet you."

The man standing in front of Bax hadn't changed much since those pictures were taken. His portly middle might have been a little rounder, his hair was a little whiter and a little thinner, but he was still distinguished looking.

Win released her hand. "So, tell me, my dear. Where have you seen a Pulitzer?"

"My dad has one. It sat on the mantle over the fireplace in our living room, the whole time I was growing up."

Win put on the glasses that hung around his neck on a thin chain and looked at Bax. "You said your last name is Baxter?" He paused for a minute, and she could see his mind working. He got a big smile on his face. "If you are who I think you are, you're being modest. Your dad has a couple of these. Are you Jack Baxter's daughter?"

Bax looked surprised. "You know about my dad?"

"Know about him?" said Win. "I know him. We worked at the *New York Times* together. He was a junior reporter, with a brand-new degree in journalism, fresh out of college and looking to set the world on fire. He certainly has done that. I was there when he won his first Pulitzer for that corruption piece on the New York Housing Authority. He could have gone to any big-city newspaper he wanted after that, but he chose the old *Rocky Mountain News* in Denver. That was quite a surprise, but I guess he made the best of it. He won one more Pulitzer in Denver, and then another one while at *National Geographic*. Last I heard he was doing outdoor adventure stories and traveling the world."

"Yes, sir. He and Mom are living the good life, and he gets to report on fun things like fishing and hunting."

"Well, the next time you see him, you tell him ole Win Lowell was asking about him. Now, what can I do for the Colorado Bureau of Investigation?"

Win invited Bax to follow him into the back office, and she grabbed a seat on the other side of a huge cluttered mahogany desk. She heard gentle snoring, and she looked around and there, sleeping soundly in the corner on a big cushion, was an old golden retriever.

"That's Charlie. We've been together a lot of

years. Best dog I ever owned and the best companion for a man of my advanced years. Spends most of his day asleep, just like you see him."

Charlie opened his eyes and looked at Bax, gave a small wag of his tail and closed his eyes again. He looked so peaceful sleeping there.

She turned back to Win. "I was told that if I wanted to know anything about the missing Native American women, you were the man to see. We're investigating the disappearance of a woman in Cortez, and I'm looking for some insight."

Win looked at Bax and must have decided that she was serious. He stood up and asked her to follow him. They passed through the back room, where the papers were printed, and into a small, well-kept residence. Win led her into a back bedroom that had been converted to an office. He opened the door and stood back so Bax could enter. She stopped short in the doorway and scanned the room. Every wall was covered with newspaper and internet articles about missing women. There must have been thousands of printouts and clippings, many dating back several years. She took it all in.

"How long have you been looking into the disappearances?" she asked.

"Since the beginning. First disappearance was a small article in a tiny newspaper in Arizona in 2008. It didn't generate much interest at the time. It wasn't till some Native American activists mentioned the number of women missing from reservations in 2016 that people finally noticed, and by then, the numbers were staggering. Now, don't get me wrong. It's possible and even likely that a lot of these women left on their own, but even if you discount, say, twenty percent as runaways. The number of missing is still huge."

Bax was walking along the walls, reading bits and pieces of the articles that were hanging there. She would stop now and then to read something that caught her attention. She turned to Win. "What do you know about the woman who went missing on her way home from Durango two weeks ago?"

He pulled out his desk chair and sat down. "I get a little winded when I get excited. Need to sit down for a minute." He took a couple of deep breaths. "Dee Hightower, right?" he asked. "I don't think she's one of these women. She doesn't fit the profile, that's why she's not on the wall." He pointed to a wooden chair covered in books and magazines, and Bax grabbed the pile, set it on the floor and sat down.

"Most of these women led hard lives—drugs, prostitution, abuse and unemployment. A lot of people think that the Indian casinos were a great boom to the reservation's economy, and it did help a lot of tribe members who were in dire straits. But it didn't help everyone. That is why it was so easy to discount the disappearances. They just wrote these women off as either having nothing for them on the reservation or that their lifestyle was a factor in their disappearance—either way, no one cared enough to look into it. That's why I looked into it. Because if I didn't, who else would?"

"Win. Is there anything that indicates that these women met their ends at the hands of one person?"

"It would be interesting to believe that a serial killer is roaming the nation's reservations, but that would be ridiculous. Many of these disappearances happened during the same time frame and in different locations. You would need an army of serial killers to pull that off. No, I think a lot of the answers would, with proper investigations, be found on the reservations."

Bax looked at the wall covering the most recent period in Montezuma County. "What about the other two women who disappeared? Are they connected?"

Win stood up, went to an old army-green filing cabinet in the corner, opened the top drawer and pulled out six files. He handed them to Bax. "Take these with you. These are six disappearances in Colorado and Utah in the last three years, including the last three that I think are a crime spree all on their own. No one has, as of yet, connected these, but I think the lack of similarities is what connects these. Do me a favor. If something comes of this, give me first crack at writing about it. When you are ready to start working the rest of these"—he waved his hand around the room—"let me know, and I will help you all I can."

Bax placed the files in her backpack. She thanked him for his time and the files and promised to let him know how things turned out. On the way out, she stopped and gave Charlie a pat on the head, which elicited a small tail wag. She thanked Win again and walked out the door. She was almost to her Jeep when her phone rang.

"Hey, Paul. What's up?" She listened for a minute. "Okay, as soon as I get back to the hotel, I'll look at it. I'm also going to send you the names of three additional women. Have someone at the office run deep background on them, and let's see if we can get phone records and their missing person files." She hung up, climbed in her Jeep and headed back to Cortez. She wondered what she was going to find in the files Win had given her.

Chapter Twenty

Buck was hesitant to sit down at a table in the restaurant for breakfast. He was tempted to get his order to go and eat in his Jeep. So far, just walking from the hotel to the restaurant, he had been approached by four different people. Each one trying to convince him that either aliens abducted the hikers, the government was involved in a vast conspiracy and was hiding the truth about how they died or that bigfoot ate them. He wasn't sure he could deal with another conspiracy theory right now. All he wanted to do was eat his breakfast without interruption.

He was tired and cranky after sitting up for three hours listening to Luther Strange talk about all the same things these people were now talking to him about. He wondered how one man with a radio show could get that many people fired up about so many things—or was it that his followers already had these crazy ideas and he just gave them an outlet? Whatever it was, he was pissed. Not only did he have pictures of the camp area and the demolished tents and pictures of the bodies and the autopsy reports, but he also had the preliminary toxicology reports. The sheriff hadn't received the tox report yet from the State Crime Lab.

Buck wasn't sure who'd leaked the information

to Luther Strange, but he was going to find out as soon as it was late enough to start calling people, and someone was in for an ass chewing. Buck finished his breakfast and checked his watch. He needed to head to the airstrip. The director had sent him a text last night that he would have a Colorado Air National Guard helicopter waiting for him at the airport by six. He paid his bill, grabbed his backpack and walked as quickly as possible to his Jeep.

He was getting ready to pull out onto Main Street when he remembered something he wanted to do, so he pulled out his phone and sent Paul a text. He wanted to know why everyone was comparing the missing students to something called the Dyatlov Pass incident. Several of Luther Strange's guests had mentioned it, as had the guy in the restaurant who slipped him the paper with the website on it. He never had a chance to look it up last night, so he wanted Paul to pull up what he could find and send it to him. After reading the autopsy reports and then listening to the podcast, he found that there were some odd similarities, and he wanted to know more.

Buck pulled onto the airstrip drive and parked near the end of runway 52, where he spotted a Colorado Air National Guard Sikorsky UH-60 Black Hawk helicopter sitting near a couple of small hangars. He grabbed his larger backpack, complete with a sleeping bag, his Carhartt winter ranch coat and his AR-15, which he'd pulled from the locked gun safe built into the floor of his Jeep.

He put on his ballistic vest, with extra ammo magazines, and put his evidence kit into a pocket on the backpack. He checked the battery for his sat phone and made sure he had his solar charger. He locked the Jeep and headed for the three people gathered by the chopper.

Eddie Shelley was standing next to the pilot and copilot, and he introduced them to Buck. Captain Elena "Cobra" Milhouse was the pilot, and Lieutenant Tommy "Tomcat" Parkinson was the copilot.

"What's your schedule, Captain?" asked Buck.

"Our orders are to be at your disposal until you release us, sir. We've arranged for accommodations for the next three nights, sir."

"Thank you, Captain, and do me a favor and call me Buck. I'm not much on formality."

The captain nodded and smiled, and Eddie handed her a paper with the coordinates for the base camp. They climbed into the helicopter, stowed their gear, put on communication helmets and strapped in. Buck hated flying in helicopters, and this one was similar to the ones he'd occasionally had to fly in when he was in the army. He double-checked his harness and sat back in the seat.

"Sir—uh, sorry, Buck. GPS says about twenty minutes to the coordinates."

"Thanks, Cobra. Let's go."

The chopper lifted off and headed south. The morning air was still and cool, and the flight was better than Buck had expected. He looked out the door when the captain indicated they were over

Goose Lake and had found an area of flatter ground at the north end of the lake. He told the captain to go ahead and set her down. Once on the ground, they unstrapped, grabbed their gear and coordinated their return flight for the following day at five p.m. Buck and Eddie stepped away from the chopper, and soon they were standing in the silence as the chopper disappeared from view.

* * *

They reached the base camp by midmorning and stopped at the edge of the clearing so Buck could get an overall view of the camp. The bodies and the electronic equipment had all been removed by the search and rescue team. The tents still lay where they were found, crushed by the heavy, wet spring snow. The site hadn't been protected because, at the time, it wasn't a crime scene. It might still not be one, but some things in the autopsies bugged Buck.

They walked into the camp and approached the first tent. Buck pulled up the autopsy file on his phone. Robert Meyers had been fully clothed when they pulled him out of the crushed tent. The rescuers had to pry the Swiss Army knife out of his frozen hands. Buck looked at the photos. You could see the terror in his eyes, which were wide open. Robert's eardrums were shattered, and his eyeballs had ruptured. It appeared that he had been scared to death. Buck looked inside the remains of the tent. There was still a lot of snow in certain spots, so he had to push some away from the tent. Inside there were shoes and clothes in various piles. Buck picked up a women's shirt, and all the buttons were ripped off. He pulled out his cell phone and took a series of pictures.

"Robert Meyers was the only one fully clothed?" he asked Eddie.

"Yep. It's like whatever happened here affected him differently than it affected the others."

Over the next three hours, they walked to each location where a body had been found. The farthest location was about a quarter mile from the base camp.

Kendra Jackson, based on the pictures, had traveled a quarter mile from camp dressed in just her underpants and a T-shirt. According to the autopsy report, her eardrums were also ruptured, and she had a fractured skull, along with multiple contusions. Speculation amongst the rescuers was that she had run blindly through the snowstorm and slammed into a tree. Two of her fingers had been gnawed off, probably by scavengers.

The next closest to camp was Sandra Moore. She was found in a ravine and had to be chopped out of the ice that formed when the snow melted and refroze. Her left eye was missing, her eardrums were shattered and she had on sweatpants, no shoes and her bra.

James Tulley was found a couple of yards from the tent. His injuries were the oddest of all. Besides ruptured ears and eyes, some of his internal organs had liquefied in a mushy gel. The forensic pathologist from El Paso County had never seen anything like it, and at first, he speculated it might be some kind of virus, but further tests found no evidence of anything biological. He was at a loss to explain what happened.

All four deaths were still listed as "undetermined," and it would be up to Buck to determine if that were appropriate, based on the evidence from the scene.

Buck and Eddie found a spot away from the camp and cooked up a dehydrated lunch of beef stew and mashed potatoes.

"What were your first thoughts when you arrived on the scene?" asked Buck.

Eddie thought for a minute between spoonfuls of stew. "My first thought was, what the hell happened? I was thinking bear or mountain lion attack, but there was no blood. When we started to find the bodies, I honestly don't know what I was thinking. I've never seen anything like this."

"Tell me about the guide they were with, Lum Gladstone."

"I've worked with and for Lum for years. He's been a fixture in this community as long as I can remember. He's honest, he's mountain smart, and he doesn't take chances, especially with his clients. I can't for the life of me figure out why he would leave, without his phone, or his rifle. And to leave his horse and those two mules exposed in that storm, with no protection. That's not like Lum. He loves that horse as much as he loves his wife. No, something bad had to happen to make Lum run off like that, something really bad."

"Okay," said Buck. "So, we have four dead around the camp. We haven't found this Professor

Carmichael, Lum or this guy Dom Rivera. Any thoughts on which way they might have headed?"

"We searched this valley completely. Search and rescue is still working the next valley, but the sheriff wants to call off the search by the end of the week. I have no idea where to look."

Chapter Twenty-One

Buck pulled his topographic map out of his backpack and spread it out on the ground. "Eddie, you know these woods. If you were running from something, where would you head?"

Eddie looked at the map, trying to think like someone being pursued. "I wouldn't head to Goose Lake. That area's too open. I'd head into the next valley. Lots of trees and good cover and higher ground. Possibly get a stray cell signal."

"Okay. You said that search and rescue were working that valley. Any reason to head farther up this valley?"

Eddie thought for a minute. "Probably as good a choice as the other, but the SAR teams already covered this area."

"Who has all their laptops and cameras?"

"We sent them to your Denver office for analysis?"

Buck pulled his sat phone out of his backpack and dialed a number. There was a lot of static on the line, but he was able to reach the director.

"Hey, Buck. Not a good connection. You okay?" asked the director.

"Yes, sir. Wondering if the tech guys have been able to get into the laptops from the dead students?"

"Let me transfer you to Marcy Turner. Her team

has been working on them since we received them. Hold on."

Buck heard a couple of clicks. "Marcy Turner."

"Marcy, it's Buck Taylor, been a long time."

"Buck, it's good to hear your voice. You sound far away. What's up?"

"I'm on the sat phone. Have you been able to get into any of the laptops of the dead students?"

"Yeah. We're still working on some of them. One of them is encrypted, which is odd. What are you looking for?"

"Marcy, did you find any logs or something like that, particularly in Professor Carmichael's computer? Since he was leading this expedition, I would assume he kept some kind of notes."

"Hang on, Buck. Let me pull up a list of what we've found so far. Here it is. He did keep a journal. You want me to send it to you?"

"No, never had good luck getting files to pull up on the sat phone. Can you look at the last entry and read it to me?"

"Sure thing. It's pretty long. He's mostly making notes about the pictures from the camera traps—nothing unusual there. Wait a minute. He seemed to have some concerns about a picture of a large bull elk that had been brought down. He had coordinates for the carcass and made a note that he should look at it himself. One of his students marked it as a black bear kill, but he didn't think so based on what he saw in the pictures. You want the coordinates?"

"Please," said Buck. Marcy read off the

coordinates, and he wrote them on the edge of the map. He thanked Marcy and asked her to email him everything they'd found so far. He also asked her to make the encrypted laptop a priority. He turned off the phone.

Eddie was already overlaying the coordinates on the map. He looked up at Buck. "What's the deal with an encrypted laptop? I thought these were all college students?"

"Yeah," said Buck. "Me too. Where do the coordinates lead us to?"

"Next valley past the valley SAR is working. Looks like it will take us a couple of hours to get there. You ready?"

They grabbed their backpacks and rifles, plugged the coordinates into Buck's handheld GPS and headed out. The first part of the hike was relatively easy and followed Fisher Creek. It gave Buck a chance to think as he walked. The encrypted laptop was playing on his mind, and the little bug that ran around in his head during a case was active again. There was something about the laptop, or the student it belonged to, that was important. He hoped Marcy would call him back with some answers.

They turned off the trail along the creek and started into a small valley that looked similar to the one the base camp was in. They had just walked into a clearing when Eddie held up his fist. They both stopped moving. Eddie pointed towards a clump of tall bushes about fifty yards in front of them, and Buck put his hands above his eyes to block the sun. He wasn't sure what he was looking at until a large rock started to move.

"Momma bear and two cubs," Eddie said softly. "She's a big one. Cubs look about two years old. We need to be careful."

Eddie led them towards the other side of the valley, away from the bear. They were just even with the bears when the momma raised her head and sniffed the air. She looked straight at Buck and Eddie, stood on her hind legs, and huffed. She dropped back down on all fours and started walking towards them. Buck and Eddie held their ground, but they both raised their rifles to waist level. The bear made two bluff charges, stopping about twenty-five yards away each time, stood on her back legs and growled, shaking her head from side to side. The third time she charged, Eddie told Buck to get behind him. At ten yards, Eddie, showing no fear, fired two rounds from his Henry Lever-Action .45-70 into the dirt in front of her. She stopped in her tracks, stood for a minute looking at them then turned and slowly walked back to her cubs.

"I guess she didn't think we're a threat. Lucky us."

Buck was impressed, both by the size of the bear and with the composure Eddie had shown. Buck had spent his whole life hunting around Gunnison, but he'd never come that close to a charging bear, and he never wanted to do it again. They lowered their weapons and, keeping an eye out for more bears, continued up the valley.

They found Lum, just before sunset. Unlike the

others, he was fully clothed, except he was missing his coat. He was lying in a fetal position next to a fallen tree. It looked to Buck that he had tried to hide from the storm. The holster on his hip was empty, and his left arm showed signs of animal predation. There were signs of blood around both ears, and his eyes were both missing. He appeared to be frozen solid and was still partially buried in a snowbank.

Buck pulled out his camera and started taking pictures of the body and the surroundings, focusing on the injuries. While he was doing that, Eddie started backtracking to see if he could find Lum's coat and gun.

The gun, a Smith & Wesson .44 magnum revolver, was lying on the ground about a hundred yards from the body. Eddie took some pictures and marked it with the blue bandanna he'd been wearing around his neck. He noted that all the bullets had been fired. Every chamber held an empty casing. The coat he found about forty yards away from the gun. All of the buttons on the coat were missing, and it looked to Eddie like someone, probably Lum, had ripped the coat off. He wondered once again what the hell had happened up here.

When he got back to the body, Buck was on the sat phone with Cobra, the helicopter pilot, arranging for them to fly up before the sun set completely to hoist out the body. Buck hung up, and Eddie showed him the pictures of the gun and coat and explained what he'd found. They surveyed the rest of the area around the body, and then, in the distance, they heard the helicopter approaching the coordinates Buck had given them.

The helicopter hovered above them, and the copilot dropped down a black poly body bag. Eddie and Buck, wearing medical-grade Nitrile gloves, placed Lum inside the body bag and strapped the bag to the sled the copilot had lowered to them. Buck had asked Cobra to fly the body to the El Paso Coroner's Office in Colorado Springs. He called the coroner's office and requested a rush on the autopsy. With the body secure in the chopper, Buck gave a wave, and the chopper headed out.

They decided to make camp near where they'd found the body, and after finding a spot sheltered from the wind that had picked up, they gathered a load of firewood and made camp for the night. In Buck's mind, the fire seemed a lot larger than he thought they needed, but it gave him a sense of security. They settled in for a cold night, wondering what tomorrow would bring.

Chapter Twenty-Two

Bax walked into the little Mexican bar and restaurant across the street from the hotel and grabbed a table near the back, so she could keep an eye on the place. She never appeared to recognize that most men, anywhere she went, took notice of her, at least until they saw the badge and gun that were clipped to her belt. Bax wasn't supermodel gorgeous, but she would be considered pretty by most people's standards. She had long blond hair that she wore in a ponytail that hung through the back of her CBI cap and amazing jade-green eyes.

She had a nice figure—not thin, but not heavy either. What used to be called a "mountain girl" figure. A little stocky, but with curves in all the right places. She carried herself with the grace of an athlete, and she moved with a certain fluidness that came from being a track star in college and from years of running marathons with her dad.

She pulled out her laptop, ordered a beef burrito with beans and rice, and a Corona with a lime wedge, and opened the email that Paul had sent her earlier. She had spent the better part of the day reading the files Win Lowell, the newspaperman, had given her, and she was more confused than ever. Win had told her that he didn't believe these six women, including Dee Hightower, had been abducted as part of a larger conspiracy against Native American women. She read and reread every word, but she was having trouble seeing how they weren't connected.

Everything about this group of six women said they were part of the thousands of native women who had disappeared during the past decade. Granted, Dee Hightower didn't fit the profile, but everything else fit. She pulled up the deep dive Paul had sent her on the six women and started reading.

She was finishing her burrito and reading the sixth file when she thought she found what Win Lowell might have been talking about. She pulled the files Win had given her out of her backpack and started flipping pages until she found what she was looking for in the first file. She worked her way through the remaining files, and then she had it. Each of these women was seen either getting into or talking to someone in a white utility van. None of the witnesses would have thought anything unusual about that. Hitchhiking was a popular mode of transportation on the reservations, especially with young people, so getting into a van would not have seemed out of the ordinary. It was only after these women were reported missing that anyone commented about the white van, but by then it was too late. These cases had already been added to the pile of other missing women and ended up lost in the shuffle.

Win Lowell had lots of time on his hands, and he was a seasoned investigative journalist. He wouldn't have missed such a tiny detail. He was all about details.

Bax pulled up the other file Paul had sent her. There were two video clips, and the note said that Buck had gotten these on the street leaving Fort Lewis College, from the night Dee disappeared. He asked Paul to see if they could enhance these, to see any details on the second one. She played the first one, and after a minute, she saw an old Subaru pass through the field of view. She realized this was a video clip from a doorbell camera. She stopped the video, and when she enlarged the frame, she could see Dee Hightower, alone in the driver's seat.

She clicked on the second video and watched as the white utility van slowly came down the same street. She checked the time stamp, and the van was about a minute behind Dee. It seemed Win Lowell might be right. There was a white van possibly connected to each of the six disappearances. Paul's email indicated that they were not able to get any more clarity out of the video of the white van. She closed her laptop, finished her beer and asked the waitress for the check. She left a twenty on the table, which covered the meal and tip, grabbed her backpack and headed for the door.

She'd just reached her car when her phone rang. She looked at the number and answered. "Hey, Scott. What's up?"

Deputy Sage said, "Hey, Bax. Hope it's not too late to call, but something's come up, and we have a possible suspect being brought up to the office. The sheriff would like you here."

"Awesome, Scott. I'm just finishing dinner down the street. I'll be there in five."

She stowed her backpack, started the Jeep and headed for the sheriff's office. Three minutes later, she pulled into the lot, parked and headed for the door. She flashed her ID to the deputy at the front desk, and he buzzed her into the back. She found the sheriff in his office as she headed for the conference room, which had become her unofficial office.

"Evening, Sheriff. What's going on?"

"Not sure myself," replied the sheriff. "We got a call that the chairman and some of the searchers that went with him found someone camped out at one of the ceremonial sites, and they are bringing him in. Should be here in about twenty minutes."

"Let's hope it's a good lead." She headed for her temporary office.

Bax was reading more of the files that Win Lowell had provided when she heard a commotion in the hallway and stepped out of the conference room to see what was going on. The chairman of the Ute Mountain tribe was coming down the hallway, followed by four Native American men half dragging, half carrying a bleeding man. The sheriff stepped out of his office and did not look pleased.

"Abe," he said, addressing the chairman. "What the hell happened?"

The chairman, with a straight face, said, "He resisted arrest, so we had to subdue him."

"Jesus Christ, Abe. He looks half-dead. Did you have to be so rough?"

Bax raced past the chairman and stopped in front of the four men. She lifted the prisoner's chin. "What the fuck, Sheriff? Is this how you treat prisoners?"

"Calm down, Bax. I'm not happy about this either." He looked at Deputy Sage, who'd just walked in. "Scott put him in the first interrogation room." Then he yelled down the hall. "Margie, have dispatch get a couple paramedics over here, ASAP!"

A voice from somewhere down the hall responded, "Right away, Sheriff."

The chairman walked up to the sheriff and Bax, who was still fuming about the prisoner's treatment. He held out a plastic grocery bag. "He had some of Dee's things." He set the bag on the floor next to the sheriff, turned and walked away. Bax stood there, flabbergasted. Not only were they cavalier about beating up some poor guy they found in a campsite, but they'd also disturbed a possible crime scene and removed the evidence. The four men left with the chairman just as two paramedics from the Cortez Fire Department ran in the door, and Deputy Sage directed them to the interrogation room.

Bax followed the sheriff into his office and slammed the door. "Those assholes should be arrested for violating that man's civil rights and for tampering with a crime scene. What the hell are you going to do about it?"

"Look, Bax. I'm sorry about what they did, but the crimes you are accusing them of happened on the reservation, which is a sovereign nation. Those four men are also deputized members of the tribal police. Now, I don't condone what they did, but tensions are running high, and we should focus on what's in front of us."

Bax was not satisfied in the least, but she was not going to let her anger get the better of her. She grabbed the evidence bag off the sheriff's desk and walked out of his office towards the conference room. She put on a pair of Nitrile gloves and removed each item from the bag. She laid them on the table. The first item was a cell phone in a black Otter Box case. She took a picture of it with her cell phone and pushed the power button, but nothing happened. She grabbed a phone charger out of her backpack and plugged it into the receptacle in the middle of the desk. The next item was a women's watch. Nothing fancy, just an old Timex. The third item was an HP laptop, which Bax tried to open, but it was also dead. She photographed the items and set them aside.

The last item in the bag was a round turquoise stone in a silver setting, on a silver chain. She photographed it and was about to put it in an evidence bag when the sheriff walked in and stopped short. He looked at the necklace on the table.

"I gave that to Dee on her confirmation day." He turned and walked back to his office and closed the door. Bax wasn't sure if she should follow him, but she decided not to. She bagged each item, sealed the bag and signed across the seal. She put those aside, grabbed her audio recorder and headed for the interrogation room.

Deputy Sage and the two paramedics were just coming out of the room. Deputy Sage gave her a funny look and thanked the paramedics.

"They think he might have a slight concussion and a possible broken arm. He also has a collection of scrapes and bruises. I asked them to come back in half an hour and take him to the hospital to get checked out further. I can't believe those guys did that. Sorry, Bax."

They stepped into the room, and the man was sitting at the desk with his arm in a sling and a bandage around his head. By morning he would have two black eyes and one hell of a headache. Bax sat down opposite him and turned on her recorder. She advised him of his rights and asked if he could answer a couple of questions before they sent him to the hospital. He said he would try and that he didn't need a lawyer because he didn't do anything wrong. The arm in the sling was his writing hand, so she had him agree that he did not need legal representation again for the recording.

"What's your name?" she asked.

"They didn't have any right to beat me up. I wasn't doin' nothing. Just mindin' my own business," he said.

"We'll discuss that in a minute, but first, what's your name? I need to call you something."

"Bob. Bob O'Brien. They coulda killed me," he said.

"Bob. Do you have any ID?"

"Lost it a while back. Used to live in Phoenix. Now I just travel, but I didn't steal that stuff they said I stole."

"Bob, where did you get the stuff they said you stole?"

Bob thought for a minute. "Found it in an old car in a ravine. After the two guys in the van ran it into the ravine and left, I thought it would be okay to sleep there for a couple of nights. You know. Get out of the cold. Found that stuff in the car."

"Bob, what did the van look like?" she asked.

"You know. One of those painter vans, but it didn't have no ladders like you usually see."

Deputy Sage asked, "What color was the van?"

"White."

"Can you describe the two men?"

Bob put his good hand up to his head and winced. He looked at Bax. "They were both white. It was dark, and I wasn't close when I first saw them. One was tall. One was short. My head hurts bad."

Bax turned off the recorder, and Deputy Sage opened the door and called the two paramedics, who had returned with a gurney. They put Bob on the gurney and headed for the hospital with Deputy Sage following close behind them. The sheriff stepped into the room.

"You think he's telling the truth?" he asked.

"Yeah. I do. His explanation makes sense, and

the white van could be the same van Buck got the video of. We need to find that van."

"I'll get one of the admins to run a DMV search for all white vans in this county and La Plata County. Let's see if anything clicks. What do we do with Bob?"

Bax thought for a minute. "Let's keep him in the hospital for a couple of days till we can check out his story." With that, she grabbed her laptop and headed for her hotel. She had a lot to do, and she wanted to talk to Buck.

Chapter Twenty-Three

Jerry removed the last of the bones from the enclosure and used a high-pressure air hose to make sure all the beetles were out. Those buggers liked to crawl into every nook and cranny in the bones, and sometimes they were hard to get rid of. He examined the bones to make sure all the tissue was gone, and then he dipped the basket in a kettle of boiling water with 6 percent hydrogen peroxide. He would leave that there for about an hour to remove any fat that might be trapped in the pores in the bones. The fat would putrefy and make the bones smell rancid. He couldn't have that.

He closed the screen top on the enclosure and went to the walk-in freezer to retrieve the next body. This one had already been cut into pieces, and a lot of the tissue had been removed. He liked it when the bodies were partially cleaned. He hated having to do that in the back room. It was messy and cold, and he needed to work fast to keep the tissue from decomposing. Once he was finished, he would refreeze the tissue, so he could feed it to the beetles in between bodies.

He cut open the plastic and started placing the bones in the enclosure. It was hard to tell, but this was once a woman. He had been doing this for so long that he dehumanized them. They were no longer people, just objects to get ready to sell. He had to work fast to keep any of the beetles from flying away. Once finished, he closed the lid and watched as the beetles and larvae started to devour the tissue. He'd spent thirty-some years working with dermestid beetles, and it still amazed him how much they could eat. He was proud of his beetles. In the past ten years, he hadn't lost a single colony to parasites or disease. That spoke to how well he cared for them. The dark basement and cooler temperature was an ideal environment to raise the colonies, and they thrived.

Dermestid beetles, also commonly called skin beetles, were his favorite method of cleaning the tissue off the bones. There were faster methods to clean bones, but those involved harsh chemicals that could damage the bones. The chemicals also elicited a lot of complaints from the neighbors, which he didn't need. As long as he removed most of the tissue from the bones before he put them in with the beetles, he didn't believe time was a factor. He was after quality. That's what people paid big money for, and his bones never disappointed. Besides, using the beetles made it feel like he was being environmentally sound. He had no idea how many beetles he had in his enclosures, but there must have been close to half a million. More beetles made faster work of the stripping process.

He checked the progress of the other enclosures and made a note of the time so that he could check again in an hour. He walked over to the vat, pulled out the basket and checked the bones. They looked good, so he used a pressure washer to rinse them off and then he laid them on the rolling table.

Willie walked over, looked at the bones and smiled. He and Jerry had been working together for longer than he could remember. They'd started when they were still in grade school, cleaning and selling the skulls and bones of small animals they shot while hunting. Word eventually got around, and hunters and taxidermists would bring them the bones after they had removed the skin, and Jerry and Willie would clean the bones using their beetles.

They developed quite a reputation, and they were doing well. Jerry had even met a girl who was a taxidermist, and they eventually married. Willie hadn't found the right girl yet. The smell of death was hard to get used to for most people. They had been at it for so long that they didn't even notice anymore, but they could see the reactions of the people around them when they went into a restaurant or bar. Willie tried everything to defeat the smell, but over time he just gave up. He hardly ever went out anymore, but that was okay with Willie. He didn't like most people anyway.

Jerry was checking another enclosure when Willie walked up. "Did you figure out when we can do it? She's been here a long time already."

"Yeah," said Jerry. "The other big enclosure should be ready in two days. Unless we get in a big order, I'll pull that one aside for cleaning. We can put her in that one. Besides, I'm not finished with her yet." The wicked smile he had on his face made

Willie cringe. He liked Jerry, but he sometimes thought that he was getting a little strange.

Willie smiled, walked over to one of the smaller enclosures and started clearing the beetles from around a bear skull. He thought about two more days with the Indian chick, and he licked his lips.

Chapter Twenty-Four

Buck woke up cold and stiff, crawled out of his sleeping bag and stretched to work out the kinks. He stepped a little closer to the fire and warmed his hands. He'd never had a problem sleeping on the ground, especially with his new pop-up air mattress, but he still sometimes thought that maybe he was getting too old for this shit. Eddie came out of the forest carrying a couple more logs and some twigs and laid them on the fire. They made themselves a breakfast of dehydrated eggs and bacon. Eddie made himself coffee, while Buck pulled a warm bottle of Coke out of his backpack.

"I think we're on the right track," said Eddie.

Buck nodded. "Yeah. My take on this is, Lum realized Carmichael hadn't come back and went to look for him, heading for the same coordinates we are. What I can't figure out is what the hell he was shooting at, and why did he tear his coat off in the middle of a storm?"

"Join the club, Buck. This whole thing has got me confused. Nothing makes sense."

"Well, we're not gonna find the answers sitting here."

They put out the fire, gathered up their gear and headed towards the coordinates from the journal. Maybe they would find the answers there.

Buck had his GPS in his hand, and he stopped in a small clearing. "This is it," he said.

They dropped their packs and started looking around. After searching the immediate area, they met back where they had dropped the loads.

"I don't see an elk carcass. Found some blood, but no carcass," said Eddie.

"I guess it could have been dragged off. I don't see any sign of Carmichael either."

The sun poked out from behind a cloud, and Buck saw what he thought was a flash just at the lower edge of the clearing. He started walking towards it. The flash turned out to be a trail camera. Buck pulled it down and handed it to Eddie. He opened the side panel and pulled out the smart card. Buck dug in the front pocket of his backpack and pulled out a card reader attached to a short cord. He pulled out his cell phone and plugged the cord into the bottom of the phone. Eddie handed him the card, and he pushed it into the reader and pulled up his card reader app.

The first couple of pictures showed the dead elk. It was a big one. "Must be close to four hundred pounds," said Eddie.

Buck ran the pictures forward and stopped.

"Fuck, Buck. That bear is huge." They were looking at a huge black bear as it started to eat the carcass. The next several pictures showed the bear dragging off the carcass. Buck opened the next picture, and there was Carmichael kneeling, looking at the blood spot, and then he went crazy, looking around like something had scared the shit out of him. He started scratching his skin, and then he ripped off his shirt. He ran out of the frame, but now they had a direction of travel. They looked at the next couple of pictures but saw nothing else. They loaded up the camera, grabbed their backpacks and headed after Carmichael.

They arrived at a ravine about forty minutes later. There was a great deal of snow in the ravine, and they almost gave up the search when Eddie spotted what looked like a finger poking out of the snow. Eddie pulled a climbing rope out of his backpack and anchored it to a tree. He slipped it around his waist and climbed down the twenty feet to the snow. He was knee-deep in snow when he reached the location of the possible finger. He brushed some snow away, and the possible became reality. Eddie continued brushing snow away while Buck used his phone and made a video.

Eddie stopped when he exposed Professor Carmichael's face. The body was frozen in place, lying up against a tree at the bottom of the ravine. It looked like the professor had fallen into the ravine and hit the tree. Eddie finished removing snow from around the body and then tied the rope around it. He climbed to the top of the ravine, and he and Buck pulled the body out of the ravine.

Buck did a cursory examination of the body. The professor's shirt was missing, and the only visible wounds were a large gash in the back of his head, from where he'd hit the tree, and several long, deep scratches on his arms and torso.

"Well. That leaves one left. Do you want to leave him here and keep searching?" asked Eddie.

In response, Buck pulled out the sat phone and called Cobra. They spoke for a few minutes, and Buck gave her the coordinates from his GPS unit. He hung up.

"Should be here in about an hour. Let's carry him to the middle of the opening, so we can get him out."

The chopper arrived as planned, and the body was placed in a black body bag and hoisted up. Buck and Eddie still had a couple of hours till their planned afternoon extraction, so they decided to keep working the area.

As they continued up the valley, Eddie asked, "Have you ever seen anything like this before?"

"No. This is new to me. I can understand the physical injuries, but what I don't understand is the blown eardrums and eyeballs. I have no idea what that's all about."

As they broke through some trees, they spotted a building in the distance, about a mile off. Buck suggested they head for it.

The first thing they encountered was a ten-foot-high chain-link fence topped with concertina wire. The fence links were rusted and looked like they had been here for a long time. Buck asked Eddie if he had any idea what kind of building this fence was protecting. Eddie shook his head. He'd never seen this place before. Buck pulled out his topo map and checked his GPS. He followed the coordinates, but there was nothing on the map.

They walked a little farther along the fence and soon came to a rusted sign hanging on it. They couldn't read it all, but what they were able to read was chilling. The sign read: Gov ment Instal n . . . U o De ly Fo e is Au h ized. They looked at each other.

"What the fuck is this place?" Eddie asked.

"Let's keep going and see if we can find a way in," said Buck.

They traveled about a quarter mile, passing additional signs, spaced out at roughly a hundred feet. Whatever this place was, it was once a high-security facility, and the use of deadly force was authorized. They made a left turn and continued for another quarter mile or so until they came to an old rusty gate, and an old two-track road. The road looked like it hadn't been used in years, except something wasn't quite right. Buck knelt next to one of the tracks. He pushed away some of the undergrowth and found what looked like recent tread marks. Possibly from an ATV.

"Hey, Buck. Come look at this," said Eddie.

Buck walked over to where Eddie was pointing at the fence. "That looks like a new padlock."

Buck examined the lock and then looked back down the overgrown road. "Found what looks like ATV tracks. Someone's been here."

Buck pulled a small leather pouch out of his jacket pocket, opened it and took out two lockpicks. Eddie looked at him. "Do I want to know why you have those?"

Buck smiled as he picked the lock. "In case I lose my house keys."

Eddie laughed, nodded and they pushed open the gate, which squeaked the whole way. They followed a shallow depression through the woods and came out into a small clearing, where they stopped and looked around.

The building in front of them was overgrown with vines and branches. It looked to be made of concrete block and was partially buried into the side of the mountain. There were no windows visible. They spotted several old broken antennas on the roof. They started walking around the building and came to a metal door. This door was also secured with an old keyed lockset, so Buck pulled out his lockpicks and started working on the lock. This door took longer to open than the padlock had. Eddie stood to one side with his rifle in the ready position, and Buck pushed open the thick, heavy door. Eddie moved right, and Buck moved left, both leading with their rifles. They scanned the room.

Buck turned on the flashlight attached to his AR-15 and moved ahead of Eddie, who had retrieved a flashlight from his backpack and attached it to his rifle. They moved cautiously, checking each room that they passed. There were four what appeared to be offices, and a large area with counters along one wall. They passed through a hallway with what appeared to be old showerheads attached to the wall and drains in the floor. The thing that stood out to Buck was the lack of dust and only a slight musty smell. He mentioned it to Eddie. They spotted a door in the distance and walked towards it.

Buck swung open the door, and Eddie led with his rifle. They were standing on a stair landing, looking down a flight of stairs that disappeared into the darkness. They started down cautiously. What they didn't see was the tiny red beam of light that spanned the top stair tread, which flashed as their feet broke the beam. They headed down the stairs.

They figured they must have gone down at least a hundred feet when they reached the bottom. The space was cave dark, and their flashlights barely cut through the darkness. They continued scanning the area, what little they could see, but they noticed lots of wires hanging from the ceiling and what looked like an old console against the far wall. They passed through what looked like an air lock and entered a huge chamber. They could make out bolts that were sticking out of the floor.

At the far end of the space was what appeared to be a roll-up metal door. Buck tapped Eddie on his shoulder, and he jumped and looked at Buck.

"Let's head back up."

They followed the same path back up and walked out into the fresh air. Buck closed the door. "I think this was some kind of missile base or something. Maybe an early Nike base."

"I don't know, Buck. I grew up around here, and I don't remember any stories about there being a government installation in the area. That's not a secret easily kept."

"What's on the other side of this ridge?" asked Buck.

"More of the same terrain, but we would be out of the Weminuche. There's some private property over there. Couple old ranchers and some summer cabins. Why?"

"That old two-track looks like it heads over the ridge. Just wondering where it might go?"

They had left the building, relocked the door and continued walking around the rest of the building when they heard a sound in the distance. It sounded like a couple of ATVs. Buck and Eddie headed deeper into the undergrowth and worked their way down the ridge. They stopped at a couple of downed trees and listened. They heard the ATVs stop at the building, and they could hear conversation, but they were too far to make out the words. They watched as four men in black uniforms and black ballistic vests walked around the building. Each man carried a pistol and an AR-15. They had a military bearing, and Buck hoped that they hadn't brought dogs with them. They spent what seemed like a long time searching the area around the building, and then Buck heard the ATVs fire up and head out. He heard them stop at the gate, heard the gate squeal and then the ATVs left. Buck and Eddie sat back and breathed a sigh of relief.

"Who the hell were those guys and where did they come from? There's no military bases around here."

"I don't know," said Buck. "They sure appeared to be military, but they had no patches on their clothes. We must have triggered an alarm when we went into the building."

"Yeah," said Eddie. "But there's nothing in the building. What are they protecting?"

Buck checked his watch. "I don't know, but we need to get out of here. We've got a rendezvous to keep."

Cautiously, they headed back towards the gate. Buck picked the lock again, and they squeezed through the fence without opening it any farther than they needed to. Buck relocked the padlock, and they headed back down the valley. When they reached the area where they'd found Professor Carmichael, they called for the chopper and took a breather. Buck wondered out loud if the reason the students were dead had anything to do with the building. He wasn't sure what they had stumbled onto, but the little bug in his brain was running around like crazy. They needed to get back to town and find some answers.

Chapter Twenty-Five

Bax and Deputy Sage had spent most of the morning interviewing people who owned white utility vans. She was amazed at how many people owned white vans. She didn't feel like they were making any progress, and so far, no one they'd interviewed jumped out at them.

She had spoken with Buck on his sat phone, and he thought they were on the right track looking at white vans. She figured that he had no idea either how many white vans were in the Four Corners area. The problem was that without a license plate number, the van Buck had the picture of could have come from anywhere within four states. She needed a faster way to eliminate vans, but unless she had pictures of every van to compare to Buck's picture, there was no way to do that.

They had grabbed lunch at a small bar Deputy Sage knew about and were sitting in his department SUV, looking at the list. "Looks like we have three more in the county."

She pointed to one that stood out. "What's this Sturgis Bones, Inc.? They have a white van registered to the company. Interesting name. I assume they sell bones?"

"Yeah, they've been around a long time. They work out of an old manufacturing facility just north of Cortez. They had to move a few years back. People in the neighborhood complained about the smell. They clean bones for clients and to sell. Let's go head up that way."

Deputy Sage pulled into the parking lot of what looked like it had once been some kind of factory. The road around the parking lot also went around the building, and it looked like the building had a lower level, so she asked Scott to drive down the ramp. She wanted to see if the white van was in the lower lot.

They drove towards a white van that was parked next to a loading dock door. There were a total of three dock doors, plus a lower door that looked like you could drive into it. She held up the picture of the van Buck had provided and looked at the van by the door. It looked similar, but the picture was so grainy it was hard to see any details. She used her phone to take a picture of the van, and they headed back up the ramp to the parking lot and found a visitor spot next to the front entrance.

She noticed it as soon as she stepped out of the SUV. There was an odor in the air. It was hardly noticeable, and if the wind was blowing in another direction, she might have missed it. It smelled like decomp mixed with bleach, and it was almost sweet. She crinkled her nose.

"See what I mean," said Deputy Sage. "Imagine having that smell in your backyard all the time."

Bax nodded and grabbed her backpack, and they headed for the entrance. Bax was surprised when they stepped into the lobby that the smell didn't appear to be inside the building. She presented her ID to the receptionist and asked to speak with the owner.

The young blond receptionist picked up her phone handset, pushed a button on her console and said, "Mr. Sturgis to the lobby, please." She hung up. "He shouldn't be long. Can I get you anything?"

They both declined and sat down in what appeared to be a waiting area. They didn't have to wait long before a tall man with silver hair and a full beard stepped up to the receptionist, spoke for a moment and then walked over to the waiting area. They both stood.

"Officers, I'm Walter Sturgis. How can I help you?"

Bax started to explain what they were looking for, and Mr. Sturgis asked them to follow him to the office. They passed through the lobby and walked past an open area with several cubicles. Each person working in the cubicle appeared to be on the phone or working on their computer. Mr. Sturgis stopped at a wooden door, pushed it open and asked them to enter. They stepped into a comfortable-looking office with a full wall of windows overlooking a factory assembly line, but this was unlike any factory Bax had ever seen. It looked like each assembly table was covered with bones.

"Officers, please have a seat."

Bax and Deputy Sage sat in the two leather visitor's chairs. "Mr. Sturgis," Bax said. "We are talking to everyone in the county who owns a white utility van, and according to motor vehicle records, your company owns a van."

She explained that the van they were looking for had been seen in the area where a crime happened ten days ago, and they were hoping to speak with the driver to see if they had seen anything.

"Can you tell me what kind of crime you are investigating?" Mr. Sturgis asked.

"Yes, sir," said Bax. "A young Native American woman disappeared on her way home from Durango."

"Ah, yes. Dee Hightower. Some of my employees are Utes, and they helped out with the search—such a tragedy. I have two older daughters. I can't imagine how her family is feeling."

"Yes, sir," said Bax. "Do you drive the van, sir?"

Mr. Sturgis explained that the van was driven by two of his employees, but most nights the van remained on the premises.

"Would it be possible to interview the two employees to see if they saw anything?"

"Agent Baxter, I will have them come to the office, but I assume they can decline your request for an interview or can request to have an attorney present if they so desire. My employees are like family, and I want to make sure they don't get themselves in trouble."

"That's not a problem, sir. We always remind people we interview of their rights and allow them to call an attorney if they want one. It would be great if you could have them come up here. Thank you."

He picked up his phone and pushed a button. "Bernie, could you have Willie and Jerry report to my office?"

He thanked Bernie and hung up. He looked at Bax. "I would be remiss if I didn't mention the smell when they arrive. We've all become used to the smell, but some people find the smell of death . . . disconcerting."

"What do these guys do for you?" asked Deputy Sage.

"They work downstairs, in what we affectionately call the crypt. They clean the bones. Been with me since we started the company. Top-notch employees and they take care of the beetles."

Bax was going to ask him to explain when there was a knock at the door. He said, "Come in," and two men entered the office. The smell preceded them, and Bax understood the warning. She had smelled death many times before, but this was almost an antiseptic smell of death. It was very unusual. Mr. Sturgis introduced them to Jerry Smallwood and Willie Robertson.

Jerry was tall and thin with angular features. His hair was light brown and cascaded around his face with curls. Willie was shorter by almost a foot. He had a bald head and was clean-shaven.

Bax explained why they were there and explained their Miranda rights. She asked them if they were okay answering questions without a lawyer, and both said they were. She asked Scott to wait outside with Jerry and Mr. Sturgis while she spoke with Willie. Willie took the seat Deputy Sage had been sitting in and looked concerned.

"Are we in some kind of trouble, ma'am?"

She explained about the investigation into the disappearance of Dee Hightower and that a white van had been seen in the area shortly before she was abducted and that they were trying to find someone who might have seen something. Willie asked where the van had been seen, and she told him near Fort Lewis College. He thought for a minute and then explained that he hadn't been in Durango for a couple of weeks. She asked him what they used the van for.

"Sometimes we have to pick up a donated body at a funeral parlor or pick up an animal from a farmer or hunter. Other times we might have to deliver the finished bones to a client or to a shipping company depending on where they are going."

Bax looked up. "You work with human bones?"

"Yes, ma'am. That's a lot of our business. Skulls make up the bulk of our business."

She cut him off. "Mr. Robertson, what is your job around here?"

Willie smiled. "We clean the bones, Jerry and me. We receive the bodies, and if we have room, we put them in with the beetles right away. They like fresh meat, you see. If we're backed up, we put them in the freezer until we have room."

Willie went on to explain the cleaning process in detail, but surprisingly he didn't make it sound gory. Bax's impression was that he enjoyed his job and had been doing it for a long time. By the time they were finished, she almost didn't notice the smell. She thanked Willie for his time and asked him to send in Jerry.

Where Willie was outgoing and gregarious, Jerry was reserved and almost tight-lipped. Bax had to drag the same information out of him. She got a different vibe from Jerry. He was almost stoic. He glanced around a lot, and he seemed extremely nervous. She finished her questioning and thanked him for his time. He left the office, and Deputy Sage and Mr. Sturgis came back in.

"Everything in order, Agent Baxter?" he asked.

"Yes. Thanks for letting me use your office. Would it be possible to see the van, maybe take a couple samples?"

"I'm sorry, Agent Baxter. The van was completely sterilized just the other day. Let me explain. Whenever we pick up a body from a local mortuary, we always sterilize the van afterwards. We have no idea how these folks died, and we need to protect our employees from disease. To that end, we sterilize everything the body touches."

Bax nodded. "You sell human bones? Is that even legal?"

Mr. Sturgis smiled. "Surprisingly, the laws about possession and sale of human remains are so vague that we've been told even lawyers can't figure them out. There are a few states back east, three for certain, that outlaw it completely and two that have tried to outlaw the practice, but the rest of the states have no real laws to prevent it. We treat everybody with the utmost respect. Most come to us from donations; some are homeless people who have died with no family; others have been donated for science. We also receive bodies from universities, medical schools, et cetera, that we clean for a fee. The rest of the bodies we sell on the internet or through our sales office, which you passed coming in. You would be amazed at the market for human remains."

"You only sell human skeletons?" asked Deputy Sage.

"Not at all, Deputy. The bread and butter of our business is skulls, whether human or animal. We are one of only a handful of companies that do this type of work, that can handle human bodies or large animals. We have the capacity to clean bears, mountain goats and pretty much anything that can be hunted. We also keep a selection of specialized bones for medical research, such as hands, feet, fingers. We have a bison downstairs being cleaned right now. We have also done cleaning for your agency, Agent Baxter, as well as the FBI and several municipalities around the country."

"Just out of curiosity," said Deputy Sage. "What does a human skeleton cost?"

"We get anywhere from six to ten thousand dollars for a fully articulated skeleton. I have one on the floor right now being assembled. Would you like to see the process?"

Deputy Sage looked interested. Mr. Sturgis stood and led them from his office to the assembly floor. The room smelled slightly antiseptic, and everything appeared to be immaculately clean. He stopped at the first table. On the table was what Bax recognized as a human hand. The assembler, a young woman dressed in a white lab coat, was looking through a lighted magnifier and was drilling tiny holes in one of the finger bones. She consulted a chart of the human hand and then, through the tiny holes, inserted the most delicate wire Bax had ever seen and connected it to the hand.

"That wire, Agent Baxter, has as much strength as an eighth-inch-thick aircraft cable. We have it specially made for us."

They moved on, passing several tables that contained individual skulls and bones that were being wrapped with shrink-wrap and were being placed in shipping boxes.

They stopped at the last table, where two employees were working on a full human skeleton. The work was meticulous. "This skeleton," said Mr. Sturgis, "is bound for the University of Pennsylvania Medical School. This was a young man who died of cancer. He was only twenty-five years old. His family decided to donate his body to science, and the university hired us to clean and reassemble it. Please follow me."

They walked down a small hallway to a freight elevator and stepped in. Mr. Sturgis closed the gate and hit the down button. "We call this the crypt. Our beetles like cool, dark areas. This is where the magic happens."

The elevator stopped, and they walked into a

dimly lit area containing several different-sized clear plastic boxes. They could see movement in the box nearest them, and they stepped up to it. Bax recoiled slightly at what she saw. Then she got closer and looked on in fascination as thousands of beetles and larvae devoured the tissue that was still connected to the bones.

She looked up and saw Jerry and Willie watching her. Deputy Sage called her over to a huge box, and she walked over. The site was amazing. There were more beetles than she had ever seen working on a bison carcass.

"This," said Mr. Sturgis, "came to us from Yellowstone National Park. Once the bones are cleaned and reassembled, they will be displayed in one of the visitor's centers."

Bax noticed the smell was stronger down here, but it wasn't overbearing. She asked what happened to the beetles when they weren't cleaning bones, and they stepped through a door into an almost cave-like space. There were several enclosures full of beetles eating what seemed like chunks of flesh. Willie explained that they kept some of the flesh frozen for later use and then fed it to the beetles.

Bax looked around the space and observed the rough stone walls and the huge freezer. They followed Mr. Sturgis back upstairs and thanked him for the tour. They left the building and walked to Deputy Sage's SUV. She looked at her watch and realized they had spent so much time at the bone company that they would need to put off the last two interviews until the next day.

"What do you think?" she asked Deputy Sage as they climbed into the SUV.

"It's a fascinating place, and I'm going to have nightmares for the next month. Watching those bugs made my skin crawl."

Bax agreed. "What was your impression of Willie and Jerry?"

"They seemed nice enough. A little creepy, but I guess if you did that kind of work, day in and day out for as long as they have, you might be a little creepy too."

He looked at Bax. "You get some kind of feeling from them?"

Bax thought for a minute. "I'm not sure. I got a weird vibe from Jerry. I just can't put my finger on it. I also thought it was a great place to dispose of a body."

"I thought so too, but when I asked Sturgis, he told me they only work with reputable people, and they keep good inventory records of every bone they receive. I don't know, Bax. I think it might have just been the place."

"You might be right, Scott. Let's head back to the office."

Deputy Sage started the SUV and pulled out of the parking lot. Bax sat there looking out the window. She knew Buck put a lot of value on what he called "the little bug" that ran around in his brain during an investigation. Right now, she thought she understood what he felt.

Chapter Twenty-Six

Buck sat at the corner table in the Moose Café and dug into his burger and fries. What he wanted was to head to his hotel room and get some sleep. The last couple of days had been a real strain, both physically and mentally, but he also needed to eat something that didn't start as dehydrated powder. He had his laptop on the table, and he was reading the information Paul had sent him about the Dyatlov Pass incident.

After reading a little bit of the summary, he understood why this was a conspiracy theorist's wet dream. This thing had everything—bigfoot, aliens, military conspiracy, and a bunch of hikers who died in mysterious ways. He set the laptop aside and finished his burger and Coke. His mind was not going to let him focus on this information. He realized he needed to be more awake to grasp all of this. He was reaching into his pocket for his cash when a shadow crossed in front of him. He pulled his hand out of his pocket and unsnapped the thumb break on his holster. He looked up to find Luther Strange sitting in the chair across from him. Luther heard the thumb break snap and raised his hands in front of him.

"I come in peace, Agent Taylor."

Buck snapped the thumb break and reached for his Coke.

Luther Strange looked relieved. "Thank you. I should know better than to startle a man of your caliber."

"What do you want, Mr. Strange? I was just heading for my hotel, and I don't need your conspiracy bullshit tonight."

"Look, Agent Taylor. I know you don't think what I do serves any value, but it does. I give people who have nowhere to turn a platform to speak to the masses. Yes, most of what they say is bullshit, as you call it, but there is also some truth in what they have to say. Look around you. Most of these people are perfectly normal. They just latch on to some crazy ideas."

He took a break to catch his breath. Buck said, "Fine, Mr. Strange. They're all normal people. What does that have to do with me?"

Luther Strange took a sip of water from the glass on the table. "I think there is something going on in the Weminuche. People have reported mysterious lights and black helicopters, and I think I am being watched. I have noticed the same people several times."

Buck cut him off. "There are three hundred people that live in this town, and you know them all. The rest of these people, your broadcast brought in. Of course they're watching you. That's why they're here."

Buck stood up and grabbed his laptop.

"Agent Taylor. I'm scared. I think I exposed

something nefarious, and you're the only one who can help me. Don't say I didn't try to warn you. Please be careful."

Luther Strange stood up, looked around the cafe and headed for the door. He didn't stop to look back. Buck watched him leave and decided to play a little game. Even though he was exhausted, he started to follow Luther Strange as he walked down Main Street. He'd hoped to get answers when they got back to town, so maybe this was the first step. He doubted anyone was following Luther Strange, but then a block from the cafe, he caught sight of two men. They were walking casually, on the other side of the street, past all the vendors selling bigfoot T-shirts and magic potions. They looked like any of the tourists that had descended on the small town, but they weren't looking at the items they picked up. They were watching Luther Strange.

Buck watched them for a few minutes as they slowly made their way down the street. He spotted Luther Strange turn down East Second Street, and he looked over at the two men. They put down the items they were looking at and picked up their pace, still not moving fast enough for anyone to take notice. Buck picked up his pace as well, continuing to watch the men. The men were about to cross Main Street when Buck heard a shrill whistle from a block or two behind him. He turned and spotted a woman a block back. She was dressed like most of the other people in town—stringy hair, baseball cap and ripped jeans—but she was wrapping a blue bandanna around her neck.

Buck turned back towards Second Street and spotted the two men turn in the opposite direction from where Luther Strange had gone. They headed down Wall Street and ran towards an industrial building.

Buck crossed the street and turned down Wall Street and slowed. He unsnapped the thumb break on his holster and put his hand on his gun. He moved cautiously through the parking lot of the industrial building, but he didn't see anyone. The streetlamps cast long shadows across the lot, and he decided he had lost them. He'd started to turn when the board slammed into his back. He hit the ground and tried to turn when someone kicked him in the back and then kicked him in the side. He covered his head and someone smashed the board against his upper arm. He heard a car pull up just as someone yelled, "Hey. What's going on out there?" He was kicked once more in the side, and he heard two car doors close, and the car sped off.

Buck started to get up, but a man and woman ran up and told him to stay put. The man pulled out his phone and dialed 911. Within two minutes, Deputy Murphy was kneeling next to Buck, checking his injuries.

"I'm okay," said Buck.

"No, I don't think so. Stay down till the paramedics get here."

The paramedics arrived a minute later, and Buck told them he felt fine. He was a little bruised, but more than anything, he felt foolish. He knew better than to chase a suspect in the dark, but he was concerned for Luther Strange. If he wasn't so tired, he might have realized his mistake before he took a beating.

They sat him on the back of the ambulance and took his vitals and made sure he hadn't been hit in the head. They checked his reflexes, and he seemed fine. They suggested he take a handful of aspirin because he was going to be sore in the morning. He stepped away from the ambulance just as Sheriff Butcher hobbled up on his walking cast.

"What the fuck, Buck. You okay?"

"Yeah, I'm fine," said Buck.

The sheriff looked at the two paramedics. "Is he fine?"

They both nodded and packed up their gear.

The sheriff turned back to Buck. "What the hell happened? The last we talked, you were going to dinner and then heading to your hotel room. What changed?"

Buck explained about his dinner visit from Luther Strange and how Luther felt he was being watched. He told him that, just for kicks, he'd decided to tail Luther, to satisfy, in his own mind, that no one was following him and it was all in his imagination. He told him about the two guys he'd spotted, and the girl who sent the warning message to them that Buck was watching them.

"Well that was a pretty damn fool thing to do, go after those guys on your own. This is a small town. Backup is, like, one minute away. Christ, Buck, what were you thinking?"

"Yeah. Problem is I wasn't thinking. I was tired,

and when I saw these guys head after Luther, I reacted. Completely my mistake."

"Are you certain they were after Luther?"

"No doubt, Carl. I was focused on the guys. Never even thought about someone watching me."

"Buck, what the hell are we into?"

"I don't know, Carl, but I'm damn sure gonna find out."

The sheriff offered Buck a ride back to his hotel, and he accepted. He could already feel the soreness coming on, and he knew he was going to dread tomorrow.

Chapter Twenty-Seven

The ringing phone woke Buck from a disturbed sleep, and as he reached for his phone, he remembered the beating he'd taken in the alley. He sat up, looked at the number and answered the phone.

"Hey, Bax. What's up?"

"I hope I didn't wake you. I wanted to run some things by you if you have a minute?"

"No problem. Hold on a sec."

He grabbed the aspirin bottle and shoved a handful into his mouth and washed them down with some warm Coke.

"Okay, Bax. I'm all yours."

She asked him how his trek into the mountains had gone, and he filled her in on the bodies they'd found and the strange building in the middle of nowhere that wasn't on any of their maps. They also talked about all the conspiracy theories floating around, and about tailing some guys who were following Luther Strange. He didn't mention the beating in the parking lot.

"Are you sure these guys were following Luther?" she asked.

"Yeah. I just can't figure out why. It's weird. He reports on crazy conspiracy stuff every day, but last night. He was scared."

"Could the building you found have something to do with it?"

"Unless he already knew about the building before we found it, I don't see how. We hadn't told anyone, not even the sheriff. I'd sure like to know who those guys were. They were there within forty minutes of us entering the building."

"But you found nothing in the building?"

"That's the funny thing. The building was empty, but it was obvious that someone had been inside recently."

"What are you going to do?" she asked.

"If you're okay without me for another day or two, the first thing I'm going to do is run over to Colorado Springs and see the coroner. I want to find out who at the tox lab leaked the findings to Luther Strange. Then I'm going to arrest that person. I also need to understand the autopsy results. Kate Milligan, besides being the coroner, is also a licensed medical examiner. I'm hoping she can answer a couple of questions for me."

Colorado was one of about a dozen states that still used the coroner system, instead of the medical examiner system. The coroner for each jurisdiction was an elected official, and that person did not have to have any experience or even be a medical professional. Anyone could run for coroner. The system was gradually evolving so that the coroner was required to complete a formal training program in death investigations, but it was a slow legislative process. Unlike in the medical examiner system, and since the coroner did not have to be a doctor, coroners would contract with a licensed forensic pathologist to handle any investigations that required an autopsy. These forensic pathologists were highly trained doctors who split their time among several jurisdictions to keep costs down. Many of the forensic pathologists were current or former medical examiners, and several were retired, working part-time to keep their hands in the game. In this case, Buck was lucky. Dr. Kate Milligan was one of the best pathologists he knew.

"So, fill me in on Dee Hightower," he said.

Bax told him about the suspect they had in custody and her belief that the guy was just in the wrong place at the wrong time. "It pissed me off the way they treated the poor guy, and the sheriff did nothing."

"I know it's hard when stuff like that happens. The problem is Reuben's in a tough spot. He has a relationship with the reservation that he's earned, and he helps patrol the reservation within limits. Still, the reservation is federal land and is governed by federal and tribal law. He can only say so much without jeopardizing his position with the tribe, and we have no jurisdiction over anything that happens on the res. And while we're on the subject. If this becomes a death investigation, the FBI will swoop in and take over in a heartbeat. I'm surprised they're not already involved."

"Thanks for the reminder, Buck."

She told him about the search for the van and that so far, nothing had panned out. Buck sensed some hesitation, and he asked her about it.

She told him about her visit to the bone factory, and about the two guys, Willie and Jerry, and the creepy feeling she got from them. "I always thought the little bug you talked about was kind of bizarre, but I can't shake this feeling that these two guys are somehow involved. I think I caught your bug."

Buck laughed. "Okay, let's talk it through. These guys clean bones for a living, and they drive a white van for work. You said the place is high end and very well organized. Any gut feeling that the owner might be involved?"

"I didn't get that vibe," said Bax. "I checked out his website, and it's all very professional. He certainly likes what he does, but I didn't get anything creepy from him."

"Could it have been a reaction to the surroundings and the smells that creeped you out and not the two guys?"

Bax thought for a minute. "I don't think so. Dead bodies don't bother me, and I spent years gutting animals when I went hunting with my dad. This was something else."

"Have you called Paul to do a deep dive on these guys?"

"I was going to call him next," she said.

"Right now, you don't have enough for a warrant. See what Paul turns up. I will call my brother-in-law and see if he can point us in the right direction. Lucy's brother used to do all the taxidermy work for her dad's hunting clients. I'd like to see if these guys have their own bone-selling site. Also, talk to Reuben and see if he can spare a couple guys for some surveillance. Tell him CBI will pay for it. That will make him happy. Let's watch these two guys and see where they go. Lastly, see if Reuben has a friendly judge who might give us a warrant for their phones and bank accounts. It's a fishing expedition, but let's see what happens."

"Got it. Thanks, Buck. Good luck with the conspiracy folks."

Bax hung up, and Buck showered and dressed. It was a four-hour drive to Colorado Springs, and he needed to get going. He clipped his badge and gun to his belt, grabbed a Coke out of the small refrigerator and headed out the door. He called the sheriff to tell him where he was going and asked if he could have Eddie look into what that building might have been used for and who owned it now.

His phone rang as he slid into the car. He saw the number, smiled and answered. "Hey, kiddo. What's going on?"

Cassandra, or Cassie to everyone she knew, was Buck's middle child, and she was every bit a middle child. In high school, she'd played soccer, ran track and played volleyball. She lettered in all three sports. She was also the one who got in trouble for violating curfew, drinking and getting into whatever other mischief she could find. Buck was surprised when she was accepted to the University of Arizona with a full scholarship for volleyball. He was even more surprised when she was accepted into law school. Cassie had never been one for regimented education.

Four years ago, she'd suddenly dropped out of

law school, and her career path took a different track. She joined the Forest Service and was now working as a wildland firefighter with the Helena Hotshots, one of the country's elite firefighting teams, based out of Helena, Montana.

Buck had not been surprised by any of this. He never saw her sitting behind a desk as a lawyer. She loved the outdoors, and she was as tough as they come. Lucy hadn't been pleased that she quit school without any discussion, and she always worried whenever Cassie was called out on a fire, but she also knew her daughter, and if this was where she was happy, then so was her mom.

"One of the guys on the crew is into all this conspiracy-type crap, and he said he heard your name mentioned on one of the podcasts he listens to."

"Let me guess," said Buck. "Strange Revelations?"

"Yeah, that's the one. Is there something I don't know about you? What's going on? Is this about a case you're working on?"

Buck pulled out of the parking lot and transferred the call to the car's communication system. He told her what was going on with the case, and they talked for a while about all the people who were in Creede, and all the theories everyone had. He told her about Luther Strange and his involvement. He didn't tell her about the incident in the parking lot.

They talked for a good bit of the drive about a lot of things. It had been a long time since they'd had a conversation about something besides him getting shot at. She told him about the fire they were working in Northern California, and they talked about David and Jason, and how things were going at home. When she hung up, Buck felt good. Ever since Lucy died, Cassie had been his sounding board, the way Lucy used to be. Another voice and another viewpoint to help him see a case more clearly. It also reminded him that he needed to call David and Jason.

Chapter Twenty-Eight

Buck pulled into the parking lot for the El Paso County Coroner's Office in Colorado Springs. He got out of his car and stretched. As Buck got older, he found it was a lot harder to spend four hours in a car, especially after someone had broken a 2×4 across his back. He winced from the pain, grabbed his backpack and headed for the entry. He presented his ID to the woman at the reception desk and asked to see Dr. Kate Milligan. The receptionist picked up her phone, spoke to someone and hung up.

"She'll be with you shortly. Please have a seat."

Buck sat down, pulled out his phone and opened his email. He found an email from Paul and opened it. The subject line read "Dyatlov Pass Incident," and the note said that this was just a sampling of what he could find. There was lots of info on the web.

Buck was about to open the attachment when a young woman approached him.

"Hi, Agent Taylor. If you'll follow me, Dr. Milligan will see you now."

Buck followed her down a corridor and into an autopsy suite. Dr. Kate Milligan was talking into the microphone hanging from the ceiling. She signed off and removed her gown and gloves.

"Buck Taylor. Don't see you much on this side

of the divide." She walked over and reached out her hand, which Buck shook.

"Hi, Kate. It has been a while, hasn't it?"

Dr. Kate Milligan was about six feet tall and rail-thin. She had an angular face and wore her dark brown hair tied up in a bun. Under her gown, she wore jeans and a pink T-shirt.

She removed her glasses. "Are you here about this poor fellow?" She pointed towards the body on the table covered by a white sheet.

"One of many, unfortunately. What's the cause of death?"

Kate looked serious. "Just like the others, undetermined. Buck, what the hell happened to these people? Any idea? Because I'm stumped."

"I wish I knew, Kate. I was hoping you'd have some answers for me."

She walked over to the table that held Lum Gladstone and pulled back the sheet. "His eardrums pretty much exploded; his one eye is ruptured. His insides look like jelly." She pointed to his arms, which had deep scratches on them. "He almost skinned himself, he scratched himself so bad. And before you ask if it was animals, the answer is no. I found skin under what was left of his nails, several of which were broken off. He looks just like the other folks from this group."

Buck walked around the body, occasionally bending over and looking at something he thought might be of interest.

"Kate, I'm gonna ask you a wild question. What do you know about infrasound?"

"Never heard of it. Why?"

"We've dealt with a lot of crazy conspiracy theories on this investigation, like bigfoot, alien abductions, stuff like that, but one case was brought to my attention that has some eerie similarities. There was a case in Russia back in the fifties involving some missing hikers, and when they were found, some of their injuries were very consistent with these. I guess there were a lot of conspiracy theories surrounding that case as well, but one theory that came up a few years back was that they might have been hit with infrasound waves. I haven't had the time yet to read about the incident, I'm just going by what I heard on a podcast, but there are a lot of similarities."

Kate looked at him. "There are two things I would have never put together, Buck Taylor and podcasts. When did you get so computer literate?"

They both laughed. Kate asked Buck to follow her, and they headed down the corridor to her office. She pointed towards the visitor's chair, sat behind her desk, and started clicking the keys on her keyboard. She stopped clicking and started reading something on the monitor. She clicked a couple more keys and read some more, then she picked up her phone and dialed a number. Since she only pushed four buttons, Buck figured it was an extension.

"Dave, do you have a minute to come to my office?" She paused to listen. "Yes. Now, if you can?"

She hung up and continued reading, clicking a

few more keys as she read. There was a knock on her door, and a short black man with a bit of a beer belly and wearing scrubs stepped into the office.

"Dr. Dave Pettigrew, Buck Taylor, Colorado Bureau of Investigation," she said without looking up.

Buck stood, and the two men shook hands.

"Dave, take a look at this," she said and stood up. Dave walked behind her desk, sat down in her chair and started reading. He scrolled down the page and then sat back in the chair.

He looked at Kate. "That could explain a lot. Are you buying this?"

"I briefly read two other papers on the subject, one from the military, and one from USC medical school. It sure explains a lot of what we found. I'll send you the links."

"What do you want to do? I mean, this is like right out of *Star Wars* or something. Sound weapons. Do we have a weapon like that?" He looked at Buck.

"I know we have prototypes of sound weapons, but what I read said they are large. The military is working on handheld versions, but as you said, this is like futuristic stuff. One thing I did find out is that infrasound is a real thing, and it can occur in nature or from a mechanical source. I briefly read about a university lab that had a problem, and the sound was coming from a bad fan. Whales and a lot of other creatures also use infrasound to communicate. The government did a study because they thought infrasound might have been what caused all our government people in the embassy in Cuba to get sick."

"Can we test for this, to be sure?" asked Dr. Pettigrew.

"From what I have learned, you can test for it. Sound below twenty hertz is below our hearing threshold, but we can feel it in our bodies. I read that nineteen hertz is the resonant frequency of the human eye and that it may be infrasound that causes people to see ghosts and other things. I understand it also needs to be a high decibel level. This is way out of my knowledge base, but just for kicks, I checked online, and you can buy a special kind of microphone that will pick up infrasound. Of course, if it were some kind of a weapon like the conspiracy folks are yelling about, it would be hard to find unless you were there when the weapon was fired."

"Incredible," said Kate. She looked at Dr. Pettigrew. "Let's not do anything regarding the cause of death just yet. I want to see if I can find an expert on this stuff, to look at what we have and see if this could ring true."

Dr. Pettigrew walked out from behind the desk and extended his hand. "Buck, nice to meet you, and thanks for the information." He walked out the door.

"Well, Buck. This could sure explain a lot. What we do with it, I'm not sure, but it sure does make for an interesting discussion. Now, do you need anything else from me?"

"Yeah, this next part is a little trickier. Who had

access to the tox report, before it was sent to the Mineral County sheriff?"

"We have two full-time techs in the lab. Why?"

"The information was leaked to a conspiracy podcast guy named Luther Strange, who put it on his broadcast before we had it."

"Shit. That's not how things work around here. I trust my guys one hundred percent. Any chance it got to this Luther Strange character from another source?"

"Not likely. He had it a full day before we got it. What about an admin person or a secretary?"

"There is one admin in the department, and she sends out the reports after the techs write them up. What do you want to do?"

"What I'd like to do is scare the shit out of all three of them and then arrest one of them. What I'm willing to do is let you handle this as a personnel matter and deal with it appropriately. Your call, Kate."

"Thanks, Buck. I'll find out what happened, and if it was one of my people, I'll deal with it. I'll let you know what I find out. I appreciate this, Buck."

Buck stood up, grabbed his backpack and shook Kate's hand. "Let me know if you find an expert in infrasound, okay? I'd love to know if this is what we are dealing with. Thanks."

He turned and walked out the door, put his backpack in the back of his Jeep and headed back towards Creede. It had been an interesting day so far.

Chapter Twenty-Nine

Bax opened her laptop and clicked on the information Paul had sent over about Willie and Jerry. As she suspected, there was no red flag that jumped out at her that said, "Hey, we kidnapped a woman."

Jerry was married and had two kids, his mortgage on his little house in Cortez was current, and he had no outstanding arrest warrants. He belonged to the local taxidermy club and for the most part lived a simple, quiet life. Bax found it interesting that his wife was also a taxidermist, and she thought about the smell when they'd walked into their boss's office. You could probably say that they were made for each other.

Willie lived alone in an apartment in Mancos. He was an only child and wasn't married. It didn't look like he ever had been. Again, Bax thought about the smell of death. She could see where that would take some getting used to. He too had a clean record with no outstanding warrants.

She closed the files and opened up her social media page. She entered their names and found them both. Jerry's page had pictures of his wife and kids. He had several dogs and was an avid hunter. There were several old pictures of Jerry as a youth, posing with skulls and skeletons of various animals.

There was also a picture of Jerry standing next to a human skeleton. She made a note of the date the picture was posted. Other than that, his posts were clean.

Willie's page gave the appearance that he didn't use social media every day. There were large gaps in posting dates. He had a few pictures of him and a good-looking bass boat that he seemed to be proud of. She only found one picture of Willie with either a skull or a skeleton. He didn't follow any taxidermy pages and there was no mention of his chosen career. He didn't seem to have much of a life outside of work.

She was frustrated. She hoped that the sheriff was having better luck. He was over at the county courthouse, trying to get a warrant for their phone information and bank accounts. She knew this was going to be a stretch. Judges tended not to like fishing expeditions, and they had little reason and no evidence to indict these two guys. They were working purely on gut instincts.

Just an hour ago, the sheriff had called off the search for Dee Hightower. Her husband was not happy, but they were out of options. Over the past ten days, they had searched the entire county, and other than the car in the ravine and the camper who had been beaten, who had a few of Dee's items, there was nothing left to do. She faced reality. Dee Hightower was either no longer in the area, she was being hidden, or she was already dead. Bax hoped it was not the last option.

She was about to close her laptop when a

thought occurred to her. She opened the investigation file and scrolled through the reports. She found the transcript of her interview with Bob O'Brien, the camper the Utes had brought in. She ran down the responses until she found what she was looking for.

Agent Baxter: "Can you describe the two men?"

Bob O'Brien: "They were both white. It was dark, and I wasn't close when I first saw them. One was tall. One was short. My head hurts bad."

One was tall, and one was short. Sounded just like Jerry and Willie. She pulled out her phone and called Paul Webber.

"Hi, Bax. What's up?"

"Hey, Paul. Buck is still tied up in Creede. Can you pull away for a couple of days? I need some help with some surveillance."

"Those two guys I researched yesterday?" asked Paul.

"Yeah. My gut is telling me there's something there, and we have an eyewitness who described two men in a white van. One was tall, and one was short. That fits the two guys you researched. As soon as the sheriff gets back, I'll talk to him about using some of his people, but I could use your help."

"No problem, Bax. I'll be there this afternoon."

"Thanks, Paul." Bax hung up.

She put down her phone and was returning to her laptop when Sheriff Garcia walked in and sat down in the chair opposite her.

"We have a very limited search warrant for both

cell and home phones and both bank accounts," he said. "The judge called what we had flimsy, and if this weren't a small community, I doubt we would have gotten anything. We are limited to only calls or money related to bones. Everything else is off the table. We also have to report back to her within seventy-two hours and let her know what we found, or she will revoke the warrants."

Bax breathed a sigh of relief. "That's better than we hoped for. Nice job, Sheriff. I'll start calling the phone companies and see what they have. Can you have Scott start checking with the banks? I also have Paul Webber from my office coming down."

"Okay, Bax. What else do we need to do?"

She explained about the description that Bob O'Brien had given her and then asked him about using some of his people for surveillance. Before he could answer one way or the other, she said, "Buck told me to tell you that CBI will pay for the overtime."

"Well, shit," said the sheriff. "That will make the city council happy at the next budget meeting." He picked up the phone on the table and asked the dispatcher to locate Captain DiNardo.

A few minutes later, Captain DiNardo walked into the conference room. The captain was a middle-aged woman with gray hair and looked sharp in her uniform. The sheriff introduced her to Bax as the commander of the patrol division and explained to her what they needed in the way of surveillance. She told the sheriff she would put together a schedule and have it on his desk within the hour. She shook Bax's hand and walked out of the conference room.

The sheriff walked out of the room as Deputy Sage walked in. Bax handed him a copy of the warrant and asked him to start contacting the banks in the county and see what kind of accounts Jerry and Willie had. He asked about internet banks, but Bax said she wasn't worried. If they were like most people, they would have that information on their phone, and they could grab it that way. It wasn't per the exact wording of the warrant, but it could be interpreted that way. Deputy Sage took the warrant and headed for his car. He felt it might be better to visit each bank in person due to the sensitive nature of what they were dealing with.

Bax pulled out her phone and started calling all the major cell phone providers so that she could get a line on their cell phones. She would also check the reverse phone directory and see if either of them had a landline. She finally felt like things were starting to move.

Chapter Thirty

Buck sat at one of the unused desks in the bullpen reading through his case file notes until the sheriff returned from an emergency meeting with the county commissioners. His phone rang with an unknown number.

"Buck Taylor."

"Buck, this is Bill Wagner with the U.S. Forest Service. Do you have a minute to talk?"

"Sure, Bill, I was going to call you today. What can I do for you?"

"We probably found your last missing person, Dom Rivera."

Bill Wagner told him that a couple hikers had stumbled on the still partly frozen body of Dom Rivera propped up against a tree. He told him search and rescue was bringing out the body and asked where he wanted the body sent.

"Bill, if you give me the coordinates, I can have an Air National Guard chopper meet them, and they will take the body to Colorado Springs. Any sign of foul play?"

"Not according to my ranger on the ground or the search and rescue team. Looks like he got caught out in the storm and just sat down and died. One odd thing. Search and rescue said the area he was found in was littered with debris from what

187

looks like a helicopter crash. They searched the site and found no human remains, so I have logged the site as another unidentified aircraft site. That's the fourth one in the last two years. Anyway, I included the coordinates in my report, and I'll send a copy to your email."

"Bill, any idea why he wasn't with the others?"

"Not really," said Bill. "Funny thing is he was found almost eight miles from the base camp, and the area was not part of their search parameters. I can't figure out what he was doing way out there."

"Bill, this may sound like an odd question, but was the survey team looking for anything else besides grizzlies?"

"No, this was all about grizzlies. Why do you ask?"

Buck explained about the bunker they had stumbled on, and about the guards in black uniforms. He also explained about finding Lum Gladstone with an empty gun.

"Buck, that's weird. I've been all over these mountains, and I don't recall ever seeing a bunker. There's no way it's new. Any idea when it was built?"

Buck was about to answer when Bill interrupted him. "Buck. What do you think happened to the professor's team? Those people were my responsibility, and I feel just awful about their deaths."

"I wish I knew, Bill. So far, the evidence says it could be natural causes, but there is some strange shit going on. I hope to have more answers today.

Contact search and rescue and send me the coordinates for a meetup, and I will get the chopper there."

Buck hung up, walked over to the refrigerator and grabbed a bottle of Coke. He had just taken a drink when Sheriff Butcher hobbled in. He sat down at the desk Buck was using and put his bad foot up on the desktop.

"Hurts like hell today. So, the county fathers are of mixed opinions. One says having all these crazies in town is bringing in a nice influx of money into our economy, and one says we are going to be the laughingstock of the state, and we should run them all out. The lone holdout wants to study the situation a little more. Please tell me we're making progress."

Buck told him about the call he'd just had with Bill Wagner, then they talked about the bunker and infrasound. Sheriff Butcher scratched his head. "Sounds like some kind of science fiction thing. What the hell is going on out there?"

Buck shook his head. "I don't know, Carl. You've been around a long time, any thoughts on this bunker?"

Buck showed him the bunker's location on the topo map, and the sheriff was quiet for a minute. "I've never heard of a bunker in the mountains around here, but I know someone who might." He stood up and told Buck to follow him. They walked outside and climbed into the sheriff's SUV.

"Paul Goodrich has lived in town as long as I can remember. People used to say he was involved in a secret government project, but he always denied it. Told folks he worked for the phone company, back then the old Ma Bell system. Let's see if he knows something."

The sheriff drove three blocks and pulled up in front of a small house with a well-manicured yard. They walked towards the back of the house, and the sheriff pulled open the screen door.

"Paul, Millie. It's Carl Butcher. You home?"

Paul Goodrich stepped into the kitchen. He was a slight man with short gray hair and piercing blue eyes, and he had on a pair of coveralls. "Hey, Carl. Come on in."

The sheriff introduced him to Buck, and he invited them to grab a seat at the kitchen table. "Been working on the furnace," he said to explain the coveralls. "What can I do you for?"

"Paul, you've been around here a while. Have you ever heard about a bunker way up in the Weminuche? Buck here found one, and it doesn't show up on any maps."

"So, you thought of me, because of those old rumors that I was some kind of spy or something," said Paul. He laughed, stood up, walked to the counter and poured a cup of coffee. He stood looking out the window for a minute, not saying a word. When he walked back to the table and sat down, his demeanor had changed. He set the cup on the table and looked at the sheriff and then at Buck.

"Mr. Goodrich," said Buck. "If you know something that might help us, we'd sure appreciate it. We've got seven dead bodies, and we are trying to get answers for their families about how they died. If that bunker is related to their deaths, it would sure help our investigation."

Paul Goodrich looked at Buck. "I doubt the bunker is related to their deaths, Agent Taylor."

"How can you be sure?" asked Buck.

The sheriff looked at Buck and then back at Paul Goodrich. "You know about the bunker?" he asked.

Paul took a sip from his coffee cup and looked down at the table. "We were never asked to sign a nondisclosure agreement about our work back then. It was just an unwritten rule amongst us all that we would never talk about it. The government was convinced that the Russians had spies everywhere, and the old saying was, loose lips sink ships. So, we kept quiet."

He looked at Buck. "The bunker was part of an incredible communications system. Today, you'd call it a relic of the Cold War. Let me tell you a little story about the continuity of government and the role we played. Have you ever heard of AUTOVON?"

Chapter Thirty-One

Paul Webber parked his Jeep in the parking lot of a small delivery company and made his way, on foot, to a shallow ravine about two hundred yards from Sturgis Bones, Inc. From his position, he had a clear view of the back door and the loading dock. He watched as several delivery trucks came and went, and he spotted Jerry and Willie leave at the end of the day. Neither one drove the white van, which still sat in a parking space next to the loading dock. He clicked the mic on his radio and reported that he was in position and settling in for the evening. He tried to be as inconspicuous as possible, which was not always easy.

Paul was a big guy, over six foot four with a muscular physique. He had joined CBI two years earlier after spending ten years with the Dallas, Texas, police department. His last post was as a homicide detective. Paul may have seemed like a giant, but those who knew him knew he was a pussycat. He was one of the most soft-spoken guys Buck had ever met. They had first worked together on an arson fire that had almost cost Buck his life when the case got bigger than just a fire. He had also been instrumental in helping Buck unmask a decades-old serial killer in Aspen a year ago. It had been Paul's diligence that led to the information that revealed that the old serial killer's granddaughter, Alicia Hawkins, had taken up her grandfather's cause. Paul was instrumental in tracking down Alicia Hawkins when she'd returned to Aspen a few months back to fulfill a sick promise she had made to her dying grandfather. A promise that would embolden her and secure both their sick legacies.

Bax checked in by radio and reported that she was parked down the street from Jerry's house. Everything was quiet. Deputy Sage was parked in a commercial parking lot across the street from Willie's apartment. So far, he had nothing to report. Two deputies, Martinez and Kellerman, were in unmarked cars, following the two suspects as they made their way from Sturgis Bones, Inc. Captain DiNardo had done an excellent job putting together a surveillance net in a short period of time and was now monitoring the surveillance operation from her office at the sheriff's department.

* * *

Earlier in the day, Paul and Bax had spent some time going over the phone records and financials of the two suspects. One thing was clear from the start. Jerry and Willie lived different lives outside of work, and she wondered how they had ever connected. Jerry appeared to be a normal family man. Most of his expenses were for the things all families need: food, utilities, and mortgage. There was little at the end of the month for luxuries.

Willie, on the other hand, was different in many ways. He paid rent on his apartment and had a car payment for a five-year-old Ford F-150 pickup truck. Other than food, most of his money went to online porn and gambling sites. Bax had looked at a couple of these sites and grown more and more disturbed by what she found. Bax was no prude, but some of these sites made her skin crawl. His debt level on the two gambling sites he favored didn't seem out of hand.

They moved on to the cell phones and internet accounts. Their cell phones showed nothing unusual until Bax took a deeper look at the dates the women in question had disappeared. She noticed that on those nights, their phones were quiet, and their internet activity seemed to stop for several hours. This would not be suspicious, except that before and after the period of the disappearance, their phones showed a lot of activity.

She picked up her phone and called the cell phone providers for both phones and asked to speak with a supervisor. Once on with the supervisor, she identified herself and referenced the warrant she had emailed to each company earlier in the day. She asked if it was possible to show where those phones had been during the specific times of the disappearances. The supervisor told her that they would be able to give her a general area, but they could not get more specific, and they would get back to her as soon as they had the information.

Paul noticed that there was little communication between the two men. They didn't seem to talk or text with each other, and he wondered if they might have burner phones. Of course, it was also possible they just didn't talk or text with each other. He did think Bax was on to something regarding the low-use periods, and he hoped the phone companies would get back to them soon.

Bax picked up one of Jerry's bank account statements and stared at it for a long time.

"You see something interesting?" asked Paul.

"It's what I don't see that's puzzling," she said. "Both these guys were involved for years in bone preservation, yet neither one sells any bones on the side. Just seems odd to me."

Then she stopped and smiled. She checked the date on the missing person report for Dee Hightower. "Gotcha." Paul looked up from the bank statement he was reading.

"What?"

Bax slid over the bank statement and pointed to a line about halfway down the page. Paul looked at where she was pointing. He laughed. "You have to be kidding me."

Bax was about to respond when Sheriff Garcia stepped into the room. "What's going on? You look like the cat that ate the canary."

Paul slid over the bank statement. "Willie spent two dollars and eighty-seven cents at a convenience store the night Dee disappeared. The store was in Durango."

"Son of a bitch," said Sheriff Garcia. "What's our next move, since this is still circumstantial?"

"Let's run the surveillance net and see if we can locate Dee," said Paul. "If they lead us to her, we can spring the trap. We still don't have anything on Jerry, but my guess is they were together."

"I'm gonna call the store in Durango," said Bax, "and see if they still have any video footage. If we can place them there together, that strengthens our case."

Bax grabbed her phone and called the store in Durango. She spoke with the manager, hung up and grabbed her backpack. "They keep the tapes for two weeks. I'm gonna run over there now and take a look."

"Paul, while she's doing that, let's get the team together for tonight's surveillance and run over the rules and expectations," said Sheriff Garcia.

Paul picked up his phone and called Buck, got his voice mail and left him a message about what they'd found and about the plans for the night. There was a little light at the end of the tunnel. He hoped Dee was still alive.

Chapter Thirty-Two

Paul Goodrich took another sip of coffee. "Back in the fifties and sixties, our biggest fear was a nuclear attack. We had the bomb, and the Russians had the bomb, and between us, we could annihilate most of the world. One of the military's concerns was being able to keep communications open between the government leaders and the military. We needed a nuclear bomb–proof communications system. Enter AUTOVON, the automatic voice network. The Department of Defense contracted with AT&T to develop a phone system for the military's use, which could override low-priority calls in the event of a nuclear attack. The system worked under normal conditions, just like the civilian phone system. It had its own area codes, and numbers and everyday calls worked like a normal system. The AUTOVON phones, however, had an extra set of four red keys on it. That was for the priority switching. The four buttons were P for priority, I for immediate, F for flash and FO for flash override. Each button could override calls placed with the button below it. The FO key was special. That was for use by the president or the National Command structure. Those calls always went through first."

"This system ran parallel to the civilian phone

system, so in the event of an emergency, a priority call would bump a non-priority call off the system. To set up the switches for this new system, the DoD built bunkers all over the U.S. and even in several foreign countries. Some of these bunkers were huge, and some were small enough to just contain switchgear, but they all had one thing in common: they were all built to withstand a nuclear blast. They were self-contained and were manned around the clock. Several of the largest bunkers are in the Washington, DC, area and were designed to also serve as continuity of government bunkers."

"You're talking about locations where government officials would be taken in the event of an emergency?" asked Buck.

"Correct. COG, continuity of government, and COOP, continuity of operations plans, were sites designed to maintain a government in case Washington was destroyed. These bunkers could house upwards of several hundred officials for up to thirty days. Thank god we never had to use the sites, but AT&T maintained the system until the early eighties when it was replaced with a more sophisticated system. By the mid-nineties, the system was abandoned and the bunkers left to decay. I have heard that several of these bunkers are being revitalized to house government server farms.

"Now we come to our bunker. Ours was a special kind of bunker. Not only did it contain AUTOVON switchgear and was a COG bunker, but ours served a unique role. Around the country, in secluded areas, four unmanned bunkers were built, and these were connected to our nuclear missile arsenal. We used to call them doomsday bunkers. They were our last resort in the event of nuclear annihilation. Every half hour, twenty-four seven, three sixty-five, a signal was sent to these four bunkers from somewhere in Washington. As long as these signals continued unabated, the system operated as a phone switch, but in the event the signals stopped for more than four cycles—so two hours—the system would override our nuclear missile fail-safe system and fire all of our missiles at their predetermined targets. The thinking was that if the Russians destroyed us, we would get in our last licks, even if we were all gone. The system was designed to override the Air Force folks stationed in those missile silos. It bypassed the presidential launch codes, and once activated, it could not be stopped. That was our doomsday weapon, our last chance to fight back."

Paul Goodrich stopped talking and sipped his now-cold coffee. Buck and Sheriff Butcher sat there, dumbfounded.

"That is why no one ever knew that bunker in the Weminuche existed. At the time, it was built on private property and was built covertly by hard rock miners. My job, along with a special team from AT&T and the Department of Defense, was to install the switchgear and the nuclear override system. Periodically, we would chopper up to the bunker to maintain the system and change out components. Always with an armed military escort. I don't know where the other three bunkers were located since there were about seventy-five bunkers in this country alone, but I know that our system was in contact with every missile silo in a thirteen-state area from Nebraska and Kansas to the Pacific Ocean. The system was removed in the late nineties. I guess having a system that could override good judgment scared some powerful people enough that they wanted the system destroyed. That was the last work I did in the bunker before I retired."

"We couldn't find any record of the bunker ever having existed, and it doesn't show up on any maps or satellite images," said Buck.

"And you won't. The last thing the government wants is for foreign governments or terrorists to find out about the bunkers and what they were used for. That is why a lot of us have never spoken about our involvement. As I said, a lot of the other bunkers are being repurposed, but I haven't heard anything about ours, so as far as I know, it's still abandoned."

"How big is the bunker?" asked Sheriff Butcher.

"It goes down three levels, so most of it is between one hundred and three hundred feet belowground. It was designed to house thirty government officials from the Denver area. It has two generators, a fresh water supply, dormitories, and even a studio to produce news stories. Further down the mountain, you'll find four very well-disguised inlet and exhaust tubes, and you might stumble over a radiation detector or two still lying around the building. It was an incredible system that was right for the times, but I have to tell you. I was never happier than when we were told to remove it. The idea of a computer overriding our entire missile defense system scared the shit out of me."

He stood up and put his coffee cup in the sink. "Now, gentlemen, if you'll excuse me, I have a furnace to work on. You can show yourselves out." He turned and walked out of the room.

Chapter Thirty-Three

Buck and Sheriff Butcher left the house and drove back to the office in silence. When they walked through the front door, they were met by Eddie Shelley, and sitting in the visitor's chair at the desk Buck had been using sat Luther Strange.

"I've been checking on ownership of that bunker we found, and I can't find any information," said Eddie. "I'll keep trying, but I've hit a wall."

"No need, Eddie. We'll fill you in later," said the sheriff. "What's with Luther?"

"He wants to talk to you both. He has a new conspiracy theory; you're gonna love this one."

The sheriff looked at Buck and raised an eyebrow. "Fuck. Let's get this over with."

"Luther," said the sheriff as they walked towards the desk. "What can we do for you?"

Luther stood up and extended his hand towards Buck. "Agent Taylor, I understand you took a beating that might have been meant for me. I am most grateful, sir, and I hope you have recovered from the unfortunate event, but I believe it proves that I am in danger."

Buck shook his hand. "No worries, Mr. Strange. I am fine; however, the beating I received doesn't prove that you are in danger. You speak about a lot of things on your podcast. Anything is possible. I would suggest you keep a low profile for a couple of days and call the sheriff if you think you are being followed."

"Is that it, Luther?" asked the sheriff. "We're pretty busy right now."

"No, Sheriff, that is not it. I have been informed by a reliable source that the remains of the last missing hiker has been found in the Weminuche and that he died under mysterious circumstances. Is this correct?"

"Look, Mr. Strange," said Buck. "You know we can't talk about an ongoing investigation. We can confirm that a body was discovered in the mountains and that the body has been transported to the El Paso County Coroner for autopsy. Once we have an autopsy report, we will make a public statement as to the cause of death. Right now, that's all we can give you. Now, if there's nothing else . . .?"

"My source said the body was discovered in a field and was surrounded by debris from a UFO crash and that government agents are being dispatched as we speak to remove the UFO debris. Confirm or deny?"

Buck looked at the sheriff and Eddie and tried hard not to laugh. "No, Mr. Strange, the body was not discovered in the middle of a UFO crash site. Well, I guess technically you're correct. There was debris in the area from an old helicopter crash, and since we do not have any information about the helicopter, I guess it is a UFO crash site, since it is unidentified, and it did at one time fly, but it is not a UFO in the sense of aliens."

Luther Strange's eyes narrowed and he stared at Buck. "Agent Taylor, you are making a mockery of my information. I think you are covering up a UFO recovery operation being performed by the U.S. government, and my followers will not stand for that."

Buck's face showed his annoyance. "The only U.S. government recovery operation going on is the U.S. Forest Service search and rescue team removing the remains of a deceased individual. A Colorado Air National Guard helicopter was dispatched, under my authority, to the area to help with the recovery and transportation of the body to the coroner. If you believe something nefarious is going on, I will be happy to give you the coordinates of the crash site, and you can send an army of your followers to the site to catch the government red-handed, but there is nothing to see. Since there were no human remains at the crash site, the Forest Service has decided to leave the remaining pieces of the helicopter right where they are. Go look for yourself."

At that moment, Buck's phone rang. He looked at the number and, without another word, walked into the sheriff's office and closed the door.

Luther closed his notebook and left in a huff. The sheriff and Eddie sat down at the desk, and the sheriff filled Eddie in on what they'd found out about the bunker. They were just wrapping up the conversation when Buck hung up his phone and opened the office door.

"That was the coroner. Dominick Rivera, our last hiker, died from hypothermia. There are no signs of foul play, and no other injuries like those of our other victims. She also told me she spoke with a doctor who is an expert on sonic injuries. She said the other bodies' injuries are consistent with injuries sustained in some kind of sonic event, but there is no way to determine if their deaths were attributable to such an event. Since we have no evidence to support that conclusion, she is going to release a statement later today indicating that the hikers died from hypothermia, which is the only thing she can prove. She'll send Rivera's samples to the toxicology department, but she saw no evidence that anything else killed him."

"Well, that will clear up one mystery," said the sheriff. "Maybe now all the crazies will go home."

"What about Luther?" asked Eddie. "He's not going to accept those findings."

"One thing you need to understand about Luther," said Buck. "He isn't going to accept any findings that come from us or the government. If we told him what he wanted to hear, he would change what he believes. He will never be satisfied."

"What surprises me is that with all his sources, he doesn't seem to know anything about the bunker, yet you were confident he was being followed when you were attacked," said Eddie.

"Maybe that's a good thing," said Buck. "No telling what he would make of that."

"But then who was following him?"

"You know what, Eddie. That's a good question. Whatever caused him to be watched must have happened in the last two weeks. Go back through his archives of shows for the last two weeks and see if anything pops up that might lead to someone wanting him followed."

Eddie nodded, stepped over to another desk and opened a laptop. While he was busy clicking keys, the sheriff and Buck stepped into the sheriff's office. "Buck, what about the people at the bunker? Nothing we heard this morning gave us any indication who they could be."

"I've been thinking about that. I need to call my boss anyway, to fill him in. Let's see if he has some ideas. We have nothing to go on to get a warrant to search the place, so we need a plan B. Oh, by the way, Kate found out that one of the interns in the toxicology lab was the one who sent the early tox reports to Luther. She has been terminated, and the information is in the hands of the county prosecutor to see if she should be arrested and charged."

Buck headed over to his temporary desk, opened his laptop and clicked on the investigation file. He clicked on the tab marked "Autopsy Reports" and looked down the list. True to her word, Kate Milligan had forwarded all the autopsy reports for the seven victims, and all the death certificates recorded hypothermia as the cause of death.

Buck was looking at the list of personal effects

that Dominick Rivera had had with him when he arrived at the coroner's office, and two items caught his attention. Rivera had several pieces of burnt metal and some shards of what appeared to be some kind of curved plastic. The coroner's note said the samples had been sent to the state crime lab for analysis.

Buck sat back in his chair. "Why would Rivera pick up pieces of an old helicopter crash?" he said to no one in particular. He pulled out his phone and hit a number in his speed dial list.

Chapter Thirty-Four

Bax pulled into the Easy GO gas station and convenience store on the corner of Highway 550 and West 29th Street and parked her Jeep. She walked into the store and asked to speak with the manager.

The second woman at the counter turned around and said, "I'm Brenda Gorman, how can I help you?"

Bax presented her ID and mentioned that she had called earlier and spoken with a Shirlee Williamson about some video footage from two weeks before.

"Right, Shirlee mentioned someone might be stopping by. Her shift ended an hour ago. Why don't you follow me."

She led Bax to a small, neat office, and she stood next to the desk while Brenda pulled up the security footage. She moved sideways and asked Bax to have a seat, the only one in the office. Bax sat behind the desk, and Brenda slowly started advancing through the frames. Bax gave her the date and time from the receipt, and Brenda's fingers flew across the keyboard, slowing as she neared the time Bax had given her. Bax watched carefully.

"Stop," said Bax, and Brenda released her finger from the mouse. She slowly advanced until Bax told her to stop again. The image on the screen was a white van parked in one of the spaces in front of the building.

Bax was able to make out the license plate and compared it to the plate number from the van at Sturgis Bones, Inc. The plate matched. Bax had her forward the image to her email. They continued watching and spotted a man exit the vehicle on the passenger side. Through the window of the store, the image was blurred out by the store lights.

"Do you by chance have video from the counter for the same time that might show this man more clearly?"

Brenda closed one screen and opened another, and Bax could see the image from behind the front counter. Brenda ran the video forward, and she stopped at the same time as the front lot video. They didn't have to wait long until Willie stepped up to the counter with his can of Sprite and a Snickers Bar. He dug through his pockets, looked back in the direction of the van and pulled a credit card out of his back pocket. He looked back at the van, put the card on the counter, signed the receipt and walked away from the counter.

Brenda saw the look on Bax's face. "Probably forgot he didn't have any cash. We see it all the time. Someone comes in for something cheap, and when they get to the counter, they're embarrassed to find they don't have any cash and have to use a card."

Bax had her forward the video clip to the same email, thanked her for her time and asked her not to delete the clips. She would get a subpoena for the video clips as soon as she could. Brenda told her she would move the entire two weeks to a separate folder in the cloud and save them for her.

Bax walked out of the store and slid into her Jeep. The video clip proved that Willie had been in Durango a few hours before the abduction, as a passenger in the van that was not supposed to be used for personal business. But she had no way to prove that he wasn't there on company business until she could confirm that with Mr. Sturgis, the owner. She couldn't prove Jerry was with him, although someone was driving the van, and she couldn't prove that them being in Durango connected directly to the abduction of Dee Hightower.

She called Buck and left him another voice message telling him what she'd found. She wondered where he was since he wasn't picking up his phone. She hoped he was having better luck with the conspiracy people than she was having.

* * *

Bax rubbed the sleepiness out of her eyes, poured another cup of coffee from her thermos and checked her watch. It had been two hours since the lights in Jerry's house went out, and since then, the place had been as quiet as a tomb. She opened her phone and re-read the text from Buck about the bunker. That was some story, and she wondered how many people in the country knew that this kind of thing had gone on.

She was still rereading the text when she spotted

movement near Jerry's house. The front porch light went out, and Jerry stepped onto the front porch and looked around. He then headed for the cars in the driveway, but instead of taking his car, he slid into his wife's blue Toyota Corolla. He started the engine and backed out of the driveway.

Bax picked up her radio. "Bax to DiNardo, I've got suspect Jerry leaving his house in a navy-blue Corolla."

"Thanks, Bax. Linda, are you still parked around the corner from Jerry's house?"

"Yes, ma'am," said Deputy Linda Martinez.

"Keep your eyes peeled for the blue Corolla and follow him."

"Roger."

A minute later, she said, "Captain, the Corolla just passed by and turned onto Highway 160 Westbound. I am four cars behind him. Wait. His directional just came on, and he's going through a drive-thru. I'm sitting in the parking lot next door. He just pulled up to the window and picked up a small bag and what looks like a bottle of water. He is back heading westbound on 160."

"Okay, Linda. Stay with him and keep me posted on where you are."

"Roger."

Bax thought to herself, "A little late for a midnight snack, and why didn't he head for home?"

Bax keyed her mic. "Scott, any movement at Willie's apartment?"

Deputy Sage replied, "Nothing. All quiet. Lights went out about twenty minutes ago."

"Thanks," said Bax.

A few minutes later, Linda said, "This is Linda. Jerry just turned north onto Highway 491. Traffic is light, so I am backing off a bit."

"This is Linda; he just turned onto Lebanon Road. I've pulled over because there is no other traffic on the road right now. I think he's heading to the bone company."

"Roger," came the response. "Paul, this is DiNardo. Looks like Jerry is heading your way."

Paul stretched and said, "Roger. I've got the back door covered."

"Scott. DiNardo. Anything yet?"

"No, ma'am. All still quiet."

"Roger."

"This is Paul. I have headlights coming down the ramp alongside the building. Stand by."

Bax was wide awake and listening. Right now, it was all on Paul. All she could do was keep an eye on Jerry's house.

"This is Paul. Jerry just unlocked the small back door and entered the premises. He appeared to be carrying a small white bag and a bottle." Paul noted the time.

Then everything stopped, and for thirty minutes, nothing happened, as Paul watched through his night-vision scope.

"This is Scott. I've got Willie leaving the apartment in his pickup truck. He's heading west on Highway 160. I'm a couple cars behind him."

"Roger, Scott," said DiNardo. "Jimmy, follow behind Scott, but keep your distance."

Deputy Jimmy Kellerman acknowledged.

"This is Scott. We're coming through Cortez on 160, still westbound."

"Roger."

"This is Paul. Jerry just came out of the building and locked the back door. He is pulling out of the parking lot."

"Roger, Paul."

"This is Scott. Willie just turned south onto 491 and pulled into a twenty-four-hour hamburger joint. I'm going past and pulling into a nearby store."

"This is Jimmy. I'm going past the location and will turn around and watch from across the street."

"This is Linda. Jerry is heading back the way we came. I think he's heading home."

Bax was sitting there, wondering what the hell was going on. None of this made sense. Both suspects decide to go out for a midnight snack. One goes to the office, and one goes to a food place.

She keyed her mic. "Scott, Jimmy. What's he doing now?"

"This is Jimmy. He's sitting at a table in the dining room, eating a burger. What do you want us to do?"

"Stay with him and let's see what happens," said DiNardo.

Bax was working on their next move when her phone rang. She looked at the number and answered. "Hey, Buck. I've been trying you all day. You okay?"

"Yeah, sorry. Things have gotten a little stranger

over here, and I wanted to catch you before I got back to my hotel. Tell me about the receipt lead."

Bax told him what she'd found at the convenience store in Durango and her uncertainty of its value as evidence of the abduction. Buck agreed it wasn't much to go on. They walked through the rest of the evidence she had on Jerry and Willie, and Buck told her that she was lucky Sheriff Reuben had a good judge. They were on thin ice so far.

"This is Jimmy, Willie just left the parking lot and is heading east on Highway 160."

"Bax. What's going on? Sounds like a stakeout."

"We decided to surveil Willie and Jerry and see if they might lead us somewhere. So far, all we've got is weird behavior." She outlined all the moves they'd made in the past couple of days and all the odd moves that Jerry and Willie had made that evening.

"This is Scott. Willie is back at his apartment. What was that all about? He passed five 'round-the-clock restaurants to go to the farthest one from town."

Just then, headlights appeared on Jerry's street, and the blue Corolla pulled into the driveway. Jerry slid out of the car and headed for the front door.

"Hold on, Buck." She put down her phone. "This is Bax. Jerry is back home."

"Roger, Bax."

"Sorry, Buck. The second suspect just returned home. As I was saying . . ."

"Bax. Did I hear you say Jerry entered his front door?"

"Yeah. Why?"

"Bax, they made you. I don't know how, but they did."

"That's not possible, Buck. We didn't make any mistakes."

"Listen to me, Bax. Call the sheriff and tell him to call the owner of the bone place and get him to meet you there right away. If he won't give you permission to enter the building, use exigent circumstances. You believe a life is in imminent danger. Kick in the door if you have to but get inside that building. Those two guys just played you all. Something's going down, and the key is in the bone shop. Keep the two deputies on the suspects' houses but get everyone else to that building and search the shit out of it."

Bax hung up and dialed the sheriff. "Sheriff, sorry to wake you." She told him what was going on and what Buck had said. "Yes, sir." Bax hung up and picked up her radio.

"This is Bax. Jimmy, Linda, stay on the suspects. Everyone else meet at Sturgis Bones, and Captain, send backup and an ambulance."

She dropped the radio on the seat and pulled the Jeep away from the curb. When she hit Highway 160, she put on her flashers and stepped on the gas. Dee Hightower might still be alive, but for how long she had no way of knowing.

Chapter Thirty-Five

Max Clinton answered the phone the way she always did when Buck called. "Buck Taylor. How's my favorite cop?"

Dr. Maxine Clinton, Max to her friends, was the director of the State Crime Lab in Pueblo. She was a matronly woman in her early sixties, about five foot five with short gray hair. She probably thought she carried around an extra fifteen pounds she didn't need, but she was still a handsome woman.

Married for forty years, Max had four children, eleven grandchildren and six great-grandchildren. She lived in a 150-year-old farmhouse in Pueblo, where she liked to tend her garden and sit on her porch and drink iced tea. She was also a bourbon girl and could easily drink most people under the table. She was loud and outspoken, but she knew her job.

Max had received her PhD in Biology from the University of Colorado and worked as a biology professor for twenty years before joining CBI and accepting the challenge of running the lab, which under her leadership had become one of the top crime labs in the country. She was a hard taskmaster, but she had a belief system that didn't allow for defeat. Her goal was to give the crime investigator, no matter which department or municipality they worked for, all the information they would need to solve any crime. She held that as a sacred obligation to the victims. She was incredibly dedicated, and her team at the lab practically worshipped her.

Buck would be included in that group. Many times, during a complicated investigation, it had been Max and her team that lit the spark that led to a breakthrough. Max was one of Buck's favorite people, and she felt the same way about him.

"Doing good, Max," said Buck. "You got a few minutes?"

Buck and Max caught up for a few minutes, and then Max asked Buck how she could help him.

"The El Paso County Coroner sent you a couple of items they found in the pockets of Dominick Rivera, the last missing hiker. I was hoping you had time to take a look and tell me what you could about them."

Buck heard some computer keys clicking. "Just got the analysis back a few minutes ago. I am uploading a copy of the report to the investigation file. Bottom line, the pieces came from a Bell 47G Agusta helicopter. According to the information I got from the boys in the metals lab, the Bell 47G was a popular two-seater helicopter, and was used from the late forties, early fifties until now. There are still a bunch flying today."

"Max, any chance this was a military helicopter?"

Max tapped a couple keys. "We found traces of

yellow and white paint on the metal, so I would say that it is unlikely. Why?"

"I'm trying to figure out if the crash of the chopper has something to do with an abandoned bunker we found in the mountains."

"I assume the bunker has some military connection?" asked Max.

"Yeah," said Buck. He told her the story they had heard about the origin of the bunker and the connection to the country's missile defense system. Max listened quietly. When Buck finished, there was silence on the other end of the phone.

"That's a hell of a scary story, Buck. I'm familiar with the AUTOVON system and worked with it early in my career. The university was involved in several research projects for the government. Because they were classified as essential to our national defense, we had a sixteen-button phone in the lab. The idea that the system was able to override all our security protocols and launch nuclear missiles on its own is frightening."

"Yeah, my thought exactly," said Buck. "I'm trying to figure out why Dominick Rivera would pick up those pieces. Seems like odd behavior."

"Well, Buck. People do strange things. According to the autopsy report, he died from hypothermia. Maybe he wasn't thinking clearly. Could be any number of reasons."

"Probably right, Max. Now for my next question. Do you know anyone I can talk to who is an expert in infrasound?"

"What's your interest?"

Buck told her about the information he had gotten from the coroner, the results of the other autopsies and the possible connection to the old bunker. The information the coroner had provided was medical; Buck now wanted to know about the science. Max thought for a minute and then told him she might know someone who could answer his questions. She told him she would call this person and then have him call Buck if he could help.

She ended the call the way she always did. "You're a good man, Buck Taylor. God will watch over you. Stay safe."

Buck hadn't been to church since he received his confirmation, but he always appreciated Max's little blessing. It wasn't that he didn't believe in God. He wasn't sure what he really believed in. He didn't like organized religion, but he never held that against anyone. A lot of people had prayed for his wife during the five years she fought metastatic breast cancer, but in the end, Lucy still died. Although he had been mad at first, he soon realized that to be angry at God, he first had to believe in God, and he could never get there. He always felt there were forces in the world that he couldn't explain, and he always thanked the river spirits whenever he had a chance to do some fly-fishing. He didn't have a place for one God in his life. He never held Max's beliefs against her. He always figured that it couldn't hurt if she believed he was worthy.

Buck sat back in his chair and thought about the

conversation with Max. The helicopter hadn't had military colors, which by itself did not exclude it from being a military chopper. Still, it made him wonder even more about why Dominick Rivera had picked up the pieces. He looked over at the next desk, and Eddie was hanging up the phone.

"Do we have a next of kin for Dominick Rivera?" he asked.

"Yep. We got it from his university profile. Even though he wasn't a student, he had to fill out all kinds of paperwork to clear the university and the Forest Service of any liability." Eddie shuffled a couple of pieces of paper around and lifted one.

"He has a sister in Denver, one in Kansas City and two in Chicago. The sheriff called Denver PD, and they made the death announcement to his sister about an hour ago. What's up?"

Buck hated disturbing someone at a time like this, but he needed an answer to his question. Eddie handed him a slip of paper, and Buck dialed the number.

A woman answered the phone. "Hello."

Buck introduced himself and offered his condolences for her loss. He explained that he had been investigating the deaths of the survey team and asked if she would be willing to answer a couple of questions about her brother. She said she would.

"Ms. Rivera, this may seem like an odd question, but did your brother have an interest in helicopter crashes?"

"Why do you ask, Agent Taylor?"

"He was found in the middle of an old helicopter crash site, and he had placed a couple of small pieces from the crash in his pocket."

There was a moment of silence on the phone, and then Ms. Rivera said, "Oh my god. He found the site."

"I'm sorry, Ms. Rivera, but can you explain what you mean by 'he found the site'?"

She explained that back in 1975, her grandfather, Edward Rivera, had disappeared without a trace while flying in the mountains somewhere near Creede, and that the crash site had never been found. She told Buck that her brother had spent several years trying to get answers from the government, or AT&T, without success. She told Buck about the million-dollar bank account that no one knew about and about the mortgage being paid off.

"Did your grandfather work for the government or AT&T?"

"He was a communications engineer for AT&T, and he worked in Denver. There was no reason he would be on a helicopter in the mountains. There were rumors that his department was working on some top-secret project, but we could never get anyone to confirm anything."

"Ma'am, is your grandmother still alive? I'd like to speak with her if possible."

"We'd all like to speak with her, Agent Taylor. Grandma was diagnosed with Alzheimer's a couple of years back, and she's completely out of it. She couldn't help if she tried. Agent Taylor, do you know what my grandfather was involved in?"

Buck hesitated for a minute. "Right now, Ms. Rivera, I can only speculate, but with what you have told me, I might be able to find out, and if I do, you'll be the first to know."

"Agent Taylor, one more thing. You said Dom had a couple of pieces of metal in his pocket from the crash, but you didn't say if there were any remains at the site, so I assume there were not. Can you tell me how many pieces of metal he had?"

Buck clicked on the lab report and read down the page. "He had five pieces of metal. Why do you ask?"

"I think he might have picked up a piece of metal for each of us to have as a memento of our grandfather. It would be like Dom to do that."

Buck could hear the tears starting to flow, and he thought he should end the call. "Ms. Rivera, again, I am sorry for your loss. If I find out any information about your grandfather, I will give you a call, and thank you for taking the time to talk with me." He hung up the phone and sat back in the chair.

Buck's phone vibrated with a text, and he saw two messages from Bax. He opened the first text and read it, and then clicked on the most recent one. She wanted to fill him in when he had a minute, but first he needed to call the director, and then he needed to talk to Paul Goodrich again. He would get back to Bax as soon as he could.

Chapter Thirty-Six

Buck dialed the director and gave him a rundown on the missing hiker case. He told him about the last body being found by a couple hikers, and then he told him about the conversation regarding the AUTOVON bunker.

"You mean to tell me that the government could override the nuclear fail-safe system with no human involvement at all?" asked the director.

"Yes, sir. Scary to think we had this system in our backyard, and no one knew it existed. Makes you wonder what else the government has been hiding all these years?"

"You sound like you've been listening to too many conspiracy people, but on another note, what about these security people you saw at this bunker? Any way to connect them to the dead hikers?"

"I'm not sure what to think, sir. It could be nothing. The guy we spoke with said the government was converting some of these bunkers to secure server farms. That may be what we saw. It's also possible, but unlikely, that these were terrorists. I just don't get that feeling."

"Okay, Buck. What do you want me to tell the governor?"

"You can tell him that the El Paso County Coroner is releasing a statement indicating that the cause of death for the seven hikers was hypothermia. That should get the conspiracy crazies to go someplace else. So far, no one has picked up on the bunker, so I don't think that will be an issue."

"What are you going to do?" asked the director.

"I've still got a couple of loose ends I want to tug on. As soon as I have those nailed down, I should be able to clear out of here. Maybe another day or so."

"Okay. Have you spoken with Bax? Any progress?"

"She's my next call, sir. Paul Webber was on his way down to give her a hand, so I think they'll be okay for another day or two. I will let you know if anything changes."

"Okay, Buck. Don't get too caught up with the conspiracy folks. Let me know if you need anything."

Buck hung up and was about to call Bax when his phone rang with an unknown Washington, DC, number. He answered. "Buck Taylor."

"Agent Taylor. Max Clinton asked me to give you a call. My name is Jim Donnelley. She told me you had some interest in infrasound weapons. How can I be of service?"

"Thank you for calling, Mr. Donnelley. May I ask first how you know Max, and what is your background in sonic weapons?"

"You can if you call me Jim. All this 'Mr. Donnelley' stuff is making me feel older than I am. Okay. Let's see. Max and I were grad students at the

University of Colorado together, and we've stayed in touch all these years. Max called me because she felt I could be trusted more than dealing with someone from the government."

"As for my background. After graduation, I spent twenty-five years working for the Defense Advanced Research Projects Agency. You might know it as DARPA. I can't go into too much detail but suffice to say that most of my time there was spent working on advanced weapons, including various types of sonic weapons. After I retired, I started a think tank here in Washington called Intellibrief Analytics. We gather intelligence from around the world, analyze the information, and then make recommendations to our various clients. Most of our clients are either incredibly wealthy, incredibly powerful or both, and they spend huge amounts of money based on the information we provide them. I like to think that we are a lot more reliable than our government counterparts, so right now, I am at your disposal."

"Thanks, Jim. I know if Max recommended you then you have to be the best at what you do. I just like to know who I'm dealing with."

"No worries, Buck. I would have expected nothing less. Now, Max filled me in on the autopsy reports for your seven missing hikers, and I must say, the coroner's description of the condition of the bodies is intriguing. She told me the coroner intends to rule that all the hikers died from hypothermia, which is as good a cause of death as any. I take it you are not convinced."

Buck explained about all the conspiracy theories he had been exposed to in the past couple of days, and that information from one of those theories seemed to closely match their findings.

"You're talking about the Dyatlov Pass incident, as it has come to be known. I noticed a similar pattern based on what I know of the case. Let me see if I can help you out. Some of the injuries in your case are similar. But let me stop there for a minute. I am sure your medical professional has told you that much of the damage in your cases is similar to injuries caused by infrasound, or even ultrasound. So far, all the medical community and we have to go on are people who have been exposed to infrasound accidentally. As of yet, no one, and I am talking individual or government anywhere in the world, has developed a battlefield infrasound weapon. There are several prototypes around, but nothing small enough or light enough to carry into battle. So, no one has been shot, for lack of a better word, by such a weapon. How much do you know about infrasound, Buck?"

"I know it is a low-frequency, high-decibel sound that can't be heard by humans, but supposedly, it can be felt through the body, and it can travel a long way through the ground. I have also been told it can occur naturally. Beyond that, I'm lost."

"Well, Buck. You know more than most of the world, so that's good. You are correct in what you know. Whales use infrasound to communicate, as do several animals, such as elephants and crocodiles. To create infrasound in a laboratory setting requires large subwoofers and a lot of other scientific equipment that you don't need to worry about. Suffice to say that it takes a lot of large equipment, which is why the weaponization has been difficult to create. Infrasound was brought to the forefront due to a couple of laboratory accidents in which it was found that a faulty piece of equipment—an air conditioner fan, in one instance—developed a resonance that hurt several lab workers and killed at least one person. It took several weeks of testing to determine the source of the problem."

"I heard that the illnesses in the embassy in Cuba might have been infrasound," said Buck.

"It's possible but unlikely. A more likely explanation is microwaves, which can cause a whole host of ill effects. Lots of conspiracy theories around that one but getting back to Dyatlov. During the initial investigation in nineteen fifty-nine, no one thought about infrasound. The autopsies revealed some odd injuries that were glossed over by the Russian investigators. That led to talk of bigfoot, aliens and even the possibility that the Russian military was conducting tests in the area and might have inadvertently hurt the hikers. For the most part, no one knows to this day what happened. The Russian government has opened several investigations over the years, including one just a couple years ago, but at this point, no one believes a word they say."

"How did infrasound get connected to that case?" asked Buck.

"The infrasound is a recent addition to a lot of theories and one that makes some sense, based on the condition of the bodies. If you discount the infrasound weapon theory, one that has been strongly suggested is a natural phenomenon. This is what you could be looking at based on what Max and I discussed. Max mentioned a strong storm with a lot of wind on the night the team disappeared. It is possible that the wind blew strong enough, or from a specific direction, and that something natural—a mountain, a rock outcropping, something of that nature—set up an infrasound resonance that was funneled into the valley. That would have had to have been a unique set of circumstances, because every element would have had to come together at the same time and in the same place to set up the perfect resonance."

"Jim, that sounds like a million-to-one chance of happening. Is it really possible?"

"I think the odds would be closer to several billion to one but remember the fan in the laboratory. It is possible, and based on everything my company has been able to determine, no one has a battlefield-ready infrasound weapon."

"Jim, I can't thank you enough for the time and the information. You've given me a lot to think about. Now I just need to see where it all goes. Thanks."

"No problem, Buck. You have my number on your phone. This is my cell number. You need anything else, just give me a call. And next time you see Max, give her a hug from me. She's an amazing woman."

Buck hung up and sat, thinking about everything he'd just learned. He had been having trouble wrapping his head around the idea of a weapon and it being tied to the bunker, but the possibility that this could have been a natural phenomenon? Now that was something that made sense.

He hadn't realized how late it had gotten, but before he headed out for a late dinner, he needed to call Bax. He dialed her number and waited, thinking about the last call and how things were starting to fit.

"Hey, Buck. I've been trying you all day. You okay?" asked Bax.

Buck told her he was fine and asked her what she found out about the receipt. She was explaining about the receipt when Buck heard her radio in the background.

"Bax. What's going on? Sounds like a stakeout."

She told him about the surveillance and outlined all the moves they'd made in the past couple of days and all the odd moves that Jerry and Willie had made that evening.

The little bug in Buck's brain started jumping up and down. Something was way off, and Buck was silent as he ran what Bax had been telling him through his brain. It suddenly clicked.

"Bax, they made you. I don't know how, but they did."

"That's not possible, Buck. We didn't make any mistakes."

"Listen to me, Bax. Call the Sheriff and tell him to call the owner of the bone place and get him to meet you there right away. If he won't give you permission to enter the building, use exigent circumstances. You believe a life is in imminent danger. Kick in the door if you have to but get inside that building. Those two guys just played you all. Something's going down, and the key is in the bone shop. Keep the two deputies on the suspects' houses but get everyone else to that building and search the shit out of it."

Bax hung up, and Buck thought about jumping in his Jeep and heading to Cortez, but by the time he got there, it would all be over. Besides, he knew Bax could handle whatever came up, and she had Paul there for backup. He changed his phone from silent to his ringtone so he would be able to hear if she called, and he headed out the door to grab some dinner. He wondered where both these cases were headed.

Chapter Thirty-Seven

Bax pulled her Jeep into the Sturgis Bones, Inc., parking lot and drove down the ramp to the rear loading dock. Paul had pulled his Jeep around and was slipping on his ballistic vest. He zipped it up, grabbed the AR-15 from the gun safe that was welded into the rear area and walked towards Bax's Jeep.

"Bax, what's going on?"

Sheriff Garcia pulled into the lot with lights flashing, followed by Deputy Sage and three Cortez Police Department patrol cars. A Cortez fire truck followed by an ambulance pulled in next. The parking area was getting crowded. The sheriff stepped up to Bax and Paul.

"Bax, you think she's in there?"

"Yes, sir," said Bax. "I think Buck hit it right on the head. Something is going down, and our suspects tried to split our forces to keep us away from here."

She opened the gun safe in her car and pulled out an AR-15 and slapped in a magazine. Just then, a black SUV pulled into the lot and Mr. Sturgis exited the vehicle. "Sheriff, is this absolutely necessary? We have nothing to hide."

"Mr. Sturgis," said the sheriff. "We have reason to believe a woman is being held against her will inside your building, and we believe her life is in danger. We would appreciate your cooperation by letting us in the building, or we can cite exigent circumstances and force our way in. It's your decision, but one way or another, we are going in."

Mr. Sturgis looked around and spotted one of the Cortez police officers holding a small battering ram. He looked at the faces of those around him and realized the seriousness of the situation.

"Let me unlock the door for you, and you have my permission to search. I only ask that you not damage the containers for the bones we are cleaning."

He pulled out his key, walked over to the service door and unlocked it. Bax asked one of the Cortez cops to wait outside with Mr. Sturgis, and with weapons at low ready, she pushed the door open and raced inside. The team fanned out across the bone cleaning room, which was lit only by a couple of small LED bulbs. She found a light switch next to the door and turned it on, bathing the space in bright lights. She noticed a lot of movement in the containers and imagined that the light must have startled the beetles.

"Search all these containers and try not to disturb the beetles," she said.

They searched for a half hour, and every container contained just what it was labeled with. She was getting frustrated when one of the Cortez police officers called out.

"Agent Baxter, I think I found something." She approached the officer, who was standing alongside a large cabinet full of chemicals, followed by the sheriff and Deputy Sage. The officer pointed towards the floor.

"Looks like this cabinet has been moved, several times, based on the scratches on the floor," he said.

Paul stepped past the officer, reached his fingers into the space between the cabinet and the wall and pulled. The cabinet slid forward with a slight squeal, and everyone stepped back and brought up their weapons. Paul pulled the cabinet so it was perpendicular to the wall and exposed a door with a metal bar and lock.

"We need bolt cutters," yelled Bax.

One of the firefighters rushed in with a pair of bolt cutters and cut through the padlock. Bax told him to stand back, and she removed the lock and slid back the bar. She pushed open the door, and the first thing she noticed was the darkness. She spotted something in the middle of the floor and turned on her flashlight. Paul was behind her and did the same thing.

They cautiously approached the large container and could see a lot of movement inside. As they got closer, they were repulsed by what they saw: inside the container was a huge wriggling mountain of beetles. There could have been millions of them. As they stepped up to the container, they noticed that the mass of beetles took on the shape of a human being.

"Oh my god!" she yelled. "There's someone in there. We need to get this container open!"

For a moment, no one moved, then one of the

firefighters raced in with an ax. He hit the plexiglass sidewall of the container and broke out a chunk. He continued hitting the sidewall as plexiglass and beetles poured out onto the floor and scattered. Paul and Deputy Sage grabbed the back of the container and tipped it forward, dumping more beetles on the floor. More flashlights came on, and everyone approached the container. As the beetle pile diminished, more and more of a naked person was revealed. The sheriff rushed to the container and peered inside.

"It's her," he yelled. "It's Dee. Get the paramedics." Despite the beetles that remained in the container, the sheriff pushed his way in and scooped them away from her body. Dee Hightower was screaming inside the tape that covered her mouth as she struggled against the bindings that held her down. The sheriff pulled out a pocketknife and started cutting through the straps. He cut them all and pulled Dee out through the side. He pulled the tape off her mouth, and she screamed like the team had never heard anyone scream before. A paramedic took her from the sheriff, wrapped her in a blanket and carried her outside to the ambulance.

Someone found a light switch, and a single bulb came on. They all looked around the room. At the far end of the room, up against a stone wall, was a rusted bed frame with a filthy mattress and an old dirty blanket. There was a bag on the floor near the door that resembled the food bag Jerry had been seen carrying into the building. They also spotted a piece of aircraft cable mounted to the stone wall that had a pair of handcuffs attached to it. The room reeked of human waste.

Mr. Sturgis walked into the room, followed by a Cortez police officer, and stood in the doorway and stared. His mouth opened, but no words came out. Bax looked up, spotted Mr. Sturgis, and asked the officer to please take him into the other room. She pulled out her phone and called the CBI office in Grand Junction and requested a full forensic team.

"Okay, folks," said Bax. "This is now a crime scene. I need everyone outside until the forensic team gets here."

They stepped out of the room, and Bax slipped the cut lock back through the bar. She looked around and noticed everyone brushing off beetles. She looked down and noticed the beetles crawling on her shoes and up the legs of her jeans. She swatted them and could feel her skin crawl. She could only imagine what Dee had been feeling with all those beetles crawling on her naked body. She shuddered.

Paul and Sheriff Garcia walked over to her.

"I've called the judge and have a deputy on the way over with a search warrant for this location. The judge will not give us an arrest warrant for Jerry or Willie. She doesn't think we have enough evidence to prove their involvement," said the sheriff.

"What does she mean we don't have enough evidence? We have Jerry entering the building, we have . . ." Bax stopped. "Fuck. Let's get Mr. Sturgis back to the office and place him in an interrogation room. At the moment, he is not under arrest. Paul, can you and one of the Cortez officers hold down the fort until the forensic team arrives?"

Paul nodded and stepped away.

"How is Dee?" she asked the sheriff.

"She has some bite marks on her skin, and they are going to need to search every orifice. The paramedic said those bugs are everywhere. What kind of sick individual does this to another human being?"

"I think we were getting too close, and they got worried. The bigger question," said Bax, "is how many other times have they done this? This was not a one-off operation. It took a lot of time and effort to set up."

The sheriff stared at her. "You think they might be serial killers. Could they be responsible for those other missing women?"

"Think about it, Sheriff. This could be the perfect crime. Hold the women until they are done with them. Kill them, feed them to the bugs, and then sell the skeletons to some university somewhere. We may never know how long this has been going on, how many victims there are or where the bodies are now."

"Why didn't they kill her outright?" asked the sheriff.

Bax thought for a minute. "If we caught them like this, they would be facing kidnapping, probably rape and attempted murder, instead of first-degree murder. If we didn't get here and rescue her, and their plan succeeded, she would have been eaten to death, and we wouldn't be any the wiser. These guys are pretty smart."

"What a couple of sick fucks. Do you think Sturgis is in on it? He looked like he wanted to pass out standing in the doorway," said the sheriff.

"I don't know. If he never had reason to come down here, he might have been kept in the dark. We'll need to be sure to ask him."

Bax stepped out onto the loading dock to get some fresh air and looked at the stars. She spotted Paul and Mr. Sturgis looking at something and having a conversation. She walked over to the MCSO SUV.

"Mr. Sturgis has been informed of his rights and has agreed to talk with us."

Mr. Sturgis opened his hand and showed Bax the large beetle he was holding. "Agent Baxter, this is not one of our beetles. This is a Scarab beetle. Our beetles eat dead, but not rotten tissue. These beetles will eat living tissue and flesh. We don't use them because they can be dangerous. There are thirty thousand species of beetles in the Scarab beetle family. I'm no expert on all the kinds of beetles, but I think these are the worst." He dropped the beetle and stepped on it. "Would you allow me to call an exterminator I have used in the past? These beetles are going to get everywhere if we don't get them cleaned up right away."

Bax agreed as long as they went into the space after her forensic people were done. In the meantime, he could get rid of any beetles that were able to escape the secret room.

Bax stepped away and took a deep breath. They had done a good thing tonight, she thought to herself. Now the real work would begin. She pulled out her phone and dialed.

Chapter Thirty-Eight

The ringing phone woke Buck out of a deep sleep. He reached for the phone on the nightstand, looked at the number and answered.

"Hey, Bax. You guys okay?"

"Yeah," said Bax. "We found Dee Hightower. She's at the hospital."

Buck took a sip of warm Coke out of the bottle on the nightstand. "Nice work, Bax. Any problems?"

Bax told him about the beetles that had covered her and how they'd had to destroy the container to get her out. She described Mr. Sturgis's response and his comments about the beetles being different from the ones they used for the business.

"Buck, I think you were right. Somehow they found out we were watching them, and they set themselves up for lesser charges." She explained her reasoning, and Buck listened quietly.

"Bax. You did a good thing. You found Dee alive. It's not our concern what they get charged with. That's up to the district attorney. You did your job, and a woman is safe, and yes, it sounds like that's what they did. But if they charge them with all the crimes you described, they're going to prison for a long time. The sad part is that we will never know if this has been going on for a long time, or just recently started. One more thing. You are going to be covering a lot of ground with the forensic team in the coming days. If you need help, we can call in the team from Denver or call in some of Max's people from the State Crime Lab."

"We may have a problem, Buck. The judge won't issue an arrest warrant for Jerry or Willie. She said we don't have any direct evidence linking them to the crime, and I think she might be right."

"Tell me what you have right now?"

"Well, we have them—at least Willie—and the van in Durango on the night of the abduction, and we have Jerry at the bone company early this morning with a bag of food. We have a witness that said the men were short and tall. They had access to the space." She stopped for a minute. "Pretty flimsy, huh?

"We also got the cell phone location data back and during the low-use periods, the phones were in either Jerry's or Willie's houses. Which means they didn't take them with them if they were kidnapping the women during those days and times."

"Yeah. Let's take those one at a time. They could have been in Durango for any reason, picking up bones, dropping off bones. We have a similar van near the college but can't identify the occupants. The eyewitness is questionable, and if he's a vagrant, you may never see him again. As far as access to the space. They can swear they never knew the room was there. It could also have been accessed by anyone in the company. Yeah, Bax. Since they work there, being in the space early might be completely normal. The cell phone data doesn't help at all. We have a lot of work to do. These guys are smart. See if you can get them to come in voluntarily, and then we need to wait and see what the science says."

"Well, you're just a ray of sunshine this morning." They both laughed.

"Bax, grab a couple of hours' sleep and give the forensic team time to do their job, but have the sheriff invite them in for a chat."

"Thanks, Buck. Hey, I heard someone found the last hiker," she said. "How's that going?"

"The coroner issued a statement indicating the cause of death in all seven cases was hypothermia. The odd symptoms could have been from infrasound, and they might have contributed to the death, but as far as the official cause of death, that's what she can prove."

"You don't sound like you buy into that all the way," she said.

"No, it's not that. The coroner has to work with the facts she has at hand. Anything else is pure supposition. It just leaves a lot of unanswered questions."

He told her about the conversation with Jim Donnelley and that there was a strong possibility that if it was infrasound that had affected them, it was most likely from a natural cause.

"Everything he said made sense, and what he made me realize is that we may have gotten a little caught up in the whole conspiracy theory thing. We focused on some odd facts and tried to find a weapon that would fit the facts when the fact is, there is no weapon like that available today."

"Yeah, but someone could be developing one that this guy, Jim, isn't aware of."

"Geez. You too, Bax? Adding to the conspiracy theory?"

Bax laughed and hung up, and Buck looked at his watch. He still had a couple of things to do today, and since he was already up, and a faint light was coming through the opening between the curtains, he figured he'd just get up and get to work. He opened his laptop and started entering information into the investigation file. The more he wrote, the crazier some of this stuff sounded. He realized they were short on facts and long on speculation, but he also accepted the fact that sometimes, that's the way things happen.

Just out of curiosity, he picked up the book the stranger in the restaurant had given him about the Dyatlov Pass incident and flipped through it, reading the captions under the pictures. It certainly was an unusual case, but the more he read, the more he found he was able to come to several conclusions other than what the author was presenting. He put the book down and sat back in the chair. There were some interesting parallels to his investigation, but in the long run, the cases were as dissimilar as they were similar.

He would hate to be the Russian investigators today, trying to put together facts from a sixty-year-old cold case, when the original investigation and the subsequent investigations had been botched so badly. He did understand how much of a treasure this kind of case would be for the conspiracy theory folks. It was like it was handmade for them. He thought about all the folks that had showed up to Creede, based on no real information, and how, in that void, they'd created facts to fit the situation. Even once the real facts were revealed, these folks still believed what they wanted to believe.

His thoughts went to Luther Strange and how his people had taken simple facts and turned them into something else, misinterpreting the information about a helicopter crash and convincing themselves that it was a UFO—which was, in fact, true, except it didn't have anything to do with space aliens. He closed his laptop. This case would have to go down as one of his strangest cases yet.

He showered, dressed, clipped his badge and gun to his belt and headed out the door. First stop was breakfast, and then another conversation with Paul Goodrich.

The first thing he noticed as he walked down Main Street was that many of the conspiracy folks had already cleared out. He wondered what new conspiracy would grab their attention. He stepped into the Moose Café and spotted Eddie Shelley sitting along the wall, eating breakfast. He walked over, pulled out the chair across from him and sat down. He looked around the restaurant and noticed it was mostly locals having breakfast this morning. He thought about the extra money the small businesses in town had earned these past two weeks, and how much it had helped the local economy. At least some good came out of all this.

"Eddie, how about we take one more helicopter ride to close this case out?"

"Sure, Buck. Where are we going?" asked Eddie.

"I'd like to get one more look at that bunker before I wrap this all up. More curiosity than anything."

Buck's mountain man breakfast arrived, and he dug into the bacon and scrambled egg platter, sipping his Coke between bites. "I need to see Paul Goodrich first, but we can head up after that."

"No problem, Buck. We can run over to Paul's house as soon as we're done here." He finished his breakfast and downed the last swallow of coffee.

He commented to Buck about the lack of conspiracy folks in town, and that the press release by the coroner and the governor must have made an impact. Buck nodded and finished his platter. He grabbed the check and paid for both meals, leaving a good tip for the waitress, who smiled at him as they stood up to leave.

Chapter Thirty-Nine

Eddie's pickup truck was parked just down the street, so they hopped in for the short drive to Paul Goodrich's house, where they pulled into the driveway. They walked around to the back door and knocked. An older woman wearing a faded housecoat and glasses opened the door.

"Hey, Eddie. Come on in," she said. She turned to Buck. "You must be the CBI agent my husband told me about. I'm Millie Goodrich, Paul's wife. Pleased to meet you."

Buck introduced himself and asked if her husband was about. She asked them if they wanted coffee—they both turned her down—and she stepped through the kitchen door and yelled for Paul. He walked in a few minutes later and looked at Eddie and Buck. He didn't look happy to see them.

"What can I do for you fellas this morning?" he asked.

"Paul, I apologize for the early visit, but we found out some information yesterday, and I was hoping you might be able to clear up a couple of things for me," said Buck.

Paul sat down at the table; his wife put a large mug of coffee down in front of him and then left the kitchen. Paul sipped his coffee slowly.

"I told you and the sheriff more than I should have yesterday. I'm not sure what I can add."

"I appreciate that, Paul, but I promise this won't take long. Did you work with a man named Edward Rivera?"

Paul looked up from his coffee and stared at Buck for a minute. "There's a name I haven't heard in a long time. Why do you ask?"

"The last missing hiker was Dominick Rivera. According to his sister, who I spoke with late yesterday, Dom, as he's called, has been searching in the Weminuche for a helicopter crash site and the remains of his missing grandfather. That would be Edward Rivera. The sister told me that Edward was an engineer with AT&T and was supposed to be working on a top-secret government project when he went missing."

Paul sat back in his chair and rubbed his temples. He sipped his coffee and slid the mug to the side.

"Ed was my boss when we were installing the systems in the bunker. He disappeared on July tenth, nineteen seventy-five. He was flying from Denver to the bunker when the chopper went down somewhere in the mountains south of here. Did his grandson find the crash site in the mountains?"

"I believe he might have," said Buck. "He was found in an area that contained fragments of metal and plastic that we believe came from a helicopter. The Forest Service search and rescue team found several metal fragments in his pocket. His sister thought they might have been mementos for her and their siblings."

"Did they find any remains?" asked Paul.

"No, sir. The rangers and the search and rescue team did a cursory search but did not find any remains. They said that there weren't any large pieces of the helicopter left, and it looked like it might have disintegrated when it hit the ground."

"We all wondered what happened to Ed. He was with Captain Mark Trainor. Mark was the DoD representative during our work at the bunker. Nice guy. He left a wife and two young sons if I remember correctly. The military searched for about a week, but no sign of the crash was ever found. We had no idea what happened to them—caused a hell of a shit storm, back in Washington. Brass at the Pentagon were worried that the Russians might have kidnapped them, or worse, maybe they took off with secret data to sell to them. When there was no sign of them, a full audit was done on the site, but the DoD didn't find anything to incriminate them. It was a damn shame. Both men were so young. Are you sure it's their helicopter?"

"No, sir," said Buck. "The lab found traces of yellow and white paint, so we assume it wasn't a military chopper."

"That would be right," interrupted Paul. "That was the color of the chopper we used. Damn." He tilted his head back and rubbed his eyes. "You say his grandson found the site?"

"That's how it appears," said Buck. "His grandmother has Alzheimer's, and before that, she never spoke about it. Her grandson was trying to figure out why his grandmother had a bank account with a lot of money in it when his grandfather only had a small life insurance policy. Their mortgage was also paid off."

Paul stood up, walked to the counter and came back with the coffeepot. He poured himself a refill and then pointed it towards Buck and Eddie. They both nodded, no thanks. He placed the pot on the counter and sat back down.

"The money was to buy her silence," Paul said. "You have to remember the times. We were still in the Cold War, and everything we did was top-secret. As an incentive, the government provided each member of the team with a million-dollar life insurance policy. In case something happened to us, they didn't want the families nosing around. The money made that a near certainty. I wasn't aware of any plans to pay off mortgages."

"Are those policies still intact?" asked Eddie.

"Absolutely, but my wife doesn't know about it. When the time comes, a representative with the DoD will come to the door with a check and a document to sign, citing the need to protect national security. The irony is that at this point, no one cares about what we did back then. Those days are long gone. We are just the last relics of the Cold War, like the bunker and the helicopter crash site.

"I'll bet you fellas weren't aware, but there are bunkers all over this country, probably a couple thousand. The public and the government were bunker crazy back then, and if you weren't destined to survive a nuclear blast in a COG bunker, then you were building one in your basement. The saddest part of all is that those of us involved in the program would have ended up surviving without our families. The government planned for essential personnel, but not for their families. Can you believe they would have expected us to leave our loved ones at a time like that, knowing they would have been incinerated? I'm not sure if I could have done it." He stopped talking and looked into his coffee cup.

"Here's a piece of trivia your conspiracy folks probably don't know. There were plans to build several super-deep bunkers, for the president and his staff to use in the event of an attack, and one of those was going to be built in an abandoned mine, right here in Colorado. It might have happened, except someone high up the food chain wanted to know who would be left on the surface to dig them out of the rubble. It would have been just a deep tomb. That's how crazy things got."

Buck could see the sadness in Paul's eyes. He and Eddie stood up from the table. "Thank you, Paul. This has been helpful." Paul looked up and nodded.

Buck and Eddie walked out the back door and headed back to Eddie's truck.

Chapter Forty

Bax didn't take Buck's advice about getting some sleep. She was angry, and she needed to channel that anger into action. She pulled into the sheriff's department parking lot, grabbed her backpack from the back of her Jeep and headed for the door. She could still feel the bugs crawling on her, and she realized that she should have gone back to her hotel and showered first.

She showed her ID to the deputy at the desk and was buzzed into the back. She stepped into the conference room, dropped her backpack on the table and pulled out her laptop. She headed for the interrogation room, where Sheriff Garcia and Deputy Sage were standing.

"He ready for us?" she asked.

"We read him his rights, again, and he signed the waiver, agreeing to talk with us. Let's see what he has to say," said the sheriff.

Bax and the sheriff stepped through the door and sat in the chairs opposite Mr. Sturgis. Bax set her laptop on the table and opened a recording app. She pressed start.

"Mr. Sturgis, I know it's been a long night, so hopefully we can make this quick and get you back home. I will remind you that this is a voluntary interview. You have been read your rights, as a formality, and have agreed to speak with us. Now, Mr. Sturgis, how long has your business been located in the building we were at tonight?"

"We've been in that building for about fifteen years."

"And where were you located before that?" asked Bax.

"We had a much smaller space closer to town, but it was in a residential neighborhood, and there were complaints from the neighbors about the smell. We didn't have the sophisticated exhaust system we have now, and the smell of decomposing flesh is difficult for most people to deal with."

"Mr. Sturgis, the room we were in this morning, where we discovered Dee Hightower. Were you aware of that space, and was it there when you moved in?"

He thought for a minute. "I don't recall seeing that space when we did the walk-through with the realtor, but I do remember the cabinets along that wall. There were a bunch of old parts boxes on the shelves. The place used to manufacture parts for cars or something."

"Who has keys to the basement space?"

"Me, the office manager, Jerry, Willie, but that's just for the loading dock door and the main door. From inside the building, you can just go down to the basement in the elevator. That's never locked."

"Did Willie or Jerry ever mention the space behind the basement?"

"Not to me. Do you think they had something to

do with this? I can't believe that; they have been with me since the beginning, and I trust them."

"Okay, Mr. Sturgis. We're not accusing anyone of anything yet. Jerry was seen arriving at the building early this morning. Is that unusual?"

"Not really. Jerry and Willie take care of the beetles, so they show up often to check on the deskinning process. If the beetles stay on the bones too long, they can damage the bones, so they have to be watched. We have a lot going on right now, so it wouldn't be unusual for one or both of them to be there at odd hours."

"Just a few more questions, Mr. Sturgis," said Bax. "We have a picture from a gas station showing your van in Durango, the night Dee Hightower was kidnapped, yet you told me that Jerry and Willie only use the van for business. Any idea why they were in Durango?"

He pulled out his phone and opened the calendar. Bax gave him the date, and he scrolled through. "Yes, here we are. They were picking up an antelope from a hunter. He's one of our best customers, and we make special arrangements to pick up his carcasses. I will be happy to send you his contact info." He scrolled through his contact list and clicked on a name, and Bax's phone chimed. She checked the text and thanked him.

"Just one more question, sir. Do you keep records of the bodies that arrive at your company and where those bodies go after they are cleaned and prepared?"

"Yes. Our records are meticulous and go back almost twenty-five years."

"So, you would know if you took in any extra bodies or sold any extra bodies."

"I would be happy to open our records to you. You will find we know from where and when each body arrived, if it is in inventory, or if it has been sold and shipped. We track the body from its source to its destination, including individual body parts that may have been sold separately from the skeleton."

"Thank you, Mr. Sturgis. You have been extremely helpful. You are free to go."

They all stood, and the sheriff escorted Mr. Sturgis out of the room and towards the front entry. A deputy was waiting to take him back to his car, which was still at the company. Bax turned off her recording app and sat back in the chair. She didn't get a sense that Sturgis was lying. She wasn't sure what she felt about him. She stood up, grabbed her laptop and walked back to the conference room. Deputy Sage was sitting at the table, and she sat down. Deputy Sage could see the frustration in her eyes.

"Sheriff said you should grab some shut-eye," said Deputy Sage. "Jerry and Willie are coming in voluntarily, with their attorneys. They won't be here until after lunch."

"I will, but first, I want to run back by the bone company and see how the forensic team is doing." She was about to stand up when her phone rang.

"Hey, Buck."

"How did the interview go?"

"Good. We just finished up with Sturgis, and I'm heading back to the bone company. Our two suspects won't be in until later. Gonna try to get some sleep."

"You said something in your report this morning that got my attention. You said one of the suspects stopped at a fast-food restaurant and took the bag into the bone company basement."

"That's right. Jerry went through the drive-thru and came away with a bag. Paul spotted him carry it into the basement. Why?"

"You're looking for an in—something to connect the two suspects to the missing woman. See if you can get the hospital to make her vomit. If you can compare the food from her stomach to the food that Jerry bought, you might be able to make that connection. It's a long shot, but it might give you something to work with."

"You know, Buck. That's not a bad idea. It might give us enough to get a warrant to search his house. Thanks, Buck."

Bax hung up and looked at Deputy Sage. "Vomit, huh. Seems like we might be grasping at straws, but I'll run over there and talk to Dee. See if she will go along, and then I'll have the doctor give her something. Who knows. It might just work."

Bax thanked him, grabbed her backpack and headed out the door. She slid into her car and was preparing to pull out when she noticed several Native Americans holding signs calling for justice for Dee. She wondered how they'd gotten the news so fast. She spotted Deputy Sage stop and talk to the group before getting into his patrol SUV. She wondered how much information he had passed along to the folks from the res and hoped this wasn't going to be a problem.

Chapter Forty-One

Paul Webber was talking with one of the forensic techs when Bax pulled into the parking lot. She slid out of her Jeep and walked up the stairs to the loading dock. She shook hands with Paul and the tech.

"Anything useful?" she asked.

"Not really," said Paul. "We sent the blanket and mattress to the lab to see if we can get some DNA. The only fingerprints they found inside the room were from Dee. They are working around the cabinet and the door to see if that yields anything, but I'm not feeling lucky."

"Paul," said Bax. "You sound as frustrated as I feel."

"Yeah, guess so. I've never seen a crime scene this violent, and this pristine. If these guys are our suspects, I'm not sure we are going to get anything on them."

"Buck said just about the same thing. How could they not leave some trace of themselves?"

He looked at her through tired eyes. "Could we have the wrong guys?"

"I wish I knew, Paul. We all feel it in our bones that these are the guys, but there is nothing to connect them with the crime. Why don't you head for the hotel and grab some sleep? I need to get ready for the interviews."

Paul went back inside to check out with the Cortez officer who was guarding the crime scene, and Bax walked to the end of the parking lot and stared into the emptiness. She had never been on a case where there was no evidence to connect the suspect to the crime. She worried about how she would be able to face Dee Hightower and her family if there was no proof that Jerry and Willie had committed the crime. Who were these guys? she wondered to herself. She didn't see them as criminal masterminds—or were they just lucky? She walked back to her car and headed towards her hotel. She needed food, and she needed to think about how to talk to these guys.

She pulled into the parking lot of a small Mexican restaurant, grabbed her backpack and headed for the door. She was just pulling open the door when she heard a voice from behind her. She turned and spotted Winston Lowell, the owner of the *Dolores Weekly Chronicle*, walking between two cars. He waved to her, and she held the door open.

"Hi, Bax. How fortuitous. I was hoping to catch up with you at the sheriff's office."

"Hey, Win. What brings you to town?"

"I heard there was a raid last night, and I was hoping to get an interview with Dee Hightower, but the hospital has her in lockdown. Maybe you and I could talk. I would be happy to buy you breakfast."

"Do you eat here often?" she asked.

"That I do. Miguel and his wife make the best breakfast burritos in this part of the state. Shall we?" He waved his arm towards the dining room.

He held the door, and Bax stepped into the coolness of the dining room. They found a table by the window, sat down and ordered two deluxe breakfast burritos and black coffee. When the waitress left, Win pulled out a small notebook. "So, what led to the raid?"

"Win, you know I can't discuss an ongoing investigation, but suffice to say, we did find Dee Hightower alive, and she is being treated at the hospital. Beyond that, we are continuing to investigate and will update the press as soon as we have anything new to report."

He slid the notebook to the side. "Forgive an old man for trying to take advantage of an acquaintance. I know you can't talk about it. My apologies."

Bax smiled. "Win, if I could tell you anything, I would. Right now, there's nothing to tell."

He could see the disappointment in her eyes, but he held his comments until the waitress set the two giant burritos on the table and refilled their coffee mugs.

"You look frustrated, Bax. Case not going well?"

"Not that. We're just beginning the investigation. It's just been a long night." She dug into her burrito, and they spent the rest of the time making small talk. She took the opportunity to ask Win if he would be willing to share the information he had in his digital cloud with her so she could continue looking into the missing Native American women in her spare time. He promised to send her a link to the information. When they were finished, he reached into his wallet for his credit card, but Bax had already placed a twenty on the table. He looked at the money and then at Bax and knew there was no arguing about her paying for her meal. They said goodbye with a promise that Bax would call him as soon as something in the case broke.

Bax climbed into her Jeep and headed back to the office. Jerry and Willie were due to arrive in the next hour, and she wanted to be as prepared as possible. As she was pulling into the parking lot, her phone rang, and she answered.

Director Jackson was checking in to see how things were going. She told him about the raid and finding Dee alive and about the frustration she felt with the lack of actionable evidence. The director knew that Bax wasn't a whiner but instead was passionate about her cases, and he knew she didn't like it when she was stuck. He offered some words of encouragement that he hoped would make her feel better.

"By the way, Bax. I talked to Max Clinton and authorized her to spend whatever she needed to get a rapid DNA test on any of the samples her lab finds on the blanket and mattress. Let's hope something pops. In the meantime, do what you need to do to get those guys talking during the interview. You are good at your job, and if there's something to find, you'll find it. Let me know if you need anything else."

She thanked the director and hung up. She always felt better after talking to him, and with a full stomach, and renewed confidence, she was ready to face the suspects.

Chapter Forty-Two

Buck and Eddie pulled into the Creede airstrip parking area, grabbed their ballistic vests, backpacks and rifles and headed for the helicopter. Cobra waved from the pilot's window, and they climbed into the back and put on their headsets.

"Good morning, Buck, Eddie, where are we heading today?"

"Good morning, Cobra. Two stops. First, we need to get as close as possible to where the last hiker was found." Eddie handed her copilot a slip of paper, and he plugged the coordinates into the nav system.

"Second?" said Cobra.

"I want to do a flyby around the bunker area and then see if we can find a close spot to drop us off. Someplace where you can park for a bit."

She nodded and started the engine. They lifted off and headed southeast towards the first set of coordinates. They flew over Goose Lake and traveled another couple minutes west. Cobra started to circle the area until she found a large enough field about a mile from where Dom Rivera's body had been found, and she set the helicopter down and shut off the engine. Buck and Eddie exited the chopper and told her they should be back in under two hours. They grabbed their rifles and headed out.

The hike took them under twenty minutes to reach the coordinates, and they set their backpacks down and looked around the area. At first, it was difficult to see the pieces of metal that were scattered all about. Thirty-five years of growth had taken over the area, but they started to see small pieces of metal here and there, and they spread out to see if they could find any larger pieces. By the time they joined back up, they had determined that the wreckage covered a large area of the side of the mountain. Buck had investigated a lot of crash sites during his career, both automobile and aircraft, and it looked like the helicopter had flown straight into the mountain.

The Colorado rockies were littered with the wrecks of aircraft that had done just that. Flying into mountains, especially if the pilot was not experienced in mountain flying, with the sudden weather and wind changes was not hard to do. Visibility during a storm could drop to zero in an instant, or a sudden downdraft from a high-based thunderstorm could slam an aircraft into the ground.

"Did search and rescue report finding a backpack that might have belonged to Dom Rivera? I doubt he was this far from their base camp without some kind of provisions," asked Buck.

Eddie wasn't sure, so he pulled out his sat phone and called the office. He thanked whoever he spoke with and disconnected the call.

"There's no mention of a backpack in the report," said Eddie. "What are you thinking?"

"I wonder if Dom found those pieces he had in his pocket near here, and just like we just did, dropped his pack to search a larger area and got disoriented. Let's see if we can find his backpack."

They spread out again, only this time they were looking for a specific target. They figured if Dom had become disoriented in the storm, he probably didn't travel far to reach the spot where he died, so they focused on several small game trails leading into the area. After a half hour of searching, Eddie came on some broken pine boughs and followed them away from the crash site. Fifty yards from the main crash site, he found a smaller debris field and, sitting next to a large blue spruce, he spotted Dom's backpack. He called for Buck.

Eddie, wearing a pair of blue Nitrile gloves, was looking through Dom's backpack and had laid a couple of items on the ground when Buck reached him. Buck knelt next to him and, after putting on his gloves, picked up the items. The first item was a map of the Weminuche Wilderness, and stapled to the map was a list of three sets of coordinates. Someone had crossed off the first two. Buck checked his pocket GPS, and they were standing at the third set of coordinates. The other two items were a pocket GPS and a small notebook computer. Buck pushed the power button, but the small computer was dead. Finding nothing else of interest, they put everything back in the backpack, took some pictures of the backpack and then Eddie picked it up.

They headed back to where they'd left their backpacks, grabbed their gear and headed back to the chopper.

They reached the chopper with a few minutes to spare and loaded their gear and the extra backpack into it. They climbed in, and Buck asked Cobra to head for the bunker. She started the engine and lifted off, heading to the northeast from their present location. Within a few minutes, she keyed her mic and told them that the bunker was just ahead.

"Let's stay about a mile out and circle the bunker," said Buck.

Cobra acknowledged, and she drifted away from the bunker and started a circular search pattern. As they crossed over the ridge, Eddie pointed to a small encampment to the west of the bunker. They could see several wooden crates loaded on a trailer and several tents with personnel moving about. At the sound of the chopper, everyone on the ground stopped and watched.

Cobra's voice came through Buck's headset. "We've just been hailed on a military frequency and told that this airspace is part of a military operations area, and we've been directed to clear the area. What do you want to do?"

"Pull back about a half mile," said Buck. "Ask them by whose authority are they closing the airspace, and let's see what they do."

Cobra acknowledged the transmission from the

ground and headed away from the camp, but slowed and hovered.

"They said we are in violation of a secure military area and we need to leave or face dire consequences. Buck, this airspace is not closed according to our map. I'm not sure who these guys are," she said.

"Okay, let's head back into the wilderness area and see if we can find a place to land. I'd like to take a closer look. Eddie, is that encampment inside or outside the Weminuche Wilderness area's border?"

Eddie held up his topo map and pointed to a spot just across the border. "They are just outside. Property belongs to the Stevenson family. Has for about a hundred years. Lloyd Stevenson refused to sell his property when the Forest Service and the state were setting up the wilderness area. He was also a vocal critic about the government trying to force him off his land, even though they didn't try. They offered to buy him out fair and square, just like all the other landowners. He's a cantankerous old goat."

"Buck," said Cobra. "Closest spot to land is about a mile and a half from the bunker, in that valley where we lifted out the guide's body. Okay?"

"Sounds good. Let's put her down."

Buck looked down as Cobra started her descent, and he had a hard time believing they would make it into such a small space, but she slid in between the trees like she was sliding a thread through the eye of a needle. They touched down, and she killed the engine.

"You guys want some company?" she asked.

"You better stay here in case we get into trouble with the locals. Might need someone to get us out in a hurry."

She handed Buck and Eddie two headsets. "We'll keep the frequency open so we can hear whatever is being said. You need us, grizzly is your secret word of the day. Just remember, if I have to go in with guns blazing to save you two, my ass is out about a mile. Be careful."

They grabbed their backpacks and rifles and headed up the valley towards the bunker. Buck hoped they wouldn't have to use Cobra as their backup plan. He didn't want her getting in trouble for something he did, but it was nice to know she was ready to help if need be.

They hadn't seen anyone with weapons when they flew near the encampment, but they knew from the last trip that the guards had them, so they needed to be discreet. They found a rock outcropping not far from the bunker that afforded them some protection but gave them great visibility. They stowed their gear and settled in to watch. Eddie had a spotting scope, and Buck had a pair of binoculars, which gave them an excellent view of the complex.

The first thing they noticed was that the gate they had passed through on their first visit no longer had a padlock on it. Instead, there was a hefty electronic slide lock that was activated by a keypad attached to a column along the road. There was also a heavy-duty arm so that the gate could slide open on its own. The second thing they noticed was that the entry door lock on the bunker was also a heavy-duty electronic lockset. Someone had gone through a lot of expense to secure this sixty-year-old bunker. They spotted a couple technicians installing security cameras around the building, and a microwave antenna had been installed on the roof. Buck wondered if this might be the source for the infrasound waves that had killed the hikers.

They switched their focus to the old dirt two-track road when they heard an ATV laboring to get up the hill. The reason was made clear when the ATV passed almost in front of them: it was pulling a trailer containing two of the wooden crates they'd seen at the encampment. There were no markings on the crates to indicate what might be inside. Buck used his phone to take some photos of the ATV and the crates.

The ATV passed through the gate and pulled up in front of the bunker entrance. Two men came out of the bunker, and the four men loaded the first crate onto a rolling pallet and they passed through the door. The men reappeared a few minutes later and did the same thing with the second crate. During the time Buck and Eddie watched, they observed this same activity take place four times. The crates didn't appear to be too heavy, just awkward.

All told, during the time they watched the bunker, they counted at least a dozen men and women coming and going. No one wore any kind of uniform, and only the four guards appeared to be armed.

Buck and Eddie grabbed their gear and headed back down into the valley. It was obvious from what they had observed that this was a large operation, but they still had no idea if this was a government operation or something else. Something dangerous.

They landed back at the airstrip in Creede, just in time for dinner, and Buck invited everyone to join him for dinner. Everyone accepted, and they climbed into Buck's Jeep and followed Eddie to the Moose Café. Buck's mind wasn't on dinner as he thought about what his next step would be.

Chapter Forty-Three

Bax and Paul decided to split up the interviews with Jerry and Willie, so Bax found herself sitting across the interview table from Jerry and his attorney, a slight, beady-eyed fellow named Harold Warren. Before Bax could start the interview, the attorney informed her, for the record, that his client was there strictly voluntarily, to try to help discover what had happened to that unfortunate woman. Bax acknowledged his statement for the record and read Jerry his Miranda rights, for his protection. The attorney did not object.

She started with some basic questions: How long have you lived in Colorado? How long have you worked at Sturgis Bones, Inc.? How long have you been cleaning bones? What did you do before working for Sturgis? Explain your job at Sturgis. They talked casually about his family and how he'd gotten interested in cleaning bones. All this was designed to make him feel at ease.

"Jerry were you aware of the locked room behind the cabinet?" she asked.

The attorney interrupted and asked her to define aware. She hadn't expected him to start right away with the definition questions, so she changed it around a little.

"Did you know there was a room behind the wall shelves at the back of the cleaning area?"

"No, ma'am," said Jerry. She was hoping for a little more from him, but she could see how this interview was going to go. She would have to drag every bit of information out of him.

"How long has Sturgis been in that building?"

"I'm not sure," he said. "Must be ten or twelve years, maybe a little longer."

"And in all that time, you never moved one of those cabinets and found the room behind it?"

"I didn't know those cabinets moved. Thought they were bolted to the floor and the wall," he said.

"Do you know who Dee Hightower is?"

Jerry looked at his attorney, who nodded.

"Only what I read in the paper when she went missing."

"Do you have any idea how Dee Hightower ended up in a locked room, behind your workspace, covered in beetles?"

"No, ma'am."

Bax's frustration was growing as the interview continued. She asked him about buying beetles on his own, and he told her that when he started working for Sturgis, he'd stopped doing jobs on his own and took all the beetles he had to the bone company.

"Jerry, do you ever sell skeletons or parts of skeletons on your own?"

"No, ma'am. Too busy at work to do any side jobs."

She pulled a photo from a manila envelope that

was sitting on the desk. It showed a man exiting his car and entering the building at eleven p.m.

"Jerry, this picture shows what appears to be a man sliding out of your car and entering the building. Why were you there so late?"

"I had a bison skull that was close to being finished, and I needed to get it out of the beetles. If you wait too long, the beetles can damage the skull."

"Why did you stop and buy a bag of food at a fast-food restaurant?"

"I was hungry. We eat early, and I stopped for a burger and fries, wasn't sure how long I was going to have to stay."

"Can you explain how your dinner bag ended up in the room with the victim?"

Jerry looked at his attorney who nodded. "I left it on one of the worktables. It probably got moved with all the people coming into the space." He smiled at Bax.

They spent a few more minutes talking about who had access to the space, which Jerry informed her was pretty much everyone who worked there, and how the Scarab beetles might have gotten there.

Jerry looked surprised that she knew about Scarab beetles. "I have no idea how they would have gotten there. We never use Scarab beetles because they are too dangerous to have around the other beetles. They can also bite. I wouldn't work with them."

The attorney asked if there was anything else, and Bax said they were good for the moment. She asked if Jerry would allow her to do a DNA swab, which he said he would, and she asked if he would allow them to send a forensic unit to his house. The attorney objected.

"Agent Baxter, my client has willingly and truthfully answered all your questions. Unless he is a suspect and you are prepared to arrest him, then we would strenuously fight any order for a search of his residence. If you have evidence that my client has committed or participated in this heinous crime, then please present it, and we can discuss further activities; otherwise, we will be leaving."

Bax held up her hands in surrender, thanked them for coming and watched them walk out the door. Paul came around the corner carrying a coffee mug. He looked as frustrated as she felt.

"Any luck?" he asked.

She told him about the interview, and he led her to the table in the conference room, where he opened his laptop and pulled up the interview with Willie. He had gone through the same procedure with Willie, first asking general conversational questions, and then asking about the hidden room. Bax watched as Willie's attorney, Gail Fairhaven, a large woman with tortoiseshell glasses and bottle-blond hair, stopped the interview several times and questioned Paul's motives.

Willie also responded that he'd thought the cabinets were bolted to the floor and the wall and confirmed that they never used Scarab beetles. Bax felt like she was watching an exact duplicate of her interview with Jerry. The problem was they had nothing to go on. She and Paul had tried to surprise them with the information about the Scarab beetles, but neither Jerry nor Willie had gotten excited or anxious. If anything, they were both incredibly calm.

Paul closed the video. Sheriff Garcia was standing in the doorway and had been watching the video behind them. He stepped into the room. "Looks like we got crap from these guys," he said. "Those lawyers left here thinking that we've got nothing. How do I tell that to Dee and her family?" He turned and walked out the door.

"He's right," said Bax. "We've got nothing. Unless we get something from the science, these guys are going to walk."

"What do you want to do?" he asked.

"I'm gonna go see Dee in the hospital and see if she remembers anything that can help us."

Paul nodded and sat down at the table and opened the investigation file on his laptop. Bax grabbed her backpack and headed out the front door. As she walked to her Jeep, she noticed a lot more Native Americans walking up and down the sidewalk with signs. She had a feeling this was going to be trouble as she slid into her Jeep and headed for the hospital.

Chapter Forty-Four

Buck got back to his hotel room after dinner and pulled out his phone. He hit the number one speed dial button and waited for the director to answer.

"Hey, Buck. You almost wrapped up in Creede?"

"Well, sir. That's why I'm calling. I need to figure out how far to push this, and I need a sounding board. Do you have a few minutes?"

"Sure, Buck. Fill me in on what's going on, and let's see if we can come up with a plan."

Buck filled the director in on the last twenty-four hours. The director knew about the last body being found and about the autopsy report from the coroner, declaring hypothermia as the cause of death. They talked about the governor being pleased, and that he was glad the conspiracy folks had mostly left Creede. The governor had received a call from one of the county commissioners thanking him for sending Buck in to review the evidence and help bring clarity to a strange situation.

He told the director about their surveillance of the bunker, the radio call to the helicopter directing them to leave the military operations area and the fact that no such area existed. They also talked about the bunker itself and the crates being loaded inside.

"Buck, is there any chance the crates held some kind of infrasound weapon?"

"I can't be sure, sir. We couldn't get close enough to see any writing on the crates, but with the beefed-up electronic locks on the gate and the bunker, anything is possible."

"No idea who these people were? No insignia or anything to indicate a military branch?" asked the director.

"No, sir. That's the problem. They could be military, and maybe they are installing a server farm like we were told is going on at several other bunkers around the country. But with the history the landowner has with the government, it's also possible that they are some kind of domestic terrorism operation. Without access to the bunker, we have no way of knowing which."

"Buck, I'm gonna call the governor and get his thoughts. If they are terrorists, he'll want them rooted out for sure, and if they are government, well, you know how he feels about Washington messing around in his state. Stick tight for one more day, and let's see what we can find out. Get some rest. We'll talk tomorrow."

Buck disconnected the call and sat for a minute, thinking. They had no evidence of wrongdoing; as a matter of fact, they still hadn't been able to find out who owned the bunker. With nothing to go on, there was no way a judge would give them a search warrant. Direct confrontation might work, but it could also evolve into World War III, and Buck had no desire to get Cobra and her copilot involved in a domestic firefight. He decided the best thing to do was wait on the governor. If anyone could get to the bottom of this, it would be him, or he would raise a shitstorm trying to find out. Buck laughed at that thought.

Colorado Governor Richard J. Kennedy—who was, in fact, one of "those" Kennedys—had won the election for governor two years ago by one of the largest margins in the history of the Colorado governor's race. Regular people loved him. During those two years, Buck had been instrumental in closing several high-profile investigations that made the governor look good, and the governor relied on Buck for his competence and discretion. He also valued the fact that Buck was completely apolitical. He treated everyone the same whether you were the governor, or you were the janitor at the state capitol, and he knew Buck would never get involved in any kind of political maneuver.

The governor was a multimillionaire businessman and a seasoned politician, having spent twenty years in the Colorado legislature before running for governor. He was his own man and was an outspoken critic of the federal government and their intrusion into state affairs. He hated when they got involved in secret situations without his knowledge, and he was not afraid to chew out any government official who he felt was not acting in the best interest of Colorado. He spoke his mind, and he didn't care much about what most people thought. If anyone could find out what was going on at the bunker, it would be the governor, and he felt bad for whoever was going to be on the receiving end of one of the governor's tirades.

Buck pulled out his laptop and opened the investigation file for the missing Montezuma County woman. He pulled up the videos of the interview with Jerry and Willie and watched each one several times. The last time through, he was no longer listening to the words, but he was looking at the body language for telltale signs of distress. After thirty-five years in law enforcement and sitting through probably a thousand interviews, Buck had developed a keen eye for the slightest movement that was out of place.

He ran the interview tape of Jerry one more time, this time with the sound off, and he focused on Jerry's eyes. Each time he spotted something odd, he would play it back with the sound so that he could gauge the reaction. He did this at several spots in the interview. Jerry was good. His responses to Bax's questions were short and to the point, but there were two spots where he caught a flaw in Jerry's composure. The first time was when she asked him if he still sold bones on the side, and the second time was when she asked if he knew Dee Hightower. His answers to both questions were well-rehearsed, and his demeanor barely changed, but his eyes said he was lying. Buck made a note in the file and copied Bax and Paul.

Buck clicked on Willie's interview and was surprised at how easy he was to read. He wasn't nearly as composed as Jerry, and he kept twitching in his seat. The movement was barely noticeable.

Buck followed the same process with Willie's interview and spotted several spots where Willie's demeanor changed. There was no doubt in Buck's mind that Willie was the weak link and that they both had something to hide.

By the time he was finished, it was well past midnight, so he decided to call it a day. He shut down his laptop, grabbed a bottle of Coke out of the small refrigerator and lay back on the bed. He had thought about maybe taking some time to unwind by reading a book on his digital device. Instead, he went through the investigation in his head. Mostly to see if he'd missed something or could have done something differently. Tomorrow would be his last day in Creede, and he was excited about getting to the bottom of the last mystery he had to deal with on this unusual investigation. He thought back to where it had all started and about all the conspiracy theories he had encountered along the way. This had to be one of the strangest—if not *the* strangest—cases he had ever worked on. He took a sip of Coke and leaned back into the pillows. He made the mistake of closing his eyes, and that was all she wrote. He would sleep soundly through the night until the ringing phone woke him just before sunrise.

Chapter Forty-Five

Bax walked down the hospital corridor towards room 210 and was surprised when she got there. Instead of a deputy guarding the door to Dee Hightower's room, she was confronted by three large Native American men, all carrying pistols of various makes and calibers. As she stepped towards the door, the men blocked her path.

"No one is allowed in."

Bax pushed her vest open and exposed the badge and gun clipped to her belt. "Ashley Baxter, CBI, please stand aside and let me pass. I need to interview Dee."

"No one goes in without Dee's permission, and you ain't on the list. So why don't you take a hike before you get hurt, missy."

Bax stared down the big man and noticed him get a little uneasy as he fidgeted from one foot to the other. The other two looked from Bax to the big guy and back again. They wondered how she would respond to the missy comment. They didn't have to wait long. Bax made a move to step around him, which left him off-balance, and in two swift moves, she pivoted, kicked out a leg and shoved with her palm. The big guy hit the floor with a thud that echoed through the corridor and caused several people at the nurse's desk to step into the hall to see what the commotion was about.

The two guys watching weren't sure what to do until Bax gave them a look that forced them to back up a step. She then grabbed the astonished big guy, who was lying flat on his back, by his shirt and stared into his eyes.

"The next time you decide to 'missy' someone, you had better understand who the fuck you are dealing with. I have no problem with you guarding Dee's room, but don't you ever think you can interfere with a criminal investigation."

She pushed his shoulders back to the floor, stepped over him and entered Dee's room. She could hear the other two guys give him shit for getting flattened by a girl, and she smiled.

Dee was sitting up in bed, eating a green Jell-O cup, and she looked at Bax. "Did you hurt him?" she asked.

"Just his pride. Maybe he'll think twice before messing with a woman again."

"You the cop who found me?"

Bax said, "One of several, but yes, I'm running the investigation." She reached out her hand as she approached the bed and introduced herself. Dee shook her hand and pulled the small 9mm pocket pistol out from under the covers and placed it on the table next to the bed. Bax looked at the gun and laughed.

"You look like the kind of woman who can take care of herself, why the bodyguards?"

"They're some of my cousins, and they wanted

to feel useful, so my husband told them to watch the room. Sometimes they're not so bright, but they mean well, and they're intimidating as hell."

Bax pulled the chair closer to the bed.

"How are you feeling?" she asked.

"Doctor says I can go home tomorrow. They think they got all the bugs out. That was as unpleasant as hell. Got a couple of small bite marks, but I survived, and that's what's important."

"Dee, what do you remember about your abduction?"

Dee sat quietly for a minute and thought about the events of that night two weeks ago. "I remember I had a funny feeling walking to the car after class. You know, like I was being watched, but I didn't see anyone. I texted my husband that I was on the way, and I headed home. I was about halfway between Mancos and Cortez when this van or truck came out of nowhere, and all of a sudden, the high beams were in my eyes, and I couldn't see. I swerved off the road and hit a fence post or something. Before I knew what was happening, the door opened, and someone threw a bag of some kind over my head. My wrists were strapped, and they—there were two of them—they dragged me and threw me in the back of a van. They tied my legs and gagged me through the bag. I could barely breathe."

She stopped talking and thought for a minute. Bax waited for her to continue.

"I think they injected me with something because the next thing I remember is waking up with a sore head. I was lying naked on a shitty old mattress that smelled like crap, and I was covered with this rough old smelly horse blanket. My one hand was tied with some kind of strap to the metal bed frame, and it was pitch black."

"You're doing good, Dee. If you need to take a break, just let me know, and we can stop for a minute," said Bax.

"No, I want to get this over with, so I don't have to think about it again."

"Dee, do you remember anything about the two men who grabbed you?"

"It wasn't two men. It was a man and a woman. The woman had rough hands like she worked for a living. She also had a musky smell, some kind of outdoorsy fragrance. The guy was heavier, and he had a thin beard, like those kids you see who aren't able to grow full beards, and it comes in all patchy. It all happened so fast, but I think I caught a glimpse of him before the mask was fully over my head."

Bax stopped typing into her laptop and looked at Dee. "Are you sure it was a man and a woman?"

"As sure as you and I are sitting here. Why?"

"Nothing," said Bax. "What do you remember about the van?"

Dee thought for a minute. "It smelled like fruit or flowers—kind of green. There was dirt or something on the floor. I could feel it under my hands. It rattled a lot as they drove over bumps in the road."

"Dee, did the van come from behind you or in front of you when the headlights came on?"

"The lights came on from in front of me. First, there was nothing but the dark highway, and then I couldn't see. I remember thinking that someone was approaching in the wrong lane. That's why I swerved."

"When were you first raped.?"

"That first night, or day, or whatever time it was after I woke up. They had quite a party, the three guys. It felt like I was raped for hours, then one of them left, and the other two continued. I could barely stand, I was so sore, I just laid on the bed and cried."

"There were three men? Can you describe the other two men?"

Dee thought back to that night. "One was tall, and one was short. They smelled like rotting flesh or something that died, but then the whole place smelled like rotting meat. It was dark the entire time, and I think they were wearing night-vision goggles. The one who liked to do it anally poked me in the back with some kind of metal frame that felt like binoculars or something."

"Dee, did they ever turn on the lights?"

"Every couple of days, they would come in and put the bag back over my head. Then the woman would come in and make me wash myself. She also brought another cover for the bed and another shitty blanket."

"Dee, can you describe the woman?" asked Bax.

"Don't know who she was, but she was only

there when the light was on. I could see little specks of light through the mask. It wasn't very bright. She made sure I washed everywhere."

Bax sat back in the chair, bewildered. Had they gotten this all wrong? They had been focused on Jerry and Willie, and it never occurred to any of them that there might be more people involved.

"Dee, did they ever speak to you? Anything about their voices or something you might have heard?"

"They never said a word. During the first couple of days, I screamed at them and asked them why, but they never responded. I was so scared."

Dee started to cry, and Bax handed her the cup of water that was sitting next to the bed. She sat silently while Dee composed herself.

Finally, Dee looked ready to continue. "Dee, did all three men rape you after that first night?"

"No, only the tall and the short one continued, and it wasn't every day. Sometimes they would go for a long period with no one raping me. Sometimes it was just one of them, and sometimes they would rape me one after the other."

"Dee, is there anything about any of the men or the woman that stands out? Anything that could help us identify them?"

Dee looked angry. "I thought you knew who did this to me. Haven't you arrested them? Tell me you didn't have them make me vomit for nothing."

"What you just told me changes a lot about this investigation," said Bax. "We have two persons of interest, but you just told us about two more people that we had no idea were involved. This changes things."

Dee glared at her. "You'd better figure this out, Agent Baxter. I made a promise to myself that if I ever got out of there alive and found the people responsible, I would kill them, and I will if I have to."

"Dee, you can't take the law into your own hands. We will figure this out."

"I'm getting tired. Please leave." Dee closed her eyes and shut Bax out. Bax closed her laptop, grabbed her backpack and walked out of the room. Dee's cousins were still on duty, and the big guy she'd dropped stared daggers at her, but they let her pass without comment. She left the hospital and walked into the cool night air. This investigation had just taken a significant turn, and it was not a good one. She headed for her hotel room to try to put the pieces back together.

Chapter Forty-Six

The ringing phone woke Buck from a sound sleep, and he checked the number and the time on his phone. There was just a hint of morning light shining around the perimeter of the curtains.

"Hey, Hank," said Buck.

"Fuck, Buck. Who the hell have you managed to piss off now? My phone hasn't stopped ringing since I woke up this morning. What the hell are you into?"

Buck cleared his head and took a sip of the warm Coke sitting on the nightstand. "What are you talking about?"

"I've been on the phone with the Department of Defense, the director, the attorney general and a half dozen generals from the Pentagon. Your governor has gotten a lot of people fired up, and it's all landing on my desk because you and I are friends."

"Hank," said Buck. "I have no idea what you are talking about. The governor was going to call some people to find out what's going on at an old bunker in the mountains. Why would that get a bunch of people fired up?"

Hank laughed. "You know how your governor is. He takes a great deal of pride in pissing off the federal government, any chance he gets. Well,

I guess he asked the wrong question and started a chain reaction."

"But why are you involved? This has nothing to do with the FBI," asked Buck.

"I'm involved because the DoD didn't think you would believe some random army officer calling you, out of the blue, and telling you everything is fine, and it's not terrorists working at the bunker. They know we've worked together, and they know that once you get your teeth into a bone, you don't easily let go. They felt you might be more receptive if the information came from someone you knew and could trust. So, the secretary of defense called my director, who called me, and then we set up a conference call with a bunch of DoD and Pentagon folks, along with your governor. What the hell is going on up there?"

Hank Clancy and Buck had worked closely together on several cases during the past couple of years, and they knew they could trust each other. Hank was the special agent in charge of the FBI's Denver Field Office and had recently been promoted to deputy director after successfully closing the Alicia Hawkins case, along with Buck and the Aspen Police Department.

Alicia Hawkins was a young woman from Aspen who found out that her grandfather, who was a quadriplegic and had Alzheimer's, had been a serial killer in the sixties, and had killed fifteen young women before being crippled in an auto accident. His sixteenth victim had been in the car with him the night of the crash and survived, with no recollection of the events leading up to the crash.

Alicia had found out about his past and was intrigued enough to set out on her own, and she soon discovered she was exceptionally good at killing people. Buck and Paul Webber, with the help of the FBI and the Pitkin County sheriff, broke the case, but Alicia had escaped to Florida. She led the FBI on a chase that eventually led back to Aspen. When Alicia found out, early on, that her grandfather's sixteenth victim was still alive and running a bar in Aspen, she made a promise to herself that she would make his sixteenth victim her sixteenth victim, as a sick tribute to him. Hank and Buck, working closely with the Aspen PD, raided a safe house she had rented and found her fifteenth victim, already dead, as well as the intended sixteenth victim, who was drugged and tied to a bed.

In a surprising twist to this case, they also found Alicia Hawkins dead. She had been stabbed in the heart by someone with mad skills. Evidence collected by the FBI at the scene led them to believe that she had joined forces with two young male protégés to help her with her diabolical plan and that one of the young men had killed both her and his partner and escaped Aspen, one step ahead of the FBI. They were confident that they were making good headway on the case and would apprehend the young man any day now.

Buck filled Hank in on his recent investigation into the deaths of the hikers and the strange circumstances surrounding their deaths. He told him about locating the old bunker, about the doomsday plans, finding it protected by armed guards and that new equipment was being loaded into the bunker, which could have some bearing on his investigation. He told him that he wasn't sure who the people at the bunker were, other than they had waved off the Colorado Air National Guard helicopter Buck had been in, and that they'd declared the airspace around the bunker a military operations area (MOA). Whoever they were, they were set up on land that belonged to a man who had previous issues with the government, and that led to the possibility of domestic terrorism.

"Infrasound weapons and nuclear weapons fail-safe overrides, huh?" said Hank. "Sounds like a hell of a case, and I can see why you might have thought terrorists. The locals must have gone nuts with all the conspiracy folks in town."

"So, what's the real story, Hank? Did we stumble on some super-secret government program? I'll bet the governor is just thrilled."

"Here's what I can tell you, and I will preface this by saying that some of this is way above my security clearance, but I was read in, and you will be too. The powers that be at the Pentagon don't want this to be something that keeps you investigating, so you will be going back to the bunker and given a tour of the project. Governor Kennedy has agreed with the plan, and the DoD has authorized your CANG helicopter to land on the pad inside the fence. You will be making this trip alone. No locals."

"So, this is something our government is doing and not a bunch of terrorists? That will make me sleep better. When are we expected at the bunker, and who am I meeting?" asked Buck.

"You need to go as soon as you can get the bird in the air. Your contact at the bunker is Major General Fitzpatrick. He was one of the generals on the call this morning. He has been authorized by the secretary of defense to give you all the details. Buck, this is serious shit, and you will be signing a nondisclosure agreement once this tour is over. You need to forget whatever you learn today."

"And the governor is okay with all this?"

"The governor has already signed the NDA. He's not happy this thing is in his backyard and no one had the courtesy to tell him, but he understands the need. Oh, by the way. Your director is not privy to any of this. He has been told by Governor Kennedy that this investigation is now concluded, and that you will be returning to the investigation you were on before this all began. Are you okay with all this?"

Buck sat quietly on the edge of the bed for a minute. "If the governor is okay with this, and you are confident that this is a legit government program, then I'm okay with it, but know this. You're the only one I trust."

"I appreciate that, Buck. In all the years we've known each other, I've never lied to you and I never will. Now finish that Coke, call your pilot and let's close this case. Bigfoot and alien abductions. Shit, Buck, you have all the fun." Hank laughed and hung up.

Buck called Cobra and told her to be ready to leave in one hour. He sat for a minute thinking about the odd turns this case had taken, and he wouldn't be able to tell anyone about it. He headed for a quick shower.

Chapter Forty-Seven

Bax couldn't sleep after the interview with Dee Hightower. The whole thing was very unsettling. She knew they hadn't wasted time investigating Jerry and Willie. She was confident they were involved, but who were the new players? She tried to sleep after entering her interview notes in the investigation file, but after repeated failures, she showered, dressed and headed back to the sheriff's office. That was where she found herself at seven a.m. Sitting in the conference room with Sheriff Garcia and Paul Webber, she reviewed Dee's answers, hoping for some insight.

"I don't get it. How could we completely miss the second set of suspects, and where did they come from? According to Dee, she was forced off the road by a van or truck coming at her. That means it had to come from Cortez or Towaoc or someplace north of there and not from the college in Durango. We checked every van in the area. What did we miss?"

Paul looked up from his laptop. "We need to pull all those van registrations back up and go over them again. Now we know we are looking for a woman and a young man, and a van that smells green."

Paul started clicking away on his keyboard. The sheriff looked mystified. "Is it possible we are wrong about Jerry and Willie? We have nothing we can pin on them."

"I don't think so," said Bax. "Those two are involved. We just have to find a way to prove it. We need to poke holes in their stories."

"How did Dee know we have a couple of suspects?" asked Paul.

The sheriff did not look happy. "My guess is Scott Sage told her, or one of her relatives. I will talk with him later today. I also think he had something to do with all the protesters out front. I am not happy about that."

Paul sat back and read through the DMV list he pulled out of the investigation file. "From what I can see, there are four vans that could fit the bill for the kidnap vehicle. One is registered to a horse ranch just outside town, and we interviewed the owner, an elderly man who claims it never leaves the ranch. The second one belongs to a painter, but the owner is six foot six and three hundred fifty pounds, so I think that rules him out. Van number three belongs to a handyman, and it was full of paint cans and lumber when we interviewed him. The last van is owned by a small landscape company, but the owner we interviewed was a young woman. She told Scott and me that the van has been in the shop getting the transmission worked on."

"I think we need to revisit those four and see if anything makes sense," said the sheriff. "Paul, why don't you and Bax work through the list. I'm gonna see how Dee is doing this morning and see if she remembers anything else. Maybe she will open up to me."

Paul put his laptop away after sending the DMV list to the printer, and he and Bax grabbed the list and headed for the parking lot. They noticed as they exited the building that the crowd of protesters had grown considerably since yesterday. Word had gotten out that Dee had been found safe, and everyone in the area and beyond wanted to be a part of the "Justice for Dee" movement. Bax hoped the sheriff was serious about having a come-to-Jesus meeting with Deputy Sage.

They slid into Paul's Jeep and pulled out of the parking lot, heading for the first address on the list. While Paul drove, Bax updated the notes in the investigation file.

The van at the horse ranch was sitting in front of the barn when they pulled down the drive. The old rancher was loading it with bales of hay, and he stopped and watched them approach. Bax and Paul stepped over to the man and shook hands. The conversation went as expected. The old man only used the van around the small ranch. When Bax asked if anyone else besides him had access to the keys, he hesitated a minute too long. He told them that he had two young fellas that helped him out around the ranch and that they lived in the spare bedroom behind the barn.

"Where do you put the keys at night?" asked Bax.

"There's a keyboard in the barn. Has all the keys to the equipment on it."

"So, someone could access those keys after you retire for the night, without you knowing?"

"It's possible, but I would have heard something. I don't sleep so good anymore," said the rancher.

"Are the young men working today?" asked Paul.

"Nah, they get one day off a week, and they like to spend it with their friends."

"Do you know if one of them has a girlfriend?" asked Bax.

"I don't think it's serious," said the rancher. "Although they do spend a lot of time working around the ring when my granddaughter is training the horses."

"Your granddaughter works here? Can we speak with her?" asked Paul.

"She went to Durango this morning to pick up some supplies. Won't be back till later. You think them kids are involved in something?" asked the rancher.

Paul asked for the names of the three kids and typed them into his laptop. They thanked the rancher and headed for stop number two.

It was early afternoon when they returned to the sheriff's office and noticed the crowd out front had gotten even larger. Bax also noticed more guns than she had before. She hoped things wouldn't start to get out of hand. They went around to the back entrance and were buzzed through the security door.

They ran into Sheriff Garcia in the hall. "Any luck?" he asked.

He followed them back to the conference room, and they filled him in on the information the rancher had given them. The other three possible suspect vans didn't pan out. The only one that made sense was the ranch van, but they didn't have enough for a warrant.

"What do you think?" he asked Bax.

"We need to talk to those kids, as the rancher called them."

Paul had been typing away on his laptop when he stopped and read a document that was on his screen. "The boys may be kids, but the granddaughter isn't. She's thirty-eight years old, twice divorced, and she has a record." Paul clicked a few more keys. "B and E when she was eighteen, spent two years in the La Plata County Jail. Auto theft a year after she was released. Did two years in Grand County for the car theft. Spent two years in the state prison in Florence for assault and was released for good behavior. Nothing for the last couple of years. Says here she learned taxidermy while in Florence."

"Now that's interesting," said Sheriff Garcia. "Any outstanding warrants?"

Paul clicked a few more keys. "Bingo. She has a failure to appear warrant from Santa Fe, New Mexico. She was a witness to a bar fight and never bothered to show up for court. It's a year old, but it's still open."

"Looks like we have probable cause to arrest and hold her. Paul, can you print out the warrant, and

Sheriff, do you have a couple deputies that can pick her up?"

The sheriff nodded and headed for the dispatch center. Maybe they'd just caught a break in the case. Bax sat back in the chair and closed her eyes. They needed a break, because so far, other than saving Dee, they were batting zero.

Chapter Forty-Eight

Bax heard the commotion before she saw the woman being led into the interrogation area by the two deputies. Tina Ronkowski had chosen not to come along peaceably and was now on an anti-police tirade. She covered everything from her displeasure with the two deputies to taking swipes at the world in general. Her yelling included her political and religious beliefs, the latter of which, based on the language she was using, was probably nonexistent. She also questioned the heritage and the immigration status of everyone she passed during the walk. She was a foul-mouthed, angry woman, and Bax wasn't sure how this would all play out.

The deputies deposited Tina in the interrogation room, and Bax grabbed her laptop and stepped through the door. Paul and Sheriff Garcia stood outside the window and observed. They had discussed the possibility before Tina was brought in that this might prove to be less than informative. They had no basis to question her regarding anything other than not showing up for a court appearance in New Mexico. She was under no obligation to answer anything, but Bax felt it was worth a shot.

Bax introduced herself and sat through five more

minutes of Tina's tirade before the woman stopped yelling.

"Why am I here?" she asked.

"You were arrested on an outstanding warrant from Santa Fe for failure to appear. The deputies were following the law. We have alerted the authorities in Santa Fe and are waiting to hear what they want to do with you. In the meantime, you will be our guest."

"Where's my lawyer? I told them, and I'm telling you, I'm not saying another word until she gets here."

Bax had to work hard not to say out loud that her silence would be much appreciated at this point, but she held back. She closed her laptop and sat back. She tried to make small talk, hoping to get Tina to open up about anything. She asked her what she did for a living and how she liked working on her grandfather's ranch. She asked her if she had any kids and about her marriages. Tina was quiet through the entire one-sided conversation.

"Did you hear about the sheriff's office saving that missing Native American woman? That was quite an ordeal that woman went through. Imagine being covered in flesh-eating beetles. God, that makes my skin crawl."

Tina sat stone-faced, but Bax could see something change in her eyes. It wasn't significant, but there was something there. She decided to keep talking.

"Your record says you studied taxidermy while you were at the state prison. Did you ever work with those beetles? It sounds fascinating, but kind of creepy."

"You can't question me without my lawyer being here," said Tina.

"No one is questioning you regarding your arrest. We're just having a nice conversation about things unrelated to your situation."

"I'm not talking to you about anything."

Tina, Bax decided, had learned her lessons well after three incarcerations. She knew her rights, and she was sticking to her guns. But Bax kept trying.

"After we found that woman, I was reading up on using beetles to clean flesh off bones. Fascinating reading. Anyway, I heard there was a bone cleaning company here in Cortez, and I was thinking about seeing if they might be willing to give me a tour. Would be kind of fun to see how it's done. I hear they have two guys over there—Jerry and Willie, I think are their names—and they are supposed to be the best around at using beetles. They might be able to help us understand how the woman came to be in the basement of the bone company."

"What are you playing at here?" yelled Tina. "Do you think because I took some stupid classes in prison, that I was part of that woman being kidnapped? Is this some kind of sham arrest to get some information?"

Just then, the door opened and in walked Gail Fairhaven, Attorney-at-Law. "That's it, Agent Baxter. You have no right to question my client without me being here. This is appalling. Trying to connect my client to a case you can't make against Willie, so you are trying to implicate Tina. This is beyond reproach, and I have half a mind to sue CBI and this department for violating my client's rights."

Bax was not surprised by the outburst. She'd expected it. What surprised her was that Tina was being represented by the same lawyer that Willie used. Interesting coincidence.

"Tina and I were just having a conversation . . ."

"Don't give me that crap. I know exactly what you were doing, and I will not allow it to continue." She set a file down on the table and pulled out the top piece of paper and handed it to Bax.

"This is an order from the judge in Santa Fe, rescinding the arrest warrant for failure to appear. The warrant should have been removed from the system right after the trial. The city attorney won the case even without Tina's testimony and accepted the fact that Tina was home sick with the flu. They are not pressing charges."

She looked at Tina. "Let's go. We're out of here." Then to Bax, she said, "If you want to talk to my client again, you will do it through me. If you approach her directly, I will sue your asses off." She looked towards the window. "You get me, Reuben?"

She picked up her file, and she and Tina walked out the door. Bax sat there looking at the order from the judge. She was mad. She felt Tina might have something to offer, but for now, that was off the table. If Tina was involved with Jerry and Willie, there was no way to prove it.

Bax walked out of the room and handed Sheriff Garcia the note from the judge. "That could have gone better," she said.

Paul walked over, sipping from a bottle of water. "I think she knows something. When you were talking about Jerry and Willie, something flashed in her eyes. I think you saw it too. Unfortunately, without any evidence, there is no way we can go after her. We are back to square one." He walked towards the conference room.

"Don't worry about Gail," said Sheriff Garcia. "She's a lot of bluster, but she's good people. We had to try and see if Tina knew anything, and I agree with Paul. You hit a nerve. Somehow she's involved. To what extent is anyone's guess. Maybe if we can find the two other guys from the ranch, we can get something on her."

The sheriff headed towards his office, and Bax headed to the conference room. She sat opposite Paul and opened her laptop. "What are we missing, Paul? Are these people just smarter than us?" She sat back in her chair and rubbed her temples.

"I don't think they're smarter than us. I think they have had a long time to perfect their crime. We may have to face the fact that this runs deeper than we know, and we may not get to the conclusion we want."

"We've gone from two bug guys to a conspiracy. How can there be no evidence? There has to be evidence. In a conspiracy, someone always talks.

What the hell is wrong with these people, and how do we stop them? I need to get some air."

Before Paul could respond, she grabbed her backpack and walked out of the conference room. Paul clicked on the investigation file and started reading. Sometimes you need to go back to the beginning and look at everything with a different slant. That's what Paul intended to do.

Chapter Forty-Nine

Cobra clicked her mic and let Buck know that they had been cleared to land at the bunker. She flew over the fence and gently set the helicopter down on the concrete pad. She shut down the engine and looked at Buck, who was removing his helmet and headset.

"Our orders are to sit here and wait for you, and to not engage with any of the people on-site. You have the radio if you need us. The word for today is renegade. We hear that word, and we will call for reinforcements. You good?"

"You sound like you don't trust these guys, Cobra. We're all on the same side."

Cobra and her copilot laughed, and Buck gave her a small salute and stepped onto the landing pad. He walked to the tall, gray-haired man standing at the side of the pad and extended his hand.

"Buck Taylor, Colorado Bureau of Investigation."

"Agent Taylor, it's a pleasure to meet you. Tom Fitzpatrick. Welcome to JEDI."

Buck looked at Fitzpatrick, who was dressed in jeans, cowboy boots and a button-down shirt. "JEDI?"

"Let's step inside the bunker," said Fitzpatrick. "Follow me, please."

The general turned sharply and headed towards the bunker entrance. Buck looked around and noticed the four security guards trying to be unobtrusive but keeping a close eye on both him and the helicopter crew. He followed the general and passed through the massive blast door into the main area. Unlike the first time he had been here, the inside was now awash with bright lights, and there was some new metal office furniture that hadn't been there before. The general stopped and faced him.

"I have to be honest, Agent Taylor. I was and still am opposed to this tour, but I am a soldier, and I follow the orders I am given. I have been directed by the SECDEF to show you everything and answer any questions you may have. You have been given special security clearance that is in effect for just this tour. Once the tour is completed, you will be asked to sign a nondisclosure agreement and try to forget everything you see today. Do you understand all of this?"

"Yes, General. I understand," said Buck.

The general's demeanor instantly changed from serious to almost childlike. "As I said at the pad, welcome to JEDI, the Joint Enterprise Defense Infrastructure. What you will see today is the beginnings of a ten-billion-dollar, public-private partnership that will create a secret data storage cloud for all our most valuable military and government secrets. This bunker is one of four sites around the country that will house a huge server farm capable of handling government files for hopefully a hundred years. Are you familiar with the term COG, or continuity of government?"

Buck nodded and said he had a rudimentary understanding, and that it involved secret locations around the country, where government leaders would be gathered in the event of a catastrophe.

Buck didn't want the general to know how much knowledge he had on the subject, so he stood quietly by while the general explained about the bunkers, secret phone systems and nuclear doomsday protection. He appreciated the fact that the general didn't try to hide anything and had even given Buck more information than he already had. He was becoming a little more at ease with this whole arrangement. The one thing the general didn't mention was the original purpose for this particular bunker as a fail-safe override for the nation's missile system. He wondered if the general was even aware of the original purpose.

"JEDI, as I explained, is a joint venture between the DoD and several companies that are currently bidding to build a digital cloud, similar to the Microsoft or Google clouds you might be familiar with. We chose a select group of old Cold War bunkers to use for this purpose because these are hardened facilities that can withstand a nuclear blast. But more importantly, the way they were constructed will protect the servers from an EMP, or electromagnetic pulse, a surge of energy designed to take out everything electronic. This is one of our biggest fears today. Some nations are developing EMP weapons that will leave everything on the surface intact, with no radiation, while sending us back to the Stone Age digitally and electronically. This facility will prevent that from happening."

"General, a question. If this pulse weapon destroys everything electronic, who will be able to access the information stored here?" asked Buck.

The general explained that there were hardened sites like this one in several locations and that government officials would have computers that were also protected. Buck wasn't sure that the general believed his answer, but he decided to let it go.

"General, how large is this bunker, and will this be staffed or remotely accessed?"

"Well, the old bunker goes down three levels under this building, about three hundred feet underground. We have only reactivated the first two subterranean levels, but we have space to grow as needed. As far as staffing, this facility will be primarily remote. There will be staff coming through from time to time to perform maintenance and upgrades on the servers. If you want to follow me, I will give you the grand tour."

They passed through another blast door and into an area that looked like a shower room, which the general explained was left over from the Cold War. "Anyone exposed to radiation could wash off before entering the facility," he said. They walked past the door that Buck and Eddie had taken that led to the next level and walked up to an elevator door. The general swiped his ID card, and the door opened. Buck and the general stepped inside.

They exited the elevator on the first underground level, which Buck had estimated to be about a hundred feet below the surface. The lights were on, and the air was less stale than on his first visit. Several people were removing large computer servers from the wooden crates Buck had seen outside the building on his last visit. It was a beehive of activity, and Buck was impressed. The space that was being used was a huge room. Somewhere in the background, he could hear a generator running.

The general explained the use of the servers and allowed him to watch some of the technicians connecting various pieces of equipment to the servers. He was allowed to ask the technicians questions and even helped move one large piece of equipment into place. He was shown some of the office spaces that were being set up for the maintenance people, along with crew sleeping quarters and a small kitchen. Buck followed the general back to the elevator, and they dropped down to the next level, which was more of the same and also included the mechanical systems. Two huge diesel generators were supplying power, and there was a huge tank marked fresh water and another marked waste. He heard the sound of an exhaust fan running and wondered if it had anything to do with the infrasound that had killed the hikers. He didn't ask the question.

The general led him once more to the elevator,

and they descended to the lowest level, which, just as the general had said, was well lit but empty. They rode the elevator back to the main floor and stood next to the blast door.

"So, Agent Taylor, as you have seen, there is nothing nefarious going on at this facility, and I am sorry that our security folks gave you the wrong impression. I appreciated your questions and your interest. As I said earlier, we would appreciate it if you would now conclude your investigation and forget everything you have seen."

The general walked over to the desk and pulled a document out of a file folder and slid it towards Buck along with a pen. Buck read the form, and other than the parts about treason and possible execution, which were disconcerting, he signed it and handed it back to the general.

They shook hands, and Buck walked back to the helipad. Cobra started the engine as soon as he boarded, and within minutes they were airborne and heading back to Creede. Twenty-odd minutes later, they landed, and Cobra shut down. They stepped onto the pad, and Buck thanked her for all the time she had been able to spend with him. She told him it was her pleasure and if he ever needed anything to give her a call. Buck walked towards his Jeep and waved a last goodbye as she lifted off and headed east.

Buck drove to the sheriff's department and walked through the front door. Eddie and the sheriff were sitting in the sheriff's office, and they waved him over.

"I got a call from Director Jackson this morning. I guess you'll be heading back to Cortez this afternoon. He said the governor is satisfied that nothing bad is going on out here, and he's glad we were able to close out the survey team deaths."

Buck smiled. "All is good, Carl. Your little piece of paradise is back to normal, and you have a new neighbor."

"Can you tell us anything about what's going on at the bunker, or if you do, would you have to kill us?"

"All I can tell you is that it's your tax dollars at work."

"Well, it can't be all bad. I got a call this morning from someone in the governor's office after I spoke with Jackson. The woman told me we would be getting a nice fat check from the Department of Homeland Security, so we can hire a couple more deputies and help make sure people stay away from the bunker. So, it looks like Eddie can become a full-time deputy."

"Congratulations, Eddie, that's great. Well deserved." He shook Eddie's hand and then the sheriffs. "It was a pleasure working with you guys again. If you need anything else, you know how to find me."

Buck grabbed his backpack off the desk and headed out the door. He stopped at the Moose for one last meal, left the waitress a big tip, slid into his Jeep and headed for Cortez.

Chapter Fifty

Buck pulled into the parking lot of the Montezuma County Sheriff's Department. He parked and sat for a moment. It had been a strange day. The governor had called while he was driving over, which was unusual all by itself, since the governor rarely called him directly. They talked for a few minutes about Buck's tour of the bunker and whether Buck felt confident that everything was on the up and up. Buck told him he hadn't seen anything odd or out of the ordinary and was satisfied that the bunker was legit. He also called his boss, Director Jackson, and told him he was on his way back to Cortez. The director asked how things had wrapped up in Creede, and he felt bad that he wasn't able to tell him the complete truth about what he had seen. He told him that all was well, and everyone was happy with the results of the investigation.

The director expressed his concerns about the lack of evidence that Bax and Paul had been able to uncover in Cortez, and he sensed a lot of frustration on Bax's part with the lack of progress. They agreed to talk after Buck had a chance to review what they had, and he ended the call.

He grabbed his backpack, walked past the ever-increasing crowd of protesters on the front sidewalk of the justice building and walked through the front door. He flashed his ID to the deputy at the front desk and was buzzed through to the back. He found Bax and Paul sitting in the conference room with Sheriff Garcia and Deputy Sage. He shook hands all around, and Sheriff Garcia introduced him to the county attorney, Roger Nolan, who was also in the room. Buck grabbed a seat next to Bax.

"So, what's going on?" he asked.

Bax was the first to speak up. "We were just going over everything we have with Roger to see if there is any way forward in this case. Paul spent the better part of the morning reviewing all the evidence, and as we were explaining as you walked in, we have nothing but circumstantial evidence and conjecture."

"Either we have been chasing the wrong suspects all along, or these guys are a lot smarter than we would have ever suspected," said Paul. "I just can't figure out which."

Bax filled Buck in on the interview with Dee Hightower at the hospital that he hadn't had a chance to review on his own yet. She told him about Dee's assertion that she had been abducted by a man and woman, and they were coming from the direction of Cortez and not following behind her from Durango. Buck pulled up the report on his laptop and took a minute to read the interview. There was no doubt in his mind, after reading the interview, that Dee was telling the truth.

They discussed the interview they had tried to do with Tina Ronkowski, and how that had turned into a monumental failure. Paul put the interview tape up on the large TV, and they all watched. When the interview was completed, Buck stood up and walked over to the refrigerator in the corner and grabbed a bottle of Coke. He took a big drink and let his thoughts settle.

"I think she is somehow involved. You got a reaction out of her when you talked about Jerry and Willie, but she is good. Damn good. Like you guys, I am curious about her choice of attorney, but choosing the same attorney as Willie is not a crime. This is a small community, and there are not that many defense attorneys around."

He sat back down. "Roger, what's your take on all this?"

Roger Nolan leaned into the table and folded his hands. "Right now, we have nothing to move this case forward. If I take this to a grand jury, they will not indict. I've looked at everything we have, and even the circumstantial evidence is light. I know there is no such thing as a perfect crime, but so far, if these suspects are involved, then they have committed the perfect crime. I wish I could offer more."

Buck thanked him for his insight. Buck looked at the sheriff. "Reuben, this is your county. What do you see as our next step?"

"Believe me when I say, I want to solve this case as much as anyone. This is my goddaughter this happened to, and I'm pissed. But the truth is, we've looked at everything, and nothing connects any of these people to this crime. I feel like we've been chasing ghosts, but I don't know where to look next."

Paul clicked a couple keys on his laptop and opened a lab report. "The lab report is back on the vomit sample we took from Dee and the sample Deputy Sage picked up at the restaurant Jerry stopped at that night." Everyone looked at Paul. "The vomited material matches the meal Jerry picked up at the fast-food drive-thru. It was laced with a healthy amount of Rohypnol. The report says there wasn't enough to kill her, but she should have been out for a while. I guess bugs crawling all over you would be enough to wake anyone out of deep sleep."

"Okay," said Buck. "We know Jerry bought a meal, and we know Dee ate a similar meal, laced with the drugs. How do we prove that Jerry is the one who put the drugs in the food and gave it to her?"

He looked around the table and got no responses from anyone. "This is the problem with this case. Every piece of evidence could lead to Jerry or Willie, and it could lead to someone else. They did a good job covering their tracks."

"What about the smells that Dee associated with the men. The rotting meat. Can we use smell as an identifier?"

Roger was the first to answer. "There have been cases where the identification of a suspect was made with a fragrance lineup. Those cases are few and far between, and none of them led to a guilty verdict based solely on the victim's sense of smell.

Dee says she smelled rotting meat. She was found in a factory where rotting meat was all around her. The smell on the two rapists could have followed them in the door. A jury will laugh that right out of court."

"What about the outdoorsy smell Dee noticed on the woman and in the van. Can we use that for a lineup and at least search the van?" asked Bax.

"Same problem," said Roger. "This is ranching country. The smell could have been in the air when they opened her door. There is no way to link a specific smell to one individual when anyone who works on a ranch would probably smell the same way."

"You're just a ray of sunshine, Roger," said the sheriff. "Do we have anything that we can use?"

"Paul, can you put up the forensic report from the back room on the big screen?" asked Buck.

Paul hit a few buttons and the large monitor filled with the report. Buck could read the information without putting on his glasses. He gave everyone a minute to read the report. "Anything stand out?"

The report held little information of evidentiary value. The forensic team had collected no prints in the room or on the latch side of the cabinet, other than Dee's. There was no DNA on the mattress or the blanket except for Dee's. They got no DNA from the rape kit, and the room, for as dark and dank as it was, held no useful evidence. They found a couple of hairs on the floor that came from Jerry and Willie, but they were located near the door and could have been caused by transference. For all the time the techs had been on-site, they found nothing that could help the team.

"So, the forensics is worthless, the food is worthless, and the fragrance is a nonstarter. What about the two suspects or the woman?"

Bax took over. "Both suspects had a reason to be in Durango the night of the abduction. We have a video of the van following her from the college, but Dee swears the van that turned on its high beams was coming from the opposite direction. Both suspects had a reason to be at the crime scene, we have no evidence the ranch van ever left the property and we can't put any of them in the room with Dee. The only eyewitness we have didn't get a good look at the suspects who dropped off the car near Ute Mountain, and there was no forensic evidence found in Dee's car."

Bax pushed her chair back, walked to the window and stared outside. Her frustration was evident to everyone, and they all felt the same way. Buck looked at his watch. "Let's call it a day, and everyone get some rest. We can meet back here tomorrow at nine and give it one more shot."

They all packed up the laptops and headed for the door. Buck signaled Reuben to follow him to his office, where he closed the door and sat in the visitor's chair.

Reuben sat behind his desk and looked at Buck. "You look like you have something on your mind, Buck."

"This has turned into a strange case, Reuben.

With what I've seen so far, I am not sure we are going to solve this. Honest opinion. How have Bax and Paul done?"

The sheriff thought for a minute. "They have been working their asses off. I couldn't have asked for better help with this. I've been with them most of the way, and there is just nothing there. I've been doing this a long time, and I have never come across a crime that had such little evidence. I'm at a loss."

"Thanks, Reuben. It's good to hear that they did a good job for you. They are both top-notch investigators, and this one has them stumped. Tell me this. If you announce that we will not be prosecuting anyone at this time, how is that going to affect the growing crowd out front? I noticed a lot of weapons when I came in this afternoon."

"I can handle them. My fear is facing Dee and telling her we have hit a wall. She is a tough girl, and she told me that she made a promise to herself that if she got out of the mess, she would hunt down the perpetrators and kill them. You know as well as I do, things tend to disappear on the reservation. If she knows the suspects' names, something bad might happen to them, and we might never know. She has some real wackos on her side of the family."

"I'd like to visit her tonight at the hospital. Can you call her and let her know I'm coming by?"

"You want company?"

"Nah," said Buck. "You go home and have dinner with your wife. I'll see you in the morning."

Buck stood, grabbed his backpack and left the office. He walked past the chanting crowd on the sidewalk and headed for his Jeep. He wasn't sure what he hoped to accomplish by talking with Dee, but he knew he needed to do it anyway. He pulled out of the lot and headed for the hospital.

Chapter Fifty-One

Buck walked down the hall towards Dee's room, and he noticed that the three bodyguards Bax had told him about were nowhere in sight. He knocked and pushed open the door. The lights over the bed were dimmed, and the medical equipment cast a reddish glow over everything. He spotted Dee sitting in a chair, looking out the window at the sun as it set over the high desert.

"I used to love this place," she said. She didn't acknowledge his presence. "When you're alone in the desert at night, with the wind blowing through your hair and the coyotes howling in the distance, you look up at the vast Milky Way, and everything feels perfect. Now I look at the coming darkness, and I feel like I've lost something. The night is no longer a perfect place, but instead, you wonder what kind of evil is lurking in the darkness, just out of your view. I wonder if I will ever feel safe again."

She turned in the chair and faced him, her face silhouetted by the setting sun. Buck spotted the semiautomatic pistol in her hand. She noticed him looking, and she set the gun on the edge of the bed. "Personal protection," she said. "I sent my cousins and family home. I needed some time to think."

"I didn't mean to disturb you," said Buck. "I'm—"

"You're Buck Taylor. My godfather called and told me to expect you. You work with the blond woman, Agent Baxter? I like her. She is full of passion and compassion. She also seemed very frustrated by this case. I forgot to thank her, earlier today, for rescuing me. Can you tell her that for me?"

Buck nodded. He pulled up the second visitor's chair and slid it next to Dee at the window. He sat down and looked out at the last rays of the sun as they set over the Ute Mountains. He stared for a few minutes, and then he turned to Dee.

"Dee, is there anything you remember about the time you spent in captivity that you haven't told us about? A sound, a voice. Anything that could help us identify the people who did this to you?"

Dee sat quietly for a minute. A shiver ran up her spine, and she pulled the blanket from the foot of the bed and wrapped it around her shoulders. "I read in one of my classes about sensory deprivation as a means of torture, and I often wondered what it would take to survive such an ordeal. Now I know. You have to take yourself out of your body. When I was sitting alone in the dark, never knowing the day, or the time, wondering what might be lurking in the darkness or when the men would come in to rape me again, I knew the only way to survive was to leave the present and let the spirits take me to a place of peace and beauty. I prayed to those spirits a lot, which is kind of crazy for a devout Catholic girl, but the spirits of my ancestors were able to take me places I had never been before, so I never felt the rape or feared the darkness. The spirits told me I would survive and that when the time came, they would reveal the evil ones to me and let me decide how to deal with them. Then and only then will I be able to take back the power they stole from me."

She turned back towards the window and closed her eyes. Buck stood up. "The investigation is not over. Sheriff Garcia and his people will continue looking at the information our teams have been able to gather, and we will not close the books on this case until we have the suspects in custody. I know Agent Baxter will never allow us to stop looking. What has happened to Native American women over the last decade has become a personal crusade for her. It may take time, but in the end, we will catch these people. That is my promise to you."

Buck stood up, slid the chair back to its original place and left the room. He headed for his hotel and a long night reviewing everything they had. It was his last shot before he closed out CBI's involvement in the case. He owed it to Bax and the team to make sure they had done everything they could to find the suspects.

Buck slid into his Jeep, pulled out his phone and dialed the director. He put the Jeep in gear and pulled out of the parking lot.

Chapter Fifty-Two

The meeting the following morning was short and to the point. Buck had been up most of the night going through the investigation file from start to finish, and there were two conclusions that he'd reached. The first conclusion was that the two suspects, Jerry and Willie, were involved in this crime, and it was probably not their first time. The second conclusion was that there was no way to convict them based on the evidence they had.

Buck walked into the conference room, grabbed a Coke out of the refrigerator and sat down at the table. He looked around the table at the dour faces and knew that the decision they all knew was coming was not going to be what any of them wanted to hear. He opened his laptop.

"I had a conversation with Dee last night. Considering what she went through, she is a remarkable woman. My gut says she will be fine, with some time, and I get a sense that she has a great support network on the reservation. I told her the investigation was not closed, and would not be until we find and convict the people responsible. I think she understands how hard everyone has worked on her behalf, and she told me she is grateful to everyone who helped rescue her."

Buck let that sink in for a minute. "I spoke with

Director Jackson last night, and we discussed the status of the investigation. He agrees with what we all already know, that at this point, it is not a good use of our time to continue a full investigation. Bax will stay in contact with Sheriff Garcia and his team, and if anything new pops up, she will head down here. Reuben, please keep in touch with Bax and keep her apprised of any changes in the investigation or if something new develops. My recommendation is that you keep loose tabs on Jerry, Willie and the woman, Tina. They will slip up eventually, and we will nail them. We also need to continue to look for the two men who work on the ranch with Tina. It seems they have disappeared."

Bax looked up from her laptop. "So that's it? We head home without a victory? It's all so pointless. There isn't a criminal out there who is this good, yet these people were able to keep it together and block all our efforts." She closed her laptop and placed it in her backpack.

Everyone stood up and moved away from the table. They shook hands and thanked one another for their efforts. Buck took Sheriff Garcia aside.

"Keep an eye on Dee and her family. She pretty much told me that they would find justice in their own way. She said the spirits told her this would be the way."

"Okay, Buck, but I have to tell you, after spending my whole life around that reservation, sometimes the spirits are right. Thanks for all your help. Travel safe."

Buck walked Bax and Paul to their cars. "You

guys did great work on this. Sometimes the good guys don't win. In the end, we will get these guys. Take a couple of days off, and let's meet next week at the office. The director said he's proud of you."

They each slid into their Jeeps and left the parking lot. Buck stood for a minute, looking at the mountain range. He looked back at the Justice Center and noticed the protesters were no longer walking in a circle by the front door. He wondered what Sheriff Garcia had said to them to make them leave. He placed his backpack on the passenger seat and slid into the driver's seat. He thought about the last week and all the twists and turns these two investigations had taken. Life was bizarre sometimes, and he was glad it wasn't like this all the time. He knew what would clear his head. A couple of days on a river fly-fishing, and he knew just the spot. He put the Jeep in gear and headed north.

Epilogue

Willie had decided that maybe it was time to have a life like Jerry had. He found a new shampoo that seemed to get rid of most of the death smell, and he started hanging out at a neighborhood bar with some of his friends from the taxidermy club. He had even spent some time talking to a woman who didn't seem to mind what he did for a living. Willie was feeling good.

The investigation into the woman the cops had found in the basement of the bone company didn't seem to be going anywhere, and he and Jerry had picked out a few new prospects, but first, they had to find a new location. Mr. Sturgis had been understanding about the situation, and he hadn't fired them since the cops hadn't connected them to the crime, but they didn't want to take any chances. Willie occasionally felt like they were being watched, but he never saw anyone that looked suspicious.

It was later than usual when Willie left the bar. Tonight was karaoke night, and he even found the courage to get up on the stage in the corner and sing a song. His voice wasn't terrible, but most of the people in the bar were drunk, so it didn't matter what he sounded like as long as everyone had a good time.

He pulled into the parking lot of his apartment building and shut off the truck. He opened the door and took a deep breath to clear his head. He climbed down out of the truck and reached back in to grab his backpack off the seat when his whole world went dark. He couldn't see anything through the black bag that had been placed over his head. Someone pinned his arms behind his back, and he felt the plastic Flexicuffs bite into his wrists. He tried to yell, but nothing seemed to come out, then he felt a needle prick his arm and his whole world turned black.

Willie started to come out of the dream fog his mind was in, and he knew something was terribly wrong. He felt the hot breeze blow past his legs and torso, and he realized that he was naked. He was surprised at how quickly his mind cleared and was equally surprised at how fast the confusion turned to fear. He still had the black bag over his head, and his hands and feet were tied to a post. It felt like he was standing on a pile of logs. But it was the chanting, the drumming, and the whoops and hollers that caught his attention. It sounded like there was a party going on around him, and he felt a warm liquid run down his leg. He thought to himself that it had been a long time since he'd peed on himself.

The chanting and the yelling grew louder as the people kept beat with the drums. The sound was reaching a fevered pitch when he felt someone standing next to him. Suddenly, without warning, the bag was ripped from his head, and his mind tried to comprehend the scene before him. There must have been a dozen Native Americans, all dressed in feathers and beads, with their faces painted to look like horrible beings out of someone's sick nightmare. They were dancing and yelling, and the drums were beating. Willie felt his bowels let go. He couldn't comprehend what kind of madness this was, and then the woman appeared.

She had her face painted with red and black stripes, but even through the paint, he could see that she was the woman that had been found at the bone company, and then reality struck, and he understood what was happening. Tears flowed down his face as he tried to plead with her over the sounds of the drums and people. She just stared at him as she drew closer. She circled him as the chanting increased, and as she climbed up on the pile of logs, he noticed the big gleaming knife in her hand.

He screamed like he had never screamed before, but it was no use. No one was listening to him. She waved the knife in front of his face and slid the flat side of the blade along his body. Then she whispered in his ear, "The spirits are waiting."

She stopped the knife blade just above his manhood, reached down, grabbed him, and sliced through it in one quick move. The scream that followed was bloodcurdling.

If you could find anyone who would admit to being there that night, they would tell you that the screams could be heard until well into the morning hours.

By dawn, the bonfire, the glow of which could be seen for miles in the darkness, had consumed all of the fuel and nothing was left but a smoldering pile of ash. The spirits had been satisfied, for now.

Acknowledgments

A special thank-you to my daughter Christina J. Morgan, my unofficial corroborator. She is my sounding board and makes sure my ideas make sense.

Also, to my daughter Stephanie M. Morgan. Stephanie is my beta reader and makes sure that what's on the page is what should be there. She helps me make the book make sense.

Thanks to my editor, Laura Dragonette whose efforts helped turn my manuscript into a polished novel. Her help is greatly appreciated. Any mistakes the reader may find are solely the responsibility of the author.

Also, I would like to thank my family for all of their encouragement. I have been telling them stories since they were little, and I always told them that someone should be writing this stuff down. I decided to write it down myself.

I want to thank my closest friend, Trish Moakler-Herud. She has been encouraging me for years to write my stories down. I hope this will make her proud.

A special thanks to my late wife, Jane. She pushed me for years to become a writer, and my biggest regret is that she didn't live long enough to see it happen. I love her with all my heart and miss her every day. I think she would be pleased.

Finally, thanks to the readers. Without you, none of this would be important.

About the Author

2019 Pacific Book Awards Best Mystery Finalist...*Crime Delayed*

2020 Pacific Book Awards Best Mystery Winner...*Crime Denied*

Chuck Morgan attended Seton Hall University and Regis College and spent thirty-five years as a construction project manager. He is an avid outdoorsman, an Eagle Scout and a licensed private pilot. He enjoys camping, hiking, mountain biking and fly-fishing.

He is the author of the **Crime** series, featuring Colorado Bureau of Investigation agent Buck Taylor. The series includes *Crime Interrupted, Crime Delayed, Crime Unsolved, Crime Exposed* and *Crime Denied.*

He is also the author of *Her Name Was Jane*, a memoir about his late wife's nine-year battle with breast cancer. He has three children, three grandchildren and Siberian Huskie. He resides in Lone Tree, Colorado.

Other Books by the Author

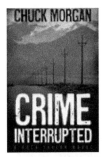

"*Crime Interrupted: A Buck Taylor Novel by Chuck Morgan is a gripping, edge-of-the-seat novel.* Right from page one, the action kicks off and never stops, gaining pace as each chapter passes." Reviewed by Anne-Marie Reynolds for Readers' Favorite.

Finalist...2019 Pacific Book Awards Best Mystery

"**This crime novel reads like a great thriller.** *The writing is atmospheric, laced with vivid descriptions that capture the setting in great* *detail while allowing readers to follow the intensity of the action and the emotional and psychological depth of the story." Reviewed by Divine Zape for Readers' Favorite.*

"Professionally written in the style of a best-selling crime novelist, such as Tom Clancy, Crime Unsolved: A Buck Taylor Novel by Chuck Morgan is a spellbinding suspense novel with an environmental flair. Intriguing subplots of fraud, survivalist *paranoia, and murder weave their way through the fabric of the plot, creating a dynamic story. This is an action-filled, stimulating tale which contains fascinating details that are relevant in our present climate." Reviewed by Susan Sewell for Readers' Favorite.*

"Chuck Morgan has a unique gift for plot,

one that makes Crime Exposed: A Buck Taylor Novel a hard-to-put-down book. From the start, readers know what happens to Barb, but they become curious as they follow the investigation, wondering if the characters will find out what happened to her. The descriptions are filled with clarity, and they offer readers great images. The prose is elegant, and it captures both the emotional and psychological elements of the novel clearly while offering vivid descriptions of scenes and characters. This is a fast-paced thriller with memorable characters and a criminal investigation that is so real readers will believe it could happen." Reviewed by Romuald Dzemo for Readers' Favorite.

Winner…2020 Pacific Book Awards Best Mystery
"It's really progressive to see a female serial killer portrayed with such intelligent writing and depth of character, and the cat and mouse chase dynamic is thrown off nicely by the switching of genders. What results is a really enjoyable thriller and crime mystery novel, and overall Crime

Denied is certain to please fans of both hard-boiled detective tales and action/adventure crime novels." Reviewed by K.C. Finn for Readers' Favorite

CPSIA information can be obtained
at www.ICGtesting.com
Printed in the USA
LVHW081000260422
717243LV00018B/264